Natalie Granville's
TOP TEN THINGS TO DO
ON YOUR NON-WEDDING DAY

10. Avoid pitying phone calls from your concerned friends and relatives. (Especially when you're the "jilter," not the "jiltee.")

9. Avoid visits from your concerned friends and relatives. (As above.)

8. Find a useful alternative for that never-to-be-worn gown. (Dressing up garden statuary is de rigueur this season.)

7. Don't wear white—unless it's decidedly *not* wedding gear. (That bikini will do the trick just fine.)

6. Drink whatever you want to calm those non-wedding jitters. (Leave the champagne cocktails for the misguided fools who *do* want to get married.)

5. Never let anyone tell you you're bitter. (Remember—you broke it off because you were getting married for the wrong reasons.)

4. Return all the presents given to you by your wealthy former fiancé. (You don't want anyone to accuse you of gaining anything but experience from this sad affair.)

3. Break all the rules you want. (After all, everyone in town is already talking about you.)

2. Celebrate your narrow escape. (You really did do the right thing.)

And the number one thing to do on your non-wedding day: Hire the gorgeous guy with the mysterious past who shows up at your door looking for work....

Dear Reader,

What a potent concept the past is! I've known people who cling to it, people who slide it under a microscope, people who run screaming from it and even a few who rewrite it. I've never met anyone who is indifferent to it.

I'm no exception. I loved being seven, eighteen, twenty-five. I revere my oldest friends, because when I say, "remember when," they do. My house is full of nicked chairs my grandmother bought. My conversations are decorated with my father's pearls of wisdom, and my conscience is buckled in tight with my mother's admonitions.

I'm free to love my past, because I'm also free to tell it to get lost. Sometimes I give away the chair that doesn't fit. Now and then I string my own pearls. Occasionally I even blow my mother a mental kiss, salute her for teaching me to think for myself, and do the thing she said I mustn't.

But what if you couldn't? What if your past owned you—instead of the other way around? That's what happened to Matthew Quinn. He's just been released from prison, but in his heart he's still locked away. He can't forget his past, not even long enough to fall in love.

It's going to take a special woman to redeem him. But Natalie Granville is a prisoner of her past, too. She's shackled to Summer House, a moldering old relic she doesn't want, can't afford and yet feels a duty to preserve.

The Redemption of Matthew Quinn is the story of how they finally manage to come to terms with the past—and to fall in love with the future. I hope you enjoy making the journey with them.

Warmly,

Kathleen O'Brien

P.S. Please write to me at P.O. Box 947633, Maitland, FL 32794-7633 or at KOBrien@AOL.com.

The Redemption of Matthew Quinn

Kathleen O'Brien

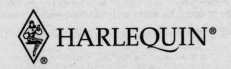

HARLEQUIN®

TORONTO • NEW YORK • LONDON
AMSTERDAM • PARIS • SYDNEY • HAMBURG
STOCKHOLM • ATHENS • TOKYO • MILAN • MADRID
PRAGUE • WARSAW • BUDAPEST • AUCKLAND

ISBN 0-373-71086-0

THE REDEMPTION OF MATTHEW QUINN

Copyright © 2002 by Kathleen O'Brien.

The Redemption of
Matthew Quinn

Books by Kathleen O'Brien

HARLEQUIN SUPERROMANCE

927—THE REAL FATHER
967—A SELF-MADE MAN
1015—WINTER BABY*
1047—BABES IN ARMS*

*Books in "Four Seasons in Firefly Glen"

Don't miss any of our special offers. Write to us at the
following address for information on our newest releases.

Harlequin Reader Service
U.S.: 3010 Walden Ave., P.O. Box 1325, Buffalo, NY 14269
Canadian: P.O. Box 609, Fort Erie, Ont. L2A 5X3

CHAPTER ONE

AT HIGH NOON when she should have been saying "I do," Natalie Granville was lounging on the cracked porch of her maggoty mansion, wearing nothing but a bikini, a smile and a light coating of perspiration.

Through the open double doors to the parlor, she listened to the answering machine. At least ten people had already called to check on her. Their messages ranged from the carefully indirect—"Hi, Nat, just wondering if you felt like talking"—to the blunt growls of her elderly cousin Granville Frome—"Dammit, girl, where are you? If you're holed up somewhere crying, I'm going to break that bastard's nose."

But Natalie ignored them all. She was a Granville, and by heaven she didn't need anybody's pity.

She hoisted herself onto the wide marble banister and lay back carefully, so that the sun could bake her entire body. She slathered sunscreen across the bridge of her nose, where those annoying freckles liked to pop up, balanced her bottle of Jack Daniel's on her stomach, and went on enjoying the heavenly day.

The would-have-been wedding day. Above her, the hot blue sky wore white lace clouds. Around her, the air sparkled like diamonds. The birds were singing schmaltzy romantic ditties.

Actually, she admitted to the bottle, trying to be honest—Granvilles were unflinchingly honest—it would have been a lovely day to get married.

Then she grinned, though her lips felt a little bit numb. Aw, who was she kidding? It was an even lovelier day to *not* get married.

Oops. Her grandfather wouldn't like that split infinitive. Granvilles always used perfect grammar. She raised the bottle over her head and, without turning her head, apologized to the glowering portrait that hung on the parlor wall.

"Sorry, Gramps. I guess I'm breaking all the rules today."

She wouldn't have called him Gramps, either, if it hadn't been for the Jack Daniel's. And the fact that he'd been dead for five years.

"Um, hello. Miss? Excuse me." A man's voice floated up to her from the driveway, which sloped away beside the terraced garden. "Sorry, but I have a delivery for Natalie Granville?"

She maneuvered herself upright carefully, straddling the banister as if it were a marble horse. "I'm Natalie Granville," she said politely. Darn, this position felt kind of awkward—the man was looking at her very strangely.

And she couldn't quite decide what to do with the Jack Daniel's. She didn't want the bottle to fall off and break. She hugged it to her side, but that didn't seem very hospitable, so she held it out. "Want some?"

The man—more like a boy, really—flushed. "No thanks," he said quickly. He held out a very large, flat box. "I just need your signature for this."

Natalie stared at the package, which looked familiar. Not the sort of thing she received for the nursery business she ran from the greenhouse, though. Too flat. Too feminine, with its shiny white corners.

Hmm. She frowned. Jack Daniel's might taste wonderful, but it didn't exactly help you to think clearly. Had she been expecting a delivery?

"I— Can you sign? It's for you. It's from Apple Blossom Bridal."

Aw, shucks. Natalie's shoulders sagged. The wedding dress.

"I don't want it," she said, closing her eyes and waving the half-empty bottle vaguely. "Could you maybe just throw it away as you leave?"

"Um...not really." The kid sounded downright nervous now. "I'll leave it here, okay?" He set the box on the banister, moving in slow motion, as if he had discovered it contained nitroglycerine. "Just right here."

Natalie sighed and had another swallow of Jack Daniel's, which, taken straight like this, was muscular enough to etch its initials in her esophagus. She shivered, loving it.

"Okay." She wiped her mouth and smiled at him. "If you have to."

Tucking the bottle under her elbow, she reached over, signed his clipboard, and then began unwrapping the box.

"It's my wedding dress," she said conversationally. "Or I guess it's technically my *non*-wedding dress. Today is my non-wedding day, you see. I told them I didn't need the dress anymore, but they wouldn't give me my money back. Don't you think that's mean? I was only getting married in the first place because I needed money so badly, and now—"

But the deliveryman was already gone. Natalie looked at the empty yard around her, the acres and acres of once-beautiful gardens, and sighed. He hadn't even waited for a tip. Didn't he know Granvilles always tipped beautifully? That was why they were constantly broke. Well, that and the gambling. And the women.

And the house. Always the house. This crazy, crumbling, hungry monster of a house.

She unfolded her gown and shook the creases out of the soft white cotton lace. It was an okay dress— not great. She'd bought the cheapest one in town, although they'd all been absurdly expensive. That was the problem with living in a community of millionaires. Price tags came in only three sizes: Big, Bigger and Downright Astronomical.

She held the pearled bodice up against her chest, trying to imagine herself wearing it. She couldn't.

She climbed down off the banister and tried again, letting the layered skirt fall all the way to her ankles.

She dipped and swayed, trying to capture the dreamy, princessy feeling she used to get as a kid, when she'd rummage through the attic trunks, pretending to be a damsel in distress. She had shuffled to the attic window, antique lace dragging behind her, and surveyed her flowering kingdom.

In her ten-year-old imagination, she had always witnessed the galloping arrival of her handsome prince, her gallant knight, her brave cavalier. Or, her personal favorite, her Pair of Moors—a phrase she'd heard the grown-ups use, though she had no idea what it really meant. A few years later, when she'd learned what a "paramour" actually was, it had been a crushing disappointment.

Still pressing the gown to her chest, she moved back to the balcony and gazed down over the ruined Summer House grounds, all the way down to where the mountain ledge overlooked the tiny kingdom of Firefly Glen.

But no prince was fighting his thorny, perilous way up the mountain path. Nothing. Not so much as a speck on the horizon. Even the deliveryman's truck had long since disappeared.

She held out the wedding dress and scowled at it. It might be a five-hundred-dollar gown, but the darn thing didn't possess five pennies' worth of magic.

"Nat, are you there?" The answering machine was at it again. It was Stu. He'd called three times already. "Want me to come over and take you out to lunch?

I don't want you lying around feeling sorry for yourself.''

She stuck her tongue out at the machine, then knocked back another swig of Jack Daniel's. How dare he? She was enjoying her afternoon alone, that was all. Granvilles didn't feel sorry for themselves.

So this would have been her wedding day. So what? She'd called it off two weeks ago. She'd told Bart Beswick to take his rough hands, his wet kisses and his big bank account and get lost. She was a Granville, and Granvilles didn't sell themselves to the highest bidder.

Bart had been surprised, but not heartbroken. He'd wanted her name and her house, and he'd been pretty sure she would count herself lucky to get his money in return.

But he must have forgotten what exactly that grand old name he lusted after really meant. Granvilles chose freedom. Exhausted, overworked, penniless freedom. Granvilles might secretly hope that some-day, somehow, the long-overdue prince would still find his way up the mountain, but they certainly didn't stand around twiddling their thumbs, waiting for it to happen.

"Feeling sorry for myself? Ha!" She slurred the *s* in "sorry" just a little, but no one could hear her. In a minute or two, she was going to go inside, drink some strong coffee and get back to peeling the mil-dewed wallpaper from the Blue Bedroom. She was going to see if anyone had answered her "Handyman Wanted" ad.

She might even practice spackling, which was actually much harder than it looked.

Yep, she was going to get busy. In a minute or two. Or three.

But she sighed, dreading it. Her dress draped over her arm, she leaned her elbows on the pitted marble banister and stared down the long, empty slope of terraced gardens.

And then, because she was a Granville, she forgot about going inside. Because she was a Granville, she kept staring, dreaming, seeing flowers where no flowers had bloomed in ten neglected years.

And because she was a Granville, she closed her eyes. And as she drifted off, she could almost hear, over the birdsong and the breeze, the distant rumble of galloping hooves.

MATTHEW QUINN peeled the perforated address strip off the "Handyman Wanted" sign and studied it carefully before putting it in his pocket.

Summer House, it said in a frilly, but shaky, calligraphy—*717 Blue Pine Trail.* And a telephone number.

Summer House. Looking at the calligraphy, Matthew pictured the owner as an eighty-year-old, silver-haired widow who would make weak tea and cookies for the handyman, but would never invite him into the musty, cluttered twilight of her Victorian sanctum.

Especially not if she knew he'd just been released from prison.

She had tacked the notice to a community bulletin board outside Firefly Glen's red brick Town Hall. The other notices on the board described a pure Norman Rockwell weekend: the Firefly High Astronomy Club stargazing seminar, the fly fishermen's annual casting contest, the Firefly Girls' Saturday car-and-boat wash, the Congregational Church chicken barbecue and white elephant sale.

And, prominently displayed, a picture of a grinning Highland terrier that read simply, "Rob Roy ran away again. If you see him, call me. Theo."

Apparently everyone knew who Theo was. Everyone but Matthew.

He felt strangely paralyzed, standing at the high end of Main Street, gazing down at the row of quaint, expensive shops. Red-white-and-blue flags flew. Yellow flowers bloomed. Windows sparkled in the summer sun.

It suddenly looked like a stage set, as if it had been painted on cardboard and could be rolled away at will, revealing the familiar dirty, weed-ridden prison yard behind.

He wondered if he had been kidding himself. Could he really ever fit into a place like this again? He had picked this destination three years ago, during his first month in prison. He'd spent long, sleepless hours looking at a map of New York State, imagining where he would go when he was free again.

He hadn't even noticed Firefly Glen the first few times. It was that small. But once he'd seen it, it had become a kind of obsession. A symbol. You couldn't imagine anything ugly happening in a place called Firefly Glen. You just knew there would be clean air, warm smiles, wholesome food, simple pleasures—all those decent things they made you empty out of your pockets when they processed you into prison.

But now that he was here—now that it was not just a symbol, but a reality—he felt as out of place as a lump of coal in a cabbage patch, as his grandfather used to say. Maybe prison had changed him too much. Maybe he didn't believe in Norman Rockwell anymore.

"Hi, there. You look lost. Can I help?"

The voice was friendly, but, when Matthew looked up, he saw that the pleasant brown eyes of the stranger in front of him were careful and wary.

"I'm Harry Dunbar," the man said. And then he added, pointing his thumb toward his shiny gold star with a smile, "I'm the sheriff of Firefly Glen."

Suddenly Harry lurched, as another man came up behind, bumping into him rudely.

"Sorry, Harry," the second man said, grinning. He seemed to be holding a third man up by the collar. "Boxer here is having a little trouble with a straight line this morning."

"Of course he is," the sheriff grumbled. "It's Saturday, isn't it?"

The second man noticed Matthew, and looked over,

smiling. "Hi," he said, putting out his free hand, briefly letting go of the bleary-eyed fellow he'd been guiding. "I'm Parker Tremaine."

Was everyone in this town so compulsively friendly? Matthew, who had lived in New York City all his life, hadn't really expected this. He wondered if this Parker guy was a sheriff's deputy. Maybe he and the sheriff were both just trying to size Matthew up, trying to decide if he was a desirable or a threat to their idyllic little Rockwell paradise.

But as Matthew shook Parker's hand, he caught more details, and he realized Parker was no public servant. He was a vastly different type. He wore a very expensive business suit. The suit was a statement. Elegant, understated, educated.

Yes, he knew Parker's type. He had even *been* Parker's type, once upon a time. Just three years ago, he'd worn suits like that, walked like that, smiled out on his world with comfortable confidence like that. Three short years. But it might as well have been a million.

"Are you trying to ticket this poor guy for leaving his car in a no-parking space?" The man smiled over at Matthew. "Harry takes his job very seriously. But don't worry. I can get you off."

Matthew flinched and his gaze flicked to the curb instinctively. He hadn't noticed any signs. He didn't break the smallest of laws anymore. He didn't speed, didn't change lanes without signaling. He didn't even jaywalk.

But the sheriff was smiling crookedly. "Parker's being funny," he said to Matthew. "The restrictive paint's been worn off that space for years. Can't get maintenance to repaint, can't get the town council to cough up money for a sign." He turned back to the man in the suit. "Why don't you take Boxer on home, Parker? He could use a shower. He's getting a little ripe in this hot sun."

Parker frowned and turned. "Oh, hell. Where *is* Boxer?" He scanned the area quickly, and then his gaze settled on the ground near the door to the sheriff's department. "Great. He's passed out again."

He sighed, then turned back and smiled at Matthew. "Welcome to Firefly Glen. Never a dull moment. I'm the local lawyer, and that guy on the ground over there is just one of our many beloved eccentric millionaires."

Matthew glanced at the heap of rumpled clothes propped up against the wall of the building. "Boxer" had begun to hum softly, leading an imaginary band with one finger. The guy sure didn't look like a millionaire. He had a black eye, a bad haircut, and he did, indeed, stink.

"Well, get him out of here, or I'm going to lock him up again." Sheriff Harry swiveled back to Matthew and his guarded look returned. "So, was I right? Are you lost? Anything I can help you with?"

Matthew considered asking him for directions to Blue Pine Trail, but at the last minute he decided against it. The two men seemed friendly enough, but in prison you didn't tell anyone anything, just on principle. Apparently the habit was going to cling to him, the same way the odor of cheap stew and strong prison bleach seemed to cling to the inside of his nose.

"No, thanks," he said, forcing himself to look Harry Dunbar straight in the eye. If he was going to stay here for the summer, he might as well make friends with the locals.

And then it hit him—his decision had been made. He *was* going to stay, assuming he could get a job. This wasn't some imaginary Oz with streets of gold, some enchanted Eden from which people like him had been forever banished. It was just a rather ordinary small town. It had grumpy sheriffs, Friday night drunks, inefficient elected officials, slick lawyers and lost dogs, just like hundreds of small towns across New York State.

And its houses needed repair. Matthew knew how to do that. He'd spent every summer during college with a hammer in his hands, and he could spend this one the same way.

"I was just having a look around." He steadied his gaze. "I'm here for the summer."

The sheriff frowned, as if the explanation didn't quite satisfy him, but suddenly Parker Tremaine let out a low curse.

"Harry, look at this," Parker said, staring at the bulletin board. "I warned Natalie not to post her address on these ads, and she's done it anyway."

Matthew wondered what the lawyer would say if he knew one of those address slips was even now tucked away in Matthew's pocket.

"She did?" The sheriff stalked over and read the notice. Then, with a grumble, he ripped it off the board and crumpled it in his fist. "Hell, now I'll have to go all over town tearing the darn things down. I tell you, Parker, Granvilles have always been too na-ive to live, and Natalie Granville is the worst of the lot."

A sudden commotion erupted from the direction of Boxer's corner. "Natalie Granville is a hell of a sweet woman, and I'll kick the ass of anyone who says she's not," the old man said, struggling to his feet. He glared at the sheriff. "In fact, I think I'll kick your ass anyhow, Dunbar, just for saying her name in that tone of voice."

"Parker—" the sheriff began tightly.

"I know, I know. I'll get him out of here. Just give me a hand."

And while the two civilized young professionals were wrestling the crusty old drunk to his feet, Mat-thew seized his chance.

No one saw him climb into his car and drive away. No one asked where he was going, and he wouldn't have told them if they had.

Because he was going to find Natalie Granville. He was going to tell her the truth about himself, and he was going to ask her for a job. Maybe she was just naive enough to believe in things like fair play and second chances—concepts he was pretty sure the suspicious sheriff would consider foolish.

Matthew pressed harder on the gas, overcome by a sudden urgency. Maybe this was why he had chosen Firefly Glen. Silver haired and sweet, the despair of cynical sheriffs yet beloved by pugilistic drunks, Natalie Granville just might be the answer to prayers Matthew hadn't even realized he was praying.

CHAPTER TWO

SUMMER HOUSE, the understated brass plaque embedded in the tall stone pillar said. But the plaque lied.

Summer House wasn't a house. It was an Italian villa, a sumptuous estate fit for a decadent prince. A baroque fantasy of pink marble and red terra-cotta and gray *pietra serena* stone. An orgy of arches and ornamentation, loggias and sculptures and formal staircases descending into shadowy gardens.

Matthew left his car by the gate and walked up the long driveway, stunned. Summer House didn't belong in Upstate New York, tucked into the dense birch and hemlock woods of the Adirondack Mountains. It belonged in the rolling hills of seventeenth century Italy, where lemon trees grew in huge clay pots, and silvery olive trees twinkled in the Tuscan sun.

And yet here it stood.

It was slightly crazy.

It was extremely beautiful.

And it was, quite literally, falling apart.

Matthew, who had finally reached the front door, was hardly an expert, but decay cried out even to the untrained eye. Half a dozen windows on both floors were cracked and taped. The stone walls were pitted in places, crumbling away to dust in others. Many of the statues had lost noses and fingers and other protruding body parts.

And Nature, which obviously had once been banished from these formal Italian gardens by an army of landscapers, was marching boldly back, reclaiming its territory inch by inch.

No one answered the bell. In fact, Matthew couldn't be sure the bell even worked. He reached up to use the ornate brass knocker, but as he touched it the thing swung free at one end, a loose screw rattling to the ground.

Good Lord. He found the screw and managed to reattach it temporarily, although the threads were nearly stripped. He backed up, and his foot landed on a small sliver of broken glass. As he bent to retrieve the pieces, he balanced himself on a terra-cotta finial, which rocked on its base, threatening to topple.

He caught it somehow and righted it, but he glanced around with a deepening doubt. This place was a minefield of disrepair, and it was way out of his league.

Natalie Granville might be the answer to his prayers, but he definitely wasn't the answer to hers. She didn't need a handyman. She needed a miracle.

He moved back down the steps, ready to leave, almost glad that no one had answered the door. He'd just get back in his car and—

But suddenly he heard a sound. A soft, fairylike singing that came from around the east side of the house. The sweet, elderly spinster, the naive Natalie, perhaps?

Curious in spite of himself, he followed the sound, crunching across broken stones with thick weeds growing in the cracks, ignoring the staring eyes of a dozen armless statues that lined the path like wounded soldiers in the war against decay.

As he approached the corner of the house, he caught a glimpse of something soft and white fluttering in the breeze. What was it? It looked like a long, white gauzy stream of lace. He squinted, confused. It looked like a ghostly wedding veil.

He moved closer. It *was* a wedding veil. A woman stood at the end of a wide back terrace, and she wore a long white wedding dress, her head crowned with the beautiful, flowing, fluttering lace.

But she wasn't a living, breathing woman. She was a stiffly silent, white marble statue.

Matthew blinked. And as he watched, the soft singing began again. Something weird and disbelieving skimmed across his nerve endings. He was the last man on earth to entertain nonsensical notions. Still, he couldn't have stopped himself then if a Minotaur had barred the way.

His gaze fixed on the marble bride, he rounded the corner.

And then, finally, he saw the other woman. The young, blond, bikini-clad beauty who was walking the balustrade like a tightrope, singing merrily to herself as she put one bare foot in front of the other.

Now that he was close enough, he could tell she had a lovely voice, but her words were badly slurred, and he noticed that she clutched a bottle of Jack Daniel's in one hand, holding it out as if for balance.

The balustrade was wide—at least eighteen inches—but it was slick in spots with mildew. And besides, the woman was clearly drunk. He saw her weave slightly, and he began to move fast. She held on for a few wobbling seconds, just long enough for him to reach the balcony.

The bottle fell first, crashing to the terrace and smashing into a hundred pieces. But, two seconds later, the woman fell the other way, and landed neatly in Matthew's arms.

For a couple of seconds she was utterly silent, her mouth open as she stared, wide-eyed, in shock and breathless disbelief. She instinctively wrapped her arms around his neck, and her face was so close to his that he could count the tiny, pale freckles scattered across the bridge of her nose.

Six.

She was ridiculously light in his arms. She probably wasn't more than five-four, maybe one-ten? She had a mass of untamed blond hair that fell in soft curls over his arm. Her skin was slippery and warm, and it smelled of coconut oil.

After a couple of seconds, he began to register just how very little she was wearing. He decided he ought to set her down, but her arms were still wrapped around his neck, so it was awkward.

Finally she recovered her breath.

"Gosh," she said. "It's a good thing you caught me, isn't it?"

He smiled. "Yes."

"I could have broken something. A leg. An arm." Her eyes widened even more. "I could have broken my neck, just the way my grandfather always used to say I would."

"Yes," he agreed, though privately he doubted it. The fall was only a couple of feet, and she was so drunk she probably would have landed limply and safely on the grass.

"So I guess it's a very good thing you were here."

"I guess so."

She nodded sagely, as if they'd solved something important. With a soft sigh, she dropped her head comfortably against his chest.

And jerked it right back up.

"Hey, wait a minute," she said, concentrating so hard her brow wrinkled. "Why *were* you here?"

He debated with himself. Since he'd changed his mind about applying for the handyman job, he probably shouldn't even mention it. On the other hand, he'd hate for her to think he was just some weirdo prowling around.

He looked into her slightly unfocused eyes. They had swirls of gold in the brown, like melted butterscotch being stirred into chocolate syrup. She was very young, very gorgeous, and he was suddenly aware of the warm thrust of her breasts against his chest.

He cleared his throat. "Do you think you're steady enough to stand up on your own?"

"Oh. Sure." She helped extricate herself, and she did pretty well, except that she had to take two steps before she found her balance. She frowned, as if trying to hang on to her train of thought. "You were going to tell me—"

"Someone put up an ad for a handyman," he said, deciding that honesty was his best course. The grandfather she'd mentioned probably took a dim view of trespassers. "I was thinking of applying."

"Really?" She tilted her head. "You don't look like a handyman," she said. Then she flushed and placed her palm against her forehead. "Oh, that was dumb, wasn't it? I mean, there isn't any particular *way* handymen look, is there? It's just that you're so…"

She bit her lower lip as she studied him, apparently searching for the telling detail. "I know. It's because you smell so good. Darryl smelled like when you open the refrigerator, and you can just tell you've left the hamburger in there way too long." She wrinkled her nose. "You know that smell?"

He couldn't help chuckling. "Darryl was a handyman, I take it?"

"The last one. I had to let him go. I couldn't bear to tell him about the hamburger smell, so I told him I was going to finish the work myself." She sighed, her gaze taking in the mess around her. "I don't think he believed me."

Matthew's mind suddenly skidded, trying to accept the implications of her pronoun choices. "I" had to let him go, she'd said. "I" was going to finish the work. Good God. Was it possible that this young, beautiful woman was Natalie Granville? Could this fragile slip of femininity really be the owner of this weird mansion, custodian of all this decrepit glory?

Surely not. She didn't look much older than a coed, a completely normal twenty-something, celebrating summer break by sunbathing and getting looped.

"Is this your house?"

She nodded. "Unfortunately, yes. I'm Natalie Granville, the last of the Granvilles, and the proud owner of every crumbling stone you see. Sorry about falling into your arms." She grinned. "But you certainly proved that you're a very handy man. Thanks."

"My pleasure." He held out his hand. "I'm Matthew Quinn."

"Hello, Matthew Quinn. You're hired."

His first thought was that the sheriff had been right. Natalie Granville was too naive to live. Hired? She didn't have any idea who Matthew was. She hadn't asked a single question, requested a single reference. She didn't even know if he could tell a pair of needle-nose pliers from a monkey wrench. For all she knew he could be jack-of-no-trades. Or even Jack the Ripper.

But his second thought was that, absurdly, he

wished he could say yes. There was something inexplicably appealing about her, and it wasn't just how great she looked in that bikini.

"I'm sorry," he said. "But I had already decided not to apply for the job. I'm afraid it's a little out of my league."

She frowned. "Oh, no, don't say that! You're perfect for it."

"No, really. I couldn't tell, from the flyer, how extensive your needs were. I'm okay at the little stuff—painting, patching drywall, replacing gutters, fixing a leaky drain, stuff like that. But this—"

"I've got plenty of leaky drains," she put in desperately. But then, catching his raised eyebrow, she sighed. "And a leaky roof. And a leaky foundation. And of course the water all leaked out of the pool years ago."

He looked at her heart-shaped face, with the sprinkle of freckles she probably despised standing out against her pale skin. She looked absolutely forlorn.

"I'm sorry," he said. "I really do wish I could help."

"You can! I'm not expecting anyone to tackle everything. Just do what you can. I'll pay whatever you ask." She bit her lower lip, catching herself. "Well, I guess I can't really promise that, because as you may have noticed this house just gobbles money. But I'll pay what I can, and you can live in the pool house for free, and I'll cook the meals—"

She stopped herself again. "Unless you like to do

your own cooking. I'd let you use the kitchen, of course, and I'd buy the groceries, so even if I couldn't pay you a whole lot in salary it would still be a good deal, and you—''

''It's not the money, Natalie,'' he said. It seemed silly to call her Ms. Granville when his fingers were still slick from holding her oiled body. ''It's that I don't have the necessary skills to do this job well.''

''I think you do. Please, Matthew.'' She squeezed her hands together. She suddenly looked very pale. ''Please say yes.''

He was amazed to discover how difficult it was to resist her. Her artless chatter and sweet smiles might merely be the result of the booze, but he didn't really believe it. He thought he could still recognize honest-to-God goodness when he saw it.

Even in his old life, back before prison, when he had been making millions in the stock market, both for himself and for a lot of other rich people, innocence had been pretty rare. He had hobnobbed with dazzling genius and indescribable beauty. He had shaken hands with raw ambition and insatiable greed. He had kissed the sleek cheeks of glamour and power and sex.

But he hadn't ever met anyone as open and guileless as Natalie Granville.

Of course, he reminded himself wryly, she was very drunk. She might be a lot more cynical when she was sober. She probably had a ten-page application for the handyman inside, requiring everything from his blood type to his shoe size.

Or she might be just plain crazy. After all, somebody had dressed that statue up in a wedding gown.

"You know," he said gently, "smelling good doesn't exactly qualify me to reroof an Italian villa."

"I know, but still." She put one hand against her heart earnestly. "I know it sounds crazy, but I know it's the right thing. I need you here. It's just a feeling I have."

A feeling that probably had much more to do with the Jack Daniel's than it did with Matthew himself. But he refrained from saying so. She had begun to look a little green around the edges, and he thought what she needed most of all might be a couple of aspirin and a long nap. When she woke up, she probably wouldn't even remember dancing on the balustrade…or begging a total stranger to live in the pool house and fix her leaky drains.

The sound of a sports car rumbling up the back driveway interrupted whatever she'd been going to say next. She looked over at the long-nosed car, a shiny model of British racing green that Matthew recognized as costing as much as a small house.

"Damnation." She groaned. "I told him not to come. Well, I didn't exactly tell him, but I didn't answer when he called, and surely he ought to know—"

"Nat?" A long, lean young man unfolded himself from the car and smiled over at Natalie, pointedly ignoring Matthew. He was dressed in the official rich young stud uniform of khakis, polo shirt and boat shoes. "I called three times, honey. But you didn't pick up."

"That's because I was busy interviewing my new handyman," she said, drawing herself erect and obviously trying to sound haughty and businesslike. The effect was spoiled somewhat by her saying "thatsh" instead of "that's" and "hannyman" instead of "handyman." And of course the wild hair and the bikini weren't exactly her most professional look.

The man took it all in. He was clearly trying to size up the situation, and finding himself unable to make the pieces fit. He looked over at Matthew narrowly. "Handyman?"

"Yes," Natalie said, working hard to get the *s* right. She tugged self-consciously at her bikini pants, trying to cover her hipbone, but merely succeeding in exposing an extra inch of thigh in the process. "Matthew, meet Stuart Leith, city councilman for Firefly Glen. Stuart, Matthew Quinn."

"Hello." Stuart's voice was flat. "Quinn, did you say? And you want to be Natalie's new handyman?" It was the same tone he would have used to say, "You want to fly to the moon on a bumblebee's back?"

For a minute, Matthew considered saying yes, just because he'd like to wipe the smug look from Stuart the Stud's face. God, had he ever looked that self-satisfied? He should have spent three years in prison for that alone.

But he couldn't play macho games right now. It wouldn't be fair to Natalie. "Actually, no," he said, forcing himself to smile politely. "I had thought of applying, but when I got here I could see I'm not quite right for the job."

"Matthew," Natalie began plaintively. A few beads of sweat had formed on her brow. She was going to be sick. He knew the signs.

"I see," Stuart said firmly, closing the door to his car carefully and coming around to stand by Natalie. "So. You were probably just about to leave, then, weren't you? Don't let me hold you up."

Natalie made a low sound of distress. "Oh, dear. I'm afraid I don't feel very good."

"Come on, honey, I'll take you inside." Stuart aimed steady eyes at Matthew. "You can find your way back to the gate, can't you?"

Matthew nodded. "Be careful," he said. "There's some broken glass on the patio."

"Thanks. I'll take care of it." Stuart bent over Natalie. "What on earth has been going on here, honey?"

"Matthew."

"Bye, Natalie," he said quietly as Stuart began to lead her away.

She groaned, but whether it was because he was leaving, or because the Jack Daniel's had finally staged its inevitable revolt in her stomach, he couldn't tell. He had already turned his back on them and was heading around to the front of the house where he'd left his car.

Goodbye, and good riddance. He had plenty of trouble in his life right now. He didn't need to take on more. And no question the lovely Natalie Granville, however adorable, was capital *T* trouble. Her crumbling mansion was trouble, her empty bottle of Jack Daniel's before lunchtime was trouble, her statue wearing a wedding dress was trouble. Even her snooty, smothering boyfriend was trouble.

Matthew slammed the car door, turned the key and shoved the gearshift into drive. He should be glad to go, glad to escape from this moldering nuthouse. What a pair! A bone-deep snob and a ditzy, tipsy, possibly crazy Pollyanna.

But maybe he was crazy, too. Because instead of feeling relieved as he watched Summer House grow smaller and smaller in his rearview mirror, he felt an unmistakable, inexplicable pinch of real regret.

SUZIE STRICKLAND SAT in the Summer House driveway for two hours that Saturday afternoon, waiting for Stuart Leith to leave.

She wanted to talk to Natalie.

And she wanted to do it alone. But she couldn't wait forever. She had summer school Monday, and she had a ton of homework.

How long could that preppy cretin hang around, anyhow? Natalie couldn't really enjoy his company, could she? He was a double-barreled knuckle-dragger, whereas Natalie was actually kind of cool.

Suzie's fingers instinctively strayed to her eyebrow, accustomed to fiddling with the little gold ring when she was nervous or irritable or worried. But the ring wasn't there. The piercing had become infected last week, and she had to wait for it to heal.

It was like a conspiracy. She needed to write an essay to go with her college application, and if she expected to have a shot at an art scholarship it would have to be good as hell, really creative. But how was she supposed to be creative when so many things were driving her crazy?

And here came one more. The lawn mower's rumble had been growing louder for the past half an hour. Mike Frome, another preppy cretin, was some kind of distant cousin of Natalie's, and he was spending the summer working on the estate.

She slouched down in the seat, but he saw her anyway. He cut off the mower and came sauntering over, wiping his face with his shirt just so he could show off his buffed-up abs.

"Hey, Suzi-freaka," he said, in that superior, sarcastic way he had. He'd started calling her that in middle school, when she had worn bell-bottoms and peace signs. He, of course, wouldn't be caught dead in anything that hadn't already received the Boring Young Conservatives Seal of Approval.

His crowd and her crowd had hated each other since puberty. She had been pretty pissed at fate when, one day last year, while shooting pictures of the basketball team for the school paper, she had discovered that he had suddenly become really cute.

And she meant *really* cute.

She sat up, acting surprised, pretending she hadn't noticed his arrival. "Well, if it isn't Mindless Mike. What are you doing here?"

"I work here." He put his elbow on the hood of her car and leaned down, smiling in at her. He was all sweaty, but he looked cute sweaty, which he undoubtedly already knew. "What are *you* doing here?"

"I work here, too, moron." Oh, brother. She shouldn't have said that. She hadn't even asked Natalie about it yet. But he always acted so darn superior, as if his money and his looks and his athletic ability guaranteed him entrée anywhere, while poor little Suzie Strickland, whose parents actually worked for a living, had to prove that she had the right to breathe the same air.

"Oh, yeah?" He looked curious. "What do you do? Are you like the maid or something?"

He was close enough that she could have reached out and punched him. But he would have had a field day with that, telling everyone at school how crazy Suzi-freaka had gone postal on him.

"No," she said icily. "As a matter of fact, I'm going to be painting a trompe l'oeil in the Summer House library." She smiled a Cheshire cat smile. "Not that you'd have any clue what a 'trompe l'oeil' actually is."

Mike looked a shade less confident. "The hell I don't. I was in your art history class last year, remember? It's a—" he wiped his face again "—a thing on the wall."

She snorted. "Yeah. Right. It's a thing on the wall. What did you get in art history class, anyway? A D minus?"

He rolled his eyes. "You know what, Suzi-freaka? I don't remember what I got. Some of us have more in our lives than obsessing about making the honor roll."

"Well, that's fortunate. Considering you haven't got a snowball's chance in hell of ever making the honor roll."

"Whatever." Mike yawned extravagantly and pretended to scan the sky with a professional eye. "I'd better get back to work before the rain comes in. I've got a hot date tonight." He raised the pitch of his voice, imitating her. "Not that you'd have a clue what a 'hot date' actually is."

Okay, now she really was going to punch him.

"The hell I don't," she countered. "It's a double-D cup with a single-digit IQ, in the back seat of your daddy's Land Rover." She gave him a dirty look. "Although frankly I would have thought you'd had your fill of all that with Justine Millner."

Oh, hell. She shouldn't have said that. He had told her about the Justine Millner problem in confidence, one night when, to their total shock, they had ended up at the same party. She had sworn never to mention it again.

But what was she supposed to do? Justine was Mike Frome's only weak spot, whereas Suzie herself had hundreds, and he knew how to jab an insult into any of them at will.

"You know what you are, Suzi-freaka?" Mike palmed the hood of her car hard in a sardonic good-bye slap. "You're some kind of serious bitch."

She watched him lope away. *Bitch.* He'd never called her that before. Well, so what? Did he really think she cared what he called her? Did he really think she gave a flying flip?

She turned the key in the ignition and started the car. That horrible Stuart Leith wasn't going anywhere. Apparently everyone on the face of the earth was having hot dates on this summer Saturday night—everyone but her.

Not that she cared. She didn't care one bit. They were mindless animals, and she was an artist.

But for the first time in her entire life, that word didn't bring any magical comfort. For the first time in her life, she would have gladly traded places with Justine Millner, or any other bimbo with a double-D cup and a reservation for two in the back of Mike Frome's father's SUV.

CHAPTER THREE

NATALIE WAS GOING TO DIE.

At least that's what she'd been hoping since she woke up this morning, and she figured she had a pretty good chance. If this screaming headache and roiling nausea didn't get her, surely the humiliation would.

But in the meantime, she had to deliver these plants to Theo. If by some awful chance she lived, she'd still have to pay the electricity bill. And the water bill. And the property taxes. And the insurance. And, and, and…

So she kept driving, even though the sun was stabbing swords of light into her eyeballs and when she hit a bump her skull almost burst from the pain.

She double-parked in front of the Candlelight Café, Theo's diner on Main Street. She glanced up toward the sheriff's office, hoping Harry was out on call. He was such a stickler about things like double parking. And she couldn't afford another ticket. She hadn't paid her last two yet.

Theodosia Burke, the seventy-four-year-old tyrannical owner of the café, must have been watching for Natalie's car. Within a very few seconds, the wiry little woman had joined Natalie at the back of the tiny Honda Civic, where the hatch had been lifted to reveal six lush rabbit's foot ferns in hanging baskets.

Though grateful for the help, Natalie was surprised that Theo had been willing to leave her customers. She ran her little diner like a five-star gourmet restaurant.

"Good morning," Theo screamed.

The words echoed in Natalie's brain like thunder. She tried not to wince, but she couldn't help putting a protective hand to her forehead to try to keep her brain from exploding.

"Morning," she whispered with her eyes shut.

"Well, I'll be darned." Theo paused, a hanging basket in each hand. "It's true, isn't it? I thought that idiot Leith was lying. What's the matter with you, girl? Don't you know why Granvilles don't drink? They can't hold their liquor worth squat."

Natalie tried to smile, but she had the feeling it looked more like a grimace. "Yes, ma'am," she said meekly. "I can confirm that."

"Idiot young people," Theo complained. "Always have to learn everything the hard way."

"Yes, ma'am." Natalie wasn't up to arguing. The sun was beating down on her, and she'd begun to perspire, which, besides being quite disagreeable, made her feel a little sick.

Theo chuckled thoughtfully. "Stu told me about the wedding dress. Sure wish I could have seen that."

Natalie didn't join in the chuckle, so Theo finally

subsided. "I guess yesterday was a little rough, huh? I hope you weren't feeling too sorry for yourself. That never did anyone a bit of good, you know."

Natalie started to protest that Granvilles didn't indulge in self-pity, but it wasn't strictly true. She was feeling fairly darn sorry for herself this morning. But not over Bart Beswick and the non-wedding day.

"Darn it," she began rather vehemently. But that was a mistake. Her head ringing, she took a deep breath and started over in a fierce whisper. "Why does everyone keep forgetting I was the one who called off this wedding? They all treat me like some pitiful jilted bride who is half dying of a broken heart."

Theo laughed out loud. "They don't think you're pitiful, girl. They think you're crazy. You just passed up the chance to marry about twenty million bucks. Which, as we all know, you could definitely use."

"But I didn't love him. And he didn't love me, not really."

"Yeah, I know. But most of the folks around here don't see what love's got to do with twenty million dollars."

Natalie sighed and gathered two baskets in each hand, shoving the hatchback shut with her elbow.

"Well, if they don't know, I can't explain it to them." She nodded toward the café. "Let's get these inside. Your customers are probably wondering where you are."

When she climbed the first step, though, she realized that Theo was lagging behind. "Come on, Theo." Her sunglasses were crawling down on her nose. She tilted her head back, trying to make them slide into place. She couldn't stand the nuclear glare of the sun. "These plants are kind of heavy, you know."

"I know. But before we go in, I probably should tell you—"

"What?"

"We've got a new customer. New in town, I mean. Good-looking guy. He's in there now."

Natalie groaned. Theo was the Glen's most energetic matchmaker. "Theo, I'm *not* in the market for a new man yet. Especially not today. Look at me. My jeans are dirty, my head is splitting, and I'm about one wrong move from either puking or fainting. I don't care how handsome he is. Please, please, please don't introduce me to him."

Theo looked strangely tongue-tied—a first for the crusty old woman. She fiddled with the ferns, untangling a couple of soft fronds, not looking at Natalie.

"I don't think I have to," she said. "I think you've already met him."

"I have?" Natalie glanced toward the glossy red door, which was flanked by tubs full of bright yellow marigolds supplied by Natalie's own nursery. "When?"

Theo looked up. "Well…tell me, girl. How much do you actually remember about yesterday?"

"I—" Natalie started. "I remember everything," she whispered.

"Everything?"

"Every embarrassing minute of it. Up to and including—" She swallowed. "Oh, no."

Theo nodded sympathetically. "Oh, yes. Up to and including the handsome Matthew Quinn."

TEN MINUTES LATER, Natalie was still trying to calm herself down with a mental barrage of reassurances.

It wasn't really such a disaster, was it? Actually, this made her day a whole lot easier. She had planned to try to track Matthew Quinn down sometime this afternoon anyhow.

It was just that she had hoped to wait a few hours, until her eyes weren't quite so bloodshot. She had wanted one more shower, to banish any lingering whiff of stale liquor...or worse.

She had planned to put on her navy-blue suit, and panty hose, and maybe even makeup. She had intended to tightly French-braid her unruly hair. She had desperately wanted to look professional, sober and sane—well, as sane as any Granville ever could.

Instead, she was going to have to meet him like this. In her working jeans, with her head made of glass and her stomach made of Slinky springs.

Oh heck. Maybe it was for the best. This was how she really looked. If she couldn't persuade Matthew Quinn to help her without the aid of a suit and panty hose, maybe he wasn't the perfect man after all.

He was sitting in the back, reading the newspaper. Probably looking at the classified ads, she thought. Hunting for a job, no doubt, now that he'd decided he didn't want the one she was offering.

She continued hanging the ferns on the hooks above the front windows. She tried not to look at him too much—it would be bad for her concentration. But she was relieved to see that he looked the same, even now that she wasn't viewing him through the rosy fumes of an entire bottle of Jack Daniel's.

He was very tall, well over six feet. Maybe a touch too thin, as if no one fed him right, but still pleasantly powerful, especially those broad, squared-off shoulders.

Healthy, thick brown hair, with a touch of wave that he didn't bother to subdue. She'd be willing to bet he didn't own a single can of mousse or hair spray. Call her old fashioned, but she hated a guy who used more hair products than she did. Which, in her case, amounted to one generic brand of combination shampoo and conditioner and a brush. Serious vanity required more time—and more money—than she could spare.

She couldn't see his eyes from here. But she remembered them. Hazel eyes, with dark, thick lashes. Gorgeous eyes, but more than that. Smart eyes. And best of all, kind eyes.

She didn't pay much attention to men's clothes— or women's either, for that matter—but she sensed that he hadn't spent a lot of money on his jeans and plain white cotton shirt. Some of the pinup boys around here could take lessons. They spent obscene amounts on their designer outfits, and they didn't look half as good as Matthew Quinn.

Of course he had the advantage of being naturally sexy as all get-out. She had dreamed about him off and on last night, and, with the whiskey pretty much acting like chloroform on her inhibitions, it had been a fairly X-rated evening.

Not that she'd ever in a million years tell him about that. It would scare him off for sure. And she didn't intend to act on her fantasies. She was looking for a handyman, not a boyfriend. It was only important because it proved that he truly was special. She didn't have X-rated dreams very often, which she now realized was rather a shame.

At that moment he glanced up. He seemed to be looking for a waitress, but, even though she was high on a chair hanging the last fern, he spotted her.

For a few long seconds he waited, as if he weren't sure whether it was polite to admit yesterday had ever happened. So, to put the question to rest, she smiled. And then, slowly, he smiled back.

Gosh. She nearly fell off her chair when her knees threatened to go soft on her. She didn't want to act like a gushing teenage groupie or anything, but he had a wonderful, summery smile. It was full of sunlight and warmth.

Oh, yes. Drunk or not, her instincts had been so right yesterday. This man *was* special. He was perfect.

And she wasn't leaving the Candlelight Café until he agreed to come and work for her.

She climbed down carefully, whisking debris from the front of her jeans. She swiped at her hair, hoping she could dislodge any small green flecks of fern from her curls. And then she made her way to his table.

"Hi," she said, suddenly aware that every woman should have her own personal scriptwriter. There must be something witty and sophisticated she could say to sweep them past this awkward moment. But her mind remained a stubborn, gawky blank. "How are you?"

"Great," he said, still smiling. He put the newspaper politely down, giving her his full attention. "How about you?"

He didn't put any particular emphasis on the question, but she flushed anyhow.

"I feel absolutely gruesome," she said. Why not be honest? She had a strong feeling that they could be friends, that they would work well together, but not if she started out with a phony facade. "And terribly embarrassed. I wanted to apologize for yesterday. You were wonderful. A real knight in shining armor. And I was a complete mess. Absolutely disgusting. I don't even think I thanked you properly for saving my life."

He shook his head. "You were cute and completely charming, not at all disgusting. And you thanked me several times, even though your life was never in the least bit of danger."

He drank some coffee, raising his eyebrows over the rim. "Actually," he said, "I got the idea that maybe the rougher stages were yet to come. Maybe your friend Stuart got the worst of it?"

She caught herself smiling. "I'm afraid he might have." She sighed. "I don't remember all of it, but I'm pretty sure I'm going to have to buy him a new pair of shoes."

"Uh-oh." But Matthew's eyes were sparkling, and she could tell he found the whole episode more amusing than appalling. That was a good sign. At least he wasn't one of those stuffy prigs who put women on pedestals and lost interest if they ever got sick or dirty or tired or bitchy. Or drunk.

Not that she got drunk very often. Yesterday was her first time ever, and it would probably be the last. But in the nursery business you were always dirty. And sometimes, not often, she did catch herself being a little bit bitchy.

Theo appeared at the table. She put a plate of banana-walnut pancakes in front of Matthew, and a large fresh orange juice in front of Natalie.

"I didn't order anything," Natalie said, glancing over at her meaningfully.

"I know you didn't." Theo crossed her arms. "But you need vitamin C for that hangover." She turned to Matthew. "And you could use two or three more pounds of meat on those bones. So no arguments from either of you. Just eat up."

Natalie lifted her glass with a resigned sigh. "You

might as well take a bite," she told Matthew. "Theo won't budge from that spot until she gets her way."

Matthew smiled suddenly. "You're Theo?"

Even the notoriously immune older woman melted a little under the wattage of that smile. She unfolded her arms. "Theodosia Burke. I own the café."

"I'm delighted to meet you," Matthew said. "I was sorry to see the flyer about your dog. Have you found him yet?"

"No, not yet." Obviously pleased by Matthew's concern, she dug in her crisp white apron and pulled out an extra copy of the picture. "Here. If you'd keep your eyes peeled for him, I'd appreciate it. The fool animal is going deaf. No telling what trouble he might get into."

Matthew took the flyer. "I'll be glad to," he said. "I know you must be worried."

"Yes. Well. Eat up." Taking Matthew's check, Theo slipped it into her apron pocket. "Breakfast's on the house," she said gruffly.

She started to move on to the next table, but suddenly she turned back and gave Natalie a steady look. "And just for the record, I don't think you're having a Granville moment, whatever Stuart Leith says. I think your judgment is just fine on this one."

Natalie flushed, hoping Matthew couldn't decode that little message. For as long as she could remember, Glenners had described her family's idiosyncrasies as "Granville moments." When her grandfather had bought a pair of giraffes to lope across the Summer House lawns, it had been a "Granville moment." The helicopter pad, the dance-hall strumpet installed as the children's governess, the bootleg whiskey fermenting in the bathtub, all historic Granville moments.

She had grown up on the story of her great-great-grandfather, who had declared war on the city of Firefly Glen and established a cannon on the mountain ledge overlooking the town. Apparently the Glenners had largely ignored it, observing placidly that the old man was clearly having a "Granville moment."

She studied Matthew's face to see what he thought of Theo's cryptic parting comment. But she couldn't quite read the expression. She didn't know him well enough, not yet. He merely seemed to be enjoying his pancakes.

Okay, it was now or never. She took a big gulp of the orange juice and launched her attack.

"Anyhow, I did want to apologize. But I also wanted to see if there's any way I can talk you into accepting the handyman position."

She saw him look up and prepare to speak, but she rushed on, hoping she could forestall another refusal. "I know it probably seemed like the job from hell yesterday, what with me acting so goofy and the house being such a mess. But I want you to know that I'm really not a lush. In fact, I don't drink at all. Granvilles never drink. They have no head for alcohol whatsoever."

He smiled. "Is that so?"

"Absolutely. So you don't need to worry that I'll be forever falling off things and landing in your arms." She swallowed, aware that this wasn't coming out quite right. "And about the house. It is pretty awful, that's obvious. But I wouldn't expect any major repairs. I can't afford anything major right now anyhow. All I can afford is some routine maintenance. Just a bandage over the wound."

"Natalie, I do appreciate the offer, but—"

"Please." She wrapped her hands around her glass hard. "Please don't say no until you've heard me out. I live out there all alone. It's a huge place, a huge responsibility. New problems pop up every day. I can do some of it. I do a lot, actually. I have for years. But right now I need help."

"Natalie, I'm really not your man. I'm not here for the long haul. I'm only in Firefly Glen for the summer, and—"

"That's okay. I'm not asking you to commit long-term. But couldn't you try it for a couple of weeks? I'll pay you a month in advance. And if you don't like it, or if you still feel it's a mistake, you can leave, no questions asked. The salary is low, but the pool-house apartment is included, and meals, too."

He was looking at her sadly, as if he hated to disappoint her. But he had stopped trying to inject a firm no into her monologue, so that had to be a good sign.

"It wasn't just the liquor talking yesterday," she said, gathering courage. He was tempted, she could tell. "I really think we could get along well together. I think we'd make a great team."

"Natalie. You don't even know me. You don't know the first thing about my skills. What if I can't even hammer a nail straight?"

"Nonsense." She shook her head. "You're not clumsy. You have strong, graceful hands, and you know how to use them."

"What if I'm weak—or lazy?"

"Give me a break. With those muscles? You forget, I know exactly how strong you are. Strong enough to catch a falling woman in midair and never miss a beat."

He smiled, but his expression sobered almost instantly. "Then what about my character? You're inviting me to live in your home without any proof I'm not a liar or a thief or a crazed serial killer. What about references? What about my past?"

"I'll call your references if you want me to. But I make my best decisions when I simply follow my instincts. I can't help it. My grandfather used to say 'Granvilles always go with their gut' and he was right. In fact, the only really bad choices I've ever made were when I ignored my instincts."

She thought about Bart. She'd known from the start that a loveless marriage was a terrible idea. But she'd allowed other people to persuade her that twenty million dollars could be awfully darn lovable. Even her grandfather, on his deathbed, had recommended Bart as the answer.

But in her heart she'd known all along it would be a disaster. Breaking the engagement was the best decision she'd ever made.

Until this one.

Matthew seemed lost in his own thoughts, too. He stared at her for a long moment, rotating his spoon slowly through his fingers, like a card player tickling an ace. She couldn't help watching—it was such a perfect example of the grace she'd mentioned earlier.

Finally he spoke.

"I have something I need to tell you," he said, his voice low and grave. "Something you should know before you push this any further."

She nodded, almost afraid to hope. But he didn't look like a man who was trying to find a way to say no anymore. He looked like a man who was trying to find a way to say yes.

He took a deep breath and began.

"It's simple, really. Simple and ugly. I just got out of prison."

She could see that he expected some reaction. A recoil of horror, perhaps? An 'eek' as if she'd seen a ghost? He must not know that her great-grandfather had been in jail four times for bootlegging, and her grandmother's brother had shot his best friend over a soprano. And the ancestor with the cannon had refused to pay taxes for decades.

Granvilles didn't scare that easily. So she just looked at him and waited.

"I got out less than a month ago," he went on

finally. "I served three years of a five-year sentence at the New York State Penitentiary."

"Why?" It seemed an inadequate reaction, but it was the only one she could come up with. "What did you do?"

"Embezzling. Grand larceny. There were actually several counts, with several fancy names. The short version is that I owned a financial consulting firm. I was good at picking investments, and I made a lot of money for a lot of people. But my partner..."

He set his jaw hard, and his brown eyes were suddenly black. "The money disappeared. All of it. Millions and millions of dollars. My partner went to South America, and I went to prison."

The simplicity of his delivery was her best clue. He was in a lot of pain, and he was afraid that if he said any more the pain might show.

"But you didn't take the money, did you? Your partner took it, isn't that right?" She leaned across the table. "You aren't an embezzler just because *he's* an embezzler."

Matthew took a long drink of coffee, as if his throat was very dry. "A jury of my peers found otherwise," he said, and she heard the dark note of bitterness under the words. "And the New York State prison system didn't seem to think there were any substantive distinctions, either. They found us equally to blame."

He set the cup down carefully and turned his shadowed eyes her way. "So, there it is."

Yes, there it was. She could almost feel the anger

and bitter resentment radiating out from him. It pulsed across the table and touched her in thick, black waves. But she felt other things, too. She felt the loneliness, the courage, the shock of betrayed trust. The pure injustice and pain.

It was a lot to take in, almost too much.

She hoped she wouldn't start crying. He would never understand. He might think she cried out of pity, when really they would be tears of indignation. What a bastard his partner must have been. How could any man leave a friend to pay so heavy a price?

"So what do you say, Natalie Granville? What is your gut telling you now?"

Somehow she managed to smile. "Right now my gut is telling me that we'd better hurry. It's a statistical fact that every eight-point-two minutes another piece of Summer House falls apart. While we were discussing this nonsense, I probably lost the entire west wall of the Blue Bedroom."

"Natalie, this isn't nonsense. It's real. I am a convicted felon. You could be—"

She sighed heavily. "For heaven's sake! Let's cut to the chase. Just give me a yes or no answer. If you accept this job, will you do your best to fix up my crazy old house?"

"I can't—"

"Yes or no answer."

He nodded cautiously. "Yes."

"Are you going to try to cheat me?"

"No."

"Rob me? Steal all my expensive stuff?"

He smiled just a little. "Do you have expensive stuff?"

She grinned. "Not a bit. But if I did, would you steal it?"

"No."

"And would you ever physically hurt me?"

He took a breath. "Never."

She stood up and held out her hand. "Then, as I tried to tell you yesterday, Matthew Quinn, you're hired."

Slowly he rose to his feet. Even more slowly, he accepted her outstretched hand. His grip was strong and sure and safe, and she smiled, thinking how lucky she was that the world's most amazing handyman had somehow found his way to her rickety old door.

She was sorry for his sake that prison had brought him to this moment, but for one fleeting instant, selfishly, for her own sake, she was glad.

"Okay, then. It's settled. Can you move in tomorrow morning?"

Gradually his own smile grew less strained. And he nodded. "I don't see why not."

"Great. I'll be waiting for you."

She picked up her glass and downed the last of the orange juice. Theo was so smart. Her hangover had completely, miraculously, disappeared.

"Natalie," Matthew called out as she started to walk away.

She paused. "What?"

"I have to know. Why was that statue wearing a wedding dress yesterday?"

She shook her head, chuckling.

"I'll tell you all about it someday," she said. "Right now I can only say that I must have been having a Granville moment."

He laughed softly. "The world will say you're having another Granville moment now, hiring me."

She shrugged, still smiling.

"Let it," she said. "The world has been wrong before."

CHAPTER FOUR

MATTHEW ARRIVED at Summer House early, not wanting to give himself time to reconsider. He had hardly slept, staring at the hotel ceiling all night as he fought a twitchy, irrational urge to bolt, just to jump in the car and head north. Or south. Or anywhere. Anywhere else.

Maybe it came from those three years caged in an eight-by-eight cell, but the idea of being tied down made him crazy. Even a casual, short-term arrangement like this job for Natalie Granville left him short of breath, as if a noose had been looped around his neck.

He should have said no.

Freedom. Freedom was everything.

But it was also relative. If he didn't work at Summer House, he still had to work somewhere. Down in Florida, his sister and her husband were waiting patiently, hoping he would accept their generous offer of a job managing one of their family restaurants. And back in New York City, his parole officer was waiting, too, less patiently. Matthew's early release had been conditioned on his finding gainful employment outside the world of finance within the month.

Yes, it was Florida—with his sister's smothering solicitude and his brother-in-law's silent disapproval—or it was some quick, anonymous job like this one.

So he'd gotten up early, called his sister to tell her he was fine but that he was taking a summer job up here, to give himself time to think things over, time to clear his head.

And then he'd driven straight to Summer House.

But apparently he was too early. Natalie had left a note on the front door, in that same frilly calligraphy that had led him to her in the first place.

"Darn! I missed you!" the note said, and Matthew could almost hear her voice in the exclamation points. *"Follow signs to pool house and settle in. Back absolutely ASAP."*

He followed the silly pink sticky notes, which were affixed every few feet to whatever was available— outstretched hands of statues, terra-cotta pots, tendrils of ivy. They led him toward the eastern side of the house, through the mildewed grotto—God, what a wreck!—and out toward the monstrous, dry hole in the ground that had once been the lavish swimming pool.

He paused there, peering in, noting its broken, cavernous walls and steeply sloping floor. An elaborate mosaic had been inlaid into the finish, but so many small pieces were missing that it looked like a half-done jigsaw puzzle, and Matthew couldn't quite tell what the picture was.

Good grief, he thought, shaking his head. The place was even worse than he'd thought. He definitely should have said no. The best handyman in the world couldn't help. Natalie Granville should just rent a bulldozer and start over.

The pool house was on the far side of the cracked deck and it was, predictably, just as run-down as the rest of the crazy old mansion.

His duffel bag held lightly in one hand, Matthew stood before the beautiful ruin. It reminded him, with its marble columns and formal pediments, of a small, abandoned temple.

Mold mottled the walls. Early-morning sunlight streamed through holes in the roof, spotlighting foot-high weeds that grew up in the cracked floor tiles. And two of the three white columns had curiously jagged missing chunks, as if a dragon had sampled them for lunch.

It was picturesque and broody and probably uncomfortable as hell. Oh yeah, he positively should have said no.

But Natalie's final pink note fluttered on the front door.

Hurray! You found it! The words were followed by three more exclamation points and a smiley face. *"Welcome home!"*

He peeled the note off and held it in his hand, shaking his head in silent amazement. Where on earth did a woman like Natalie Granville, who should have been thoroughly oppressed by her dilemma, find so much enthusiasm?

And besides, Summer House wasn't his home. He didn't have a home.

"I know. It's awful, isn't it?"

He turned toward the sound of the voice. It was Natalie, looking clean and sober and surprisingly professional in a pale blue linen suit. In fact, she looked so different from the disheveled, half-naked eccentric who had fallen into his arms that at first he hardly recognized her.

Nothing could change the fact that she was beautiful. But all these efforts to look "normal"—the young exec uniform, the safe pink lipstick, the curls scraped back and tamed into a tight ponytail—took away some of her quirky magic.

What a shame. He had kind of liked her drunk and disorderly.

But just then the balmy summer breeze kicked up, and a few of those soft, shining corkscrew curls lifted free. She wrinkled her nose and, with a sheepish smile, yanked the clip from her hair. Then she bent down, peeled off her high heels and flexed her bare foot with a relieved groan.

"God, I hate shoes. Don't you?" She turned toward him and grimaced. Somehow she even managed to make a grimace look cheerful. And suddenly he realized that the magic was still there. It would take more than a linen suit to make Natalie Granville "normal."

"Don't let the mess out here scare you off," she said. She dropped her purse and shoes on the broken flagstones and reached out to take his hand. "I didn't get to the outside yet. But wait until you see inside. It has a few good points, I promise."

Before he could protest, she pulled open the door and led him into the cool interior. She bustled around, apparently nervous, flicking at imaginary specks of dust, nudging picture frames a millimeter to the left or right, smoothing the fall of curtains around the picture window that looked out onto the spectacular mountain view.

The place was bigger than it appeared from the outside. It was bright and airy and smelled of fresh paint. Natalie had left all the curtains open wide, and all the lights on, too. For a moment Matthew wondered whether she guessed how much he valued sunshine these days.

"It's not perfect, of course." She smiled at him, wrinkling her nose again. "The pictures are hideous. The roof needs some attention, but rain's not actually dripping in yet. And it has a fabulous, very modern Roman bathroom. Which is more than I can say for the main house."

"It's fine," he said, meaning it. He didn't give a damn about the pictures.

She looked around, obviously searching for a few good points to mention.

"Oh, yes! I forgot to explain about the bed."

It did need explaining, he had to admit. A huge

walnut four-poster, it dominated the central part of the room. It faced the picture window, and the sunlight exposed an elaborate jungle of birds and butterflies and snakes carved into every inch of exposed wood.

"I know it's a little big for this place, but it's a fantastic bed. Rumor is my great-great grandfather won it a hundred years ago in an arm-wrestling contest with the king of Tahiti." She smoothed the soft white bedspread. "The king was only twelve at the time. Doesn't really seem very fair of my grandfather, does it?"

Matthew smiled. "Or very smart of the king."

She looked up. "That's exactly what I've always thought," she said happily, as if delighted to discover they shared a common outlook on something so important.

"Anyhow, it's comfortable, which is why we've always kept it, even though it eats up all the space. But let's see...other than this main room, there's a kitchenette, which is pretty awful, and the bathroom, which, as I said, is fantastic. In fact, we used to wonder if my grandfather used to have assignations down here. Great bed, great Roman tub...and almost nothing else. Makes you think."

He smiled. Sounded pretty good to him.

"Time for a full disclosure, I guess. The left burner on the stove won't heat. You have to jiggle the handle to make the toilet stop running. The overhead light in here makes a hissing noise when it rains. And the faucet in the kitchen sink has a very annoying tendency to drip when you're trying to sleep.''

She sighed, apparently having come to the end of her litany of drawbacks. "I'm sorry." She gave him a tilted smile. "My only hope is, I figure it's got to beat prison, right?''

Matthew had hardly been listening. He'd been looking out the window, enjoying the limitless expanse of blue sky and the way the green oaks and hemlocks seemed to swarm down the mountainside into the cozy hamlet of Firefly Glen. But her last sentence got his attention.

He turned around slowly. "Beat prison?''

"Oh, dear." Natalie's high brow furrowed and she twisted a curl in her forefinger. "Maybe I'm being stupid. I should have realized. You probably were in one of those country club prisons, weren't you?''

For a second he didn't know how to answer. Except for his parole officer, Natalie was the first person since his release to say the word "prison" in his presence. Everyone else, even his sister, had locked it away with other shameful words you'd never mention in polite society, like hemorrhoids or cannibalism or incest.

They meant well, of course. They pretended it hadn't ever happened because they thought he wanted to forget. They just didn't get it. Prison was a part of him now, burned into him like a brand. It had happened, all right. And he would never forget.

But now, as he heard Natalie Granville say the

word so naturally, he realized that she wasn't afraid of it. She didn't think it made him dirty. He wondered whether it might be possible someday to talk to her about it. About the degradation and the panic, about the claustrophobia and the fury and the shame, and finally the creeping numbness that had come over him.

But what was he thinking? He squeezed his eyes shut hard, trying to force himself back to reality. He hardly knew her, for God's sake. Maybe he was as crazy as she was. Maybe "Granville moments" were contagious.

When he opened his eyes, he saw that Natalie was watching him anxiously. After a second, she groaned and pressed her knuckles against her brow.

"Oh, this was so dumb! I've got ten bedrooms up at the house. I should have put you in one of them. It's just that—I just thought you might like more privacy. More freedom. I guess I thought that, after prison, privacy would be more important than drippy faucets."

He shouldn't have waited so long to say something. Apparently he had lost the knack for normal conversational rhythms, along with everything else.

"No, it is," he said quickly. "You were absolutely right. Privacy is more important to me right now than almost anything. This place is terrific."

He had begun to notice little things. A fresh vase of Queen Anne's Lace stood on the nightstand, probably picked from her own side yard. And beside the flowers she'd neatly arranged a couple of paperback mysteries, a pitcher of water and a crystal glass.

Welcome home.

"It's beautiful. And trust me. Even with drippy faucets, it's got prison beat by a million miles."

"You mean it?" She wrinkled her nose again. "You don't have to say—"

"I mean it. It's perfect. In fact, it may be the most unselfish thing I've seen anyone do in about ten years."

Still frowning, she studied his eyes earnestly. But her face gradually relaxed, and soon she was smiling that sweetly lopsided smile.

"It's not really unselfish at all, you know." She touched his hand. "I just want you to be glad you said yes."

He looked down at her hand. Her fingers were small, tanned from working in the sun. Her short, unpolished nails were white crescent moons, feminine in the most simple and honest of ways.

Oh, hell. To his horror, a sudden, fierce sexual reaction shot through him. He eased his arm away and bent over his duffel stiffly. *Damn it all to hell.*

Had he really turned into such a pathetic cliché? *Watch out, ladies. He's a lonely, sex-starved drifter just out of prison...*

Well, he wouldn't let it happen, that was all. He made a silent vow to himself right there on the spot. He would *not* let it happen.

"It's getting late," he said firmly. "I'd better get

to work. How about if I unpack, and then I'll come find you, and you can tell me where to start?''

She might be naive, but she could take a hint.

"Okay," she said, smoothing the bedspread one last time. "I'll leave you alone. I'll be in the kitchen when you need me. Big door at the back." She fluffed the flowers and headed for the door.

But at the last second she turned around.

"Hey, wait a minute," she said in a thoughtful tone. "When you said this was the most unselfish thing you'd seen anyone do in ten years…" She tilted her head. "I thought you said you were in prison for three years. Not ten."

He didn't turn around. "That's right," he said, unfolding T-shirts. "I was."

"Oh." He heard her chuckle softly as she figured it out. "Oh, I see. Well, then I guess it's a good thing you came to Firefly Glen, Matthew Quinn. Obviously you're way overdue for a fresh start."

SHUCKING HER UNCOMFORTABLE business suit with relief—God, she hated wooing new clients—Natalie changed into shorts and T-shirt at lightning speed, then scurried down to the kitchen.

She surveyed her pantry thoughtfully. It wasn't ten in the morning yet. Matthew had arrived so early he probably hadn't had any breakfast. She intended to fix that. She'd make the best breakfast he'd ever seen.

As she gathered eggs, fresh fruit, whole wheat bread, sausage and homemade apple butter and plopped them on the huge kitchen island, she had to admit she might be overdoing things a little. She'd spent all day yesterday painting the pool house, hanging new curtains, washing windows till they sparkled. And now this feast, fit for a king, not a handyman.

But she wanted to treat him well. Something in his eyes told her that no one had treated him like a king in a long, long time.

Besides, she wanted to show him she was actually competent at some things. She wanted to assure him that she wasn't as half-baked and hapless as she must have seemed when they first met.

She cringed, remembering the booze, the bikini, the wedding dress on the statue. Arms full of more food, she nudged the refrigerator door shut with her forehead. Heck, he probably thought she was nuts. Which was annoying, because actually, for a Granville, she was pretty darn practical.

Her nursery business was thriving, which took a lot of know-how. She made money. Heck, if she didn't have this money pit to take care of, she'd practically be solvent.

And she was a darn good cook. She began to hum as she cracked eggs against her grandmother's big stainless steel mixing bowl. Matthew would see soon enough that he hadn't made such a terrible mistake after all.

When she heard the knock on the back door, she slid the egg-and-sausage casserole into the oven and rushed over to let him in.

"Hi," she called out, licking apple butter from her fingers and then patting her hair, praying it wasn't flying everywhere. "I hope you're hungry!"

But the face on the other side of the door didn't belong to Matthew Quinn. It belonged to Bart Beswick, the handsome young millionaire she had spent last Saturday not getting married to.

Right now, though, that handsome face was as sour as old milk. "Obviously you were expecting someone else," Bart articulated icily, hardly moving his lips. "Who?"

Natalie sighed. "Hi, Bart," she said, standing away from the door so he could enter. "You know, sweetie, it's exactly that kind of question, asked in exactly that tone of voice, that made me decide not to become Mrs. Beswick."

Bart entered the kitchen stiffly. "I'm glad you can joke about it, Natalie. God knows I can't."

"Sure you can," she said, bending down to check on the casserole. "You just won't. At least not until that big hole I shot in the side of your ego mends."

Bart pursed his lips. "It wasn't my ego. It was my heart."

"Nonsense." Natalie spoke around her index finger, which had once again become covered in apple butter. "But if you'll stop scowling, I'll let you stay for breakfast."

"I can't. I've got a meeting. And besides...you are *obviously* expecting company." He paused, but as she remained firmly silent he gave up and went on. "I just came by to ask you about my mother's bracelet."

He unfolded a couple of typewritten sheets from his breast pocket and began looking them over. "It's not here. I've checked three times. I even had my accountant check. It wasn't among the things you returned."

Natalie wiped her hands on a damp towel and wandered across the room to look over his shoulder. "You made a list?" She shook her head. "Good grief, Bart. You actually kept an inventory of the gifts you gave me?"

"Well." He cleared his throat. "It seemed prudent."

For a minute she almost lost her temper. What exactly was he implying? Did he think she'd steal the nasty bracelet, which was much too vulgar for anyone to wear?

But then she calmed down. This was just Bart. They had been friends since preschool, and he'd always been the ultraorganized class nerd. At three years old, he'd cried if his stuffed toys weren't lined up right. At twelve, he had demanded that every pencil in his pencil case be exactly the same length. Was it any wonder that, at thirty, he kept a typewritten list of his love offerings, their appraised values, dates given, and dates returned?

"Okay, whatever." She moved away. "It's just that I honestly thought I gave everything back."

He tapped the empty spot on the "date returned"

list. "Not this one. Not my mother's bracelet. You remember. The *diamond* bracelet. Rather large diamonds, in fact."

"Yes, of course I remember it," she said, sliding bread into the toaster. Darn. This could be sticky. If it hadn't been in the box she gave him when they called the wedding off, she didn't have a clue *where* the blasted thing was. "I'll look for it. Want a muffin?"

"No, thank you. Maybe you could look for it now? I'll wait."

"Bart." She took a deep breath. "I'm cooking. I'll look for it later, and I'll call you."

"Actually, I'd rather—"

"Listen." She put her hands on her hips. "I know you're just itching to put that last check mark on that lovely list, but I'm busy right now. I will find it, I promise. But you might want to be a little less gestapo about it. Technically I don't *have* to return it. Look 'gift' up in the dictionary."

"You wouldn't keep my mother's bracelet!" He looked so horrified that she was almost ashamed of herself. In spite of his methodical love of detail, Bart was a very nice man. And she had once believed that his hyperrigidity might be a good counterweight to her own impulsive nature.

Besides, his last fiancée—Terri the schoolteacher, the one woman he had *really* loved—had kept every gift he'd ever given her, right down to the last karat and gram. No wonder he was a little gun-shy.

"Of course I wouldn't," she said reassuringly. "Tell you what. Watch the casserole for me, and I'll go see if it's upstairs. Oh, and if Matthew comes in, give him a cup of coffee, okay?"

Bart's eyebrows slammed together. "Matthew?"

"The new handyman," she said, sliding a wedge of cantaloupe into her mouth and heading for the door. "He just started this morning."

"Oh, the handyman." Bart's frown eased, and he finally smiled. "I thought that you—all this food—well, you know what I thought. But if it's just the handyman, why are you putting on such a spread?"

She growled under her breath, resisting the urge to toss the cantaloupe rind onto his head. "Reason number seven hundred and twelve why it's a good thing we didn't get married, Bart. You're such an unbelievable snob."

WHEN, TWENTY MINUTES LATER, Matthew stuck his head in the kitchen door, Natalie was nowhere in sight. The only person in the room was a man who stood staring out the far window, one hand holding a coffee mug, the other drumming impatiently on the countertop.

It wasn't the same guy who had helped Natalie inside the other day—the preppy Stuart with the unfortunate shoes. This man was more solid, with tidy sandy hair and the conservative, finicky clothes of a fifty-year-old banker. Stuart had been the sports-car-

and-tennis type. This one was probably a silver Mercedes sedan and eighteen holes of bad golf.

Not that Matthew cared. But it was interesting to note that wherever Natalie Granville went, men seemed to show up like moths.

Matthew rapped politely against the door, even though it was already open. The man turned around, and Matthew was shocked to discover that he wasn't fifty at all. He was probably in his late twenties. Not much older than Natalie herself.

"Good morning," the man said, setting his coffee mug down carefully. "You must be the handyman. Matthew, I think it was?"

Matthew nodded. He held out his hand. "Matthew Quinn," he said.

The other man's eyes flickered, and one tiny beat passed before he held out his own hand.

"Bart Beswick," he said in a formal tone, as if the name should impress.

God, did he always look as if he'd been lashed to a broomstick, or was something annoying the man? Oh, right. Of course. Matthew realized too late that he'd forgotten to don his *yes-master* tone. He'd automatically approached Bart Beswick man-to-man, eyeball-to-eyeball, and Beswick didn't like it.

The guards in prison hadn't liked it, either.

But too bad. He wasn't in prison anymore. And he'd be damned if he'd start his new life by genuflecting to every millionaire he met. Apparently Firefly Glen was lousy with them, and they apparently all had rotten manners. Even in his highest-flying days, Matthew had never treated an employee with this kind of condescension.

"So." Matthew moved toward the coffeepot. "Is Natalie around?"

"No, she's upstairs," Bart said, taking his own mug and tossing its contents into the sink. "She went to look for something, but that was—" he looked at his Rolex and groaned, temporarily forgetting to be pompous "—for God's sake. It was close to half an hour ago."

So that accounted for the impatient drumming of fingers, Matthew thought. Bart had been kept waiting, and he didn't like that, either.

"Maybe she couldn't find it," Matthew suggested helpfully.

Bart grunted. "She probably completely lost track of what she went up there for. She could be repotting a gardenia or cleaning her closet or teaching herself the tango. The damn Granvilles haven't had a linear thought in six generations."

But then he caught himself, perhaps realizing this wasn't the kind of conversation you had with the hired help

"Listen…Quinn, you said?" He frowned, rapidly scanning Matthew's jeans and work shirt. He probably recognized the labels, left over from the days when Matthew had spent a sinful amount of money on clothes. "I mean… You did say you were the handyman, didn't you?"

"That's right."

"Sorry. You just don't look like any handyman I ever saw." Then he shook his head, as if recognizing the rudeness. "Sorry. I'm out of sorts and running late, and she's driving me crazy this morning. Like what else is new. Where the hell *is* she, for God's sake?"

He ran his hands through his hair, stared impatiently at the kitchen door, paced a few steps, then came back to the island. "I have a meeting to attend. A very important meeting. She never thinks about these things. You might as well know that, if you're really going to be working here. Granvilles live in their own time zone. On their own planet. And they think everyone else should just be flattered to be invited for a visit now and then."

Matthew took a sip of the amazingly good coffee, but his response was just a noncommittal murmur. He sensed that some real emotion lay behind Bart's last sentence, and he wasn't sure he wanted to invite further confidences.

Bart waited about fifteen more seconds, then sighed heavily. "Oh, hell. I'm not her houseboy. Listen, Quinn, would you mind watching the damn casserole for her?"

Matthew glanced at the oven. "No problem."

"Thanks." Bart began gathering up papers and stuffing them into his jacket pocket. "And hey, look. I'm sorry I was a little brusque earlier. I was—well, I've got a lot on my mind."

"No problem," Matthew said again. But he added a little warmth. Apologizing twice in one morning probably was a record for this guy.

"Oh, and one last thing. If you see a diamond bracelet in the eggs, or in the garbage, or in her hair, make her call me immediately. It's expensive, and it belongs to me."

Matthew raised one eyebrow quizzically. "Diamonds for breakfast. A special Granville recipe? From their home planet?"

Looking up, the other man offered Matthew his first genuine smile. It transformed his face, and Matthew found himself smiling back instinctively.

"Hey, if that's the weirdest thing that happens while you're at Summer House," Bart said as he headed out the door, shaking his head wryly, "consider yourself a very lucky man."

CHAPTER FIVE

"NATALIE?" Though he wasn't sure he should, Matthew climbed the Summer House stairs slowly. "Natalie? Are you okay?"

Something wasn't right. He'd been waiting in the kitchen for at least thirty minutes, which meant Natalie had been gone for more than an hour. The casserole had long since passed golden brown and was rapidly approaching charbroiled black.

His anxiety just beginning to prick to life, he had adjusted the oven thermostat and put the milk and fruit and apple butter back in the refrigerator. Then, when there was still no sign of her, he had started to look around the house.

She wasn't on the first floor, he was pretty sure of that. Poking around, calling her name, he'd opened a dozen weird, half-furnished rooms. One gilded parlor was filled with neatly stacked cardboard boxes marked "fertilizer." One magnificent mirrored chamber had nothing in it but a huge silver harp and a single goldfish circling pointlessly in a round glass bowl.

He'd found parlors and dining rooms and studies,

stained glass and stained ceilings, mottled murals and dusty chandeliers. But he hadn't found Natalie.

Granville moments or no Granville moments, this didn't feel right. So, though he knew he was overstepping a handyman's bounds—that prig Beswick would probably have had him arrested—he was going to check upstairs.

"Natalie?" He noticed a couple of unsteady treads beneath his feet. Better put that at the top of the to-do list before someone got hurt. "Natalie, are you all right?"

No answer. He reached the second floor and began opening doors. A blue bedroom, then a pink one. A dressing room, a luxurious wood-paneled man's bathroom, a sunny, golden sitting room...

And then, suddenly, he opened the right door, and he found her. She was kneeling beside an old-fashioned oak dresser, at the far end of a cluttered green playroom.

All the dresser's drawers gaped open, their colorful contents foaming over the edges, spilling exuberantly onto the floor. But Natalie herself was the picture of dejection, kneeling there, her head in her hands, encircled by the chaotic debris.

She heard him enter. When she looked up, her face was streaked and her eyes were red and swollen. She'd been crying.

He moved into the room quickly. "Natalie. What's the matter?"

She took a shaky breath and brushed roughly at her

cheeks. "Nothing. Nothing, really. I'm just so irritated with myself. I was looking for Bart's stupid bracelet, and I let myself get stuck in here."

"Stuck?" He knelt beside her, ignoring the mounds of linens and jewelry and toys. "How?"

"I always forget about the door," she said, picking up a random handkerchief embroidered with small purple violets and blowing her nose noisily. "That dumb door. It just shuts on its own and—"

She looked toward the door, her eyes widening. "Oh, no. Matthew, watch out—"

But it was too late. The ornately carved door, which obviously was seriously off plumb, had silently swung shut behind him. It settled into place with a firm click that Matthew suspected was not a good omen.

He looked back at Natalie. "Let me guess. It won't open from the inside."

She shook her head, sniffing. "Nope. It's been broken for years. I keep meaning to fix it, but—" she smiled crookedly "—it just never seemed to make it to the top of the list."

Matthew could understand that. What was one broken door compared to the leaking roof, rotting staircase and busted windowpanes?

"I tried to call down to you and Bart, but in a house this size it's pretty pointless. No one can hear you."

He hadn't heard anything. Of course, this place was as big as a small city, so that was no surprise. He wandered over and inspected the door's hinges. They were on the outside, of course. Just his luck.

"Usually when I come in here I prop a chair against the door," she said sadly. "And ever since I fell down the basement stairs last year and broke my ankle, I usually keep a roam phone with me, so I can call Harry if anything goes wrong. Harry's the sheriff. He always lectures me about how unsafe it is to live here alone, but eventually he sends someone to help me out."

"But this time? No chair? No phone?"

She sighed heavily. "That's why I was so disgusted with myself. This time I was all stirred up, mad at Bart because he was being such a jackass about the bracelet, and I just forgot to—" She paused. "Oh, God, the casserole. Did you meet Bart?"

Matthew had to smile. Her conversation was a little like playing mental hopscotch. "Yes, I did."

"I hope he was nice to you," she said doubtfully. When Matthew didn't answer, she groaned. "He wasn't, was he?"

Matthew shrugged. "He was fine. He didn't stay long. He said to tell you he had an important meeting."

"I knew it. He was rude, wasn't he? God, that man can be such an insufferable snob sometimes. But don't take it personally. He's just grumpy because we were supposed to get married on Saturday, and now he's convinced I've lost his mother's diamond brace-let, which I haven't, I just can't find it."

She ruffled through the clothes one more time, and sighed again. "And also he probably thinks I've just hired you because you're so good-looking, and now he'll sink into a jealous snit for weeks. But really, ordinarily he's a very sweet guy."

Matthew chuckled. "I'll take your word for that," he said. He looked around the room. "I'm more interested right now in figuring out how to get us out of here."

She stood up finally, handkerchiefs and hair bows and little sparkling doodads tumbling from her lap and settling into the sea of color on the floor. She had changed into a pair of denim shorts and a T-shirt that didn't quite cover her navel. She was sexy and adorable, and he didn't dare let himself look too long.

"Oh, well. There's only one way out now," she said somberly, with a touch of drama.

He waited.

She pointed. "Through the window. Over the roof. Across the gable and then down the hemlock tree. It's a little tricky, but I've done it before. I'm pretty good at it now. The first time I broke my left elbow."

"You know, I was afraid you'd say that."

She wrinkled her nose. "I was only eleven at the time. I told you I'm much better now.'"

Matthew walked over to the window, raised the glass and stuck his head out for a look. They were only two stories up, but these Italian palaces had fourteen-foot ceilings, and the marble terrace below seemed a very long way down. It would hardly cushion a fall.

Even worse, the roof clearly wasn't stable. It sloped dramatically, and was pocked with missing tiles. God only knows how many others were loose, ready to kick free at the lightest pressure, or how many soft spots the roof had that were likely to crumble under you.

Still, if it was the only way... He turned around, ready to instruct Natalie to wait there, that he'd climb down, then come back up and open the door from the outside. But she was already slipping off her shoes.

"It's better if you're barefoot," she said. "That way it's easier to hang on with your toes."

"Natalie, I don't think you—"

"Matthew." She turned serious eyes on him. Her hair was a mess of curls, and her eyes were still slightly puffy, though the tears had completely dried. She looked brave and beautiful and utterly foolish.

"Please don't go all Stone Age on me and say I should just wait here while you perform the heroics. I'm the one who got us stuck in here, and I want to be the one who gets us out. My self-respect requires it." She touched his arm and smiled. "You can understand that, can't you?"

And of course, he could.

NATALIE HELD ON to the gable with her knees and cursed like a sailor. Wouldn't you just know it? The hemlock had lost several branches in last winter's freeze, and one of them was the branch she needed.

Behind her, she heard Matthew laughing. "Sorry," she said sheepishly, swiveling her head to look at him. He was only a foot or two behind her, riding the gable as comfortably as if he did this every day. "My grandfather would have a fit if he heard me say that word."

"I imagine your grandfather would have an even bigger fit if he saw you straddling that gable." He maneuvered closer, so close she could feel the bracing warmth of his knees around her hips. She hated to admit she appreciated the security of knowing he was there, especially after that comment about Stone Age chauvinism.

He peered over her shoulder. "Can I assume from your colorful vocabulary that we've encountered a small hitch?"

"The branch is gone. It must have broken off in last year's ice storm." She chewed her lip, surveying the remaining branches. She might be able to jump to that big one over there, but she had a feeling Matthew would never let her try. "Darn. It's very inconvenient."

"Maybe we should throw it in reverse and look for another way down."

She hated to give up—that alternate branch was only a couple of feet away—but she knew when she was beaten.

"Okay," she said as gracefully as she could.

"You're probably right. Maybe we can find a way down on the pool side of the house."

But they had to get off this gable first. Grabbing the tiles with her toes for traction, she began to shimmy backward. After a few awkward shuffles, she realized uncomfortably that he had a close-up view of her rump, which probably looked awful in these tacky old shorts. Too bad she had insisted on going first.

Awkwardly self-conscious, she wasn't as careful as she should have been. Her foot slipped on a loose tile, and, off balance, she started to keel over sideways.

"Oh, no," she cried. Her heart jumped like a leap-frog toward her throat, and a sizzle of fear burned through her veins.

She clawed out for something, anything, but her fingers met only air. Oh, hell, she thought, time strangely melting into slow motion, she was going to fall, and she was probably going to break every bone in her body.

But she didn't fall. Suddenly Matthew's strong hands were around her waist, pulling her up, centering her safely against the solid wall of his body. "Steady," he said. "You're okay."

She sank against him, momentarily helpless as she tried to swallow her heart back down where it belonged. When she could, she laughed shakily. "Thanks. That would have been the Granville moment to end all Granville moments."

But her voice was trembling, and he obviously heard it. Tightening his arms around her, he rested his cheek against her hair and made a soothing noise. "You're okay," he said again softly.

She could feel his heart beating rather fast against her shoulder blades. Her near miss had obviously unnerved him, too. Well, of course it had. It would have been a little tricky to explain why the ex-con was up on the roof, staring down at Natalie Granville's broken body.

"Maybe we could just sit here for a minute," she said. "Till my stomach stops doing cartwheels."

"We can stay all day if you like." He shifted her so that she fit against him comfortably. "It's probably the best view in the city."

She nodded.

"I'm sorry about this, but things fall apart on this house faster than I can repair them," she said. "I inherited quite a bit of money to help with the upkeep, but with taxes what they are, and repairs so expensive…it just doesn't go far enough."

"I can imagine," he said. He sounded sympathetic.

"And of course you can't ever repair anything on the cheap, because it all has historical value, and if I ever wanted to break down and apply for a historical site restoration grant, I'd need to keep everything authentic."

"That sounds like a good idea. Has no one ever considered that?"

"Good heavens, no. My grandfather always threatened to have a stroke if anyone mentioned it. He said if you asked the government for money, then they owned you. Granvilles are notoriously independent. They don't like to have to answer to anyone.''

She sighed. ''And I've seen it happen to a couple of houses around here. Elspeth Grant, she's the head of the historical society, is a real pill. She's the kind who would come snooping around complaining that you've put a historically inaccurate kind of soap in your bathroom.''

He chuckled, but she realized she was doing an awful lot of whining, which must be pretty boring. Probably he was just indulging her, hoping that getting mad would take her mind off the scare she'd just had.

He really was a nice man, wasn't he? And he was remarkably easy to be with, even when you were making a fool of yourself. He seemed to take the Granville personality in stride, which a lot of men simply couldn't do.

They didn't speak for quite a while, strangely at ease together in this odd, stolen moment. It was as if the real world wasn't real at all. From here, it looked more like an elaborate toy train display—charming and creative, but ultimately unimportant.

Vanity Gap, the main road in and out of Firefly Glen, threaded a tiny silver path down to the toy town set among the thick green trees. Nearer by, wildflowers made a colorful patchwork quilt of the mountainside—the red of fireweed, then the soft pink of meadowsweet, and over there the yellow carpet of sundrop.

The breeze was strong, and it brought them summer smells of newly cut grass, roses and steaming asphalt. Far away a dog barked, and closer, in the branches of the hemlock, an unseen bird sang, the sound floating toward them like notes from a golden wind chime.

After a few moments, a funny little brown bird with white stripes on his wings came very close, studying them curiously. Its song was strange, more like a mewing, almost like a kitten.

"Cute," Matthew said softly against her ear. "I think he's talking to you."

"Oh, Matthew," she whispered, thrilled that the shy bird would dare to come so near. She'd never seen one up so close before. "A yellow-bellied sapsucker!"

Matthew chuckled. "What did you call me?"

She smiled, ridiculously charmed—by his silly joke, by the bird, by the pure, empty beauty of being up here like this.

"Let's don't ever go down," she said impulsively, wrapping his arms more tightly around her waist. "Let's forget all about leaking faucets and unpaid bills and Bart's horrible bracelet. Let's hide up here forever. They'll never find us."

But she spoke too soon. In the stillness, they both clearly heard the sound of a car coming up the driveway.

"Forever isn't going to last very long this time, I'm afraid."

She looked down. Below them, a car door slammed, and feet scraped against the driveway. They had been discovered already.

"Natalie Granville? Dammit, girl, what in tarnation are you doing up there on that roof? And who the hell is that up there with you?"

She groaned, letting her head fall back against Matthew's chest. "I knew it was too good to last," she said tragically. "It's my cousin Granville Frome, and it looks as if he's brought Ward Winters with him. I must really be in trouble now."

And then she raised her voice. "Hi, Granville," she called down. "Hi, Ward. You guys are just in time. I got stuck in the green nursery. You know how that door is."

The two old men had finally come into view. Granville was glaring up at her, though from this perspective he looked less intimidating than usual. "Yes, I know how that door is," he said, "and so do you, girl. Why the hell did you let that happen again?"

"Sorry," she said meekly. "But isn't it lucky you happened by?" She paused. "Why are you here, by the way?"

"We came to check out that new handyman you hired. God knows you probably didn't do any checking yourself. Word in town is you're letting him live here." The old man put his hand over his eyes to shade out the sun. "Have you got the fellow up there with you on the roof now?"

"Yes," she said, trying not to laugh. "He's right behind me."

"I see that." Granville's tone left no doubt what he thought about the arrangement. "Well, I'm going to get a ladder. You two come down here so I can get a look at him."

She turned to Matthew. "I'm sorry," she said. "He doesn't mean anything. That's just the way he talks. He's the only family I have left, you see, and he's a bit overprotective."

"No problem," Matthew said with a small smile. "But, just out of curiosity, how many more jealous, overprotective friends, relatives and ex-fiancés do you have hanging around?"

"Well." She wrinkled her nose. "It's a small town, and we all tend to look out for one another around here. Pretty much everyone in town is going to want to check you out sooner or later."

"And the population of Firefly Glen now stands at..."

"Just under two thousand."

Matthew sighed. "Then we'd better get started. This could take a while."

SUZIE STRICKLAND sat in the art room at Glen High, staring at Mrs. Putnam, the head of the art department, in undisguised disbelief.

"You've got to be kidding," she said. "You really won't write me a recommendation?"

Mrs. Putnam looked pained. "Not *won't*, Suzie. Can't. I'm sorry, but I honestly can't in good conscience recommend you for a scholarship."

Suzie scowled belligerently. "That's crazy. You know I've got more talent than anybody in this high school. In this town."

The art teacher spread her hands eloquently. "I'm afraid talent isn't everything."

Suzie snorted. What kind of garbage was this? "Of course it is."

"No, it isn't. To earn a scholarship, a student also must excel at teamwork, citizenship, interpersonal relationships. A student must demonstrate commitment, dedication, cooperation. And an ability to follow directions."

"I want an art scholarship, Mrs. Putnam. Not a Girl Scout badge."

Mrs. Putnam drew herself up, offended. She'd probably been a Girl Scout all her life. "Maybe it's time you learned that being talented isn't license to thumb your nose at authority. It doesn't give you permission to be rude to your classmates, or to refuse to do assignments."

Suzie sat up stiffly, too, holding the scholarship forms so tightly she tore one corner. This wasn't fair. She hadn't *ever* refused to do an assignment. Sometimes she interpreted the assignments a little liberally, just to make them more interesting, but that hardly amounted to educational mutiny.

And she wasn't rude to her classmates. If anything, it was the other way around. She'd been taunted by the preppy crowd for so long she hardly even taunted back anymore. But she'd bet a million bucks nobody was telling that obnoxious Mike Frome that he couldn't have any scholarship he wanted.

Not that Mike Frome *needed* a scholarship. His daddy probably owned a passel of Ivy League colleges. That's how unfair it was in this stupid town. The rich kids basked in perpetual sunlight, while the kids from the wrong side of the tracks just stood around in the rain.

Most of the time she didn't care. She didn't want to be a cheerleader. She didn't want a brand-new red convertible or hundred-dollar blue jeans. She didn't want to be on the student government or the homecoming court or the dean's list.

But she wanted this scholarship. Dammit, dammit, *dammit.* She wanted it more than she had ever wanted anything in her life.

She stood up, suddenly feeling a little shaky. She had to get out of here. She'd eat worms before she'd cry in front of Mrs. Putnam.

"Yeah. Well, thanks anyhow," she said roughly. "See you in class tomorrow."

The art teacher sighed, signaling her gentle dismay that she couldn't get through to this difficult student. "You know, Suzie, you might try smiling occasionally. Wear a pretty dress. Take some of that metal out of your ears. You're not an unattractive girl. You'd be surprised how much more cooperative the world is if you don't start out by spitting in its face.''

Suzie paused, incredulous. So that's what it came down to? If she'd just buy a lacy pink miniskirt, like the kind Justine Millner used to wear, people would love her? If she'd smile and bat her eyes and purr like a kitten, scholarships would just fall in her lap?

She tried to think of something scathing to say in response, but her throat seemed too tight, all clogged up with fury, and she couldn't speak at all. She turned and walked out, bumping into the door in her blind haste.

Just her luck, in the parking lot, she ran into Mike Frome, who was arriving to play a game of basketball with his Neanderthal buddies.

She walked right past him, praying this would be one of the days when he ignored her. But of course, it wasn't.

Spinning the basketball thoughtfully on one finger, he watched her storm toward her car and struggle with the lock. He never had to unlock his shiny SUV with a lowly key, of course. He had one of those annoying little chirpy things that did it for him.

''Hey, Suzie-freaka, whazzup,'' he said in that infuriatingly superior tone, as if she should be grateful that he even acknowledged her existence.

Well, not today. She lifted her head and tried to

turn him to stone with her gaze. If he noticed that her eyes were wet, she'd kill him on the spot.

"Whoa." He backed up, frowning. "Where did *that* come from? Damn, Strickland. What the hell did I do to piss you off?"

Finally her key fit the lock. She glared at him one more time, willing her anger to burn all traces of moisture away. Apparently, though, it didn't work. She saw him notice. A small, concerned frown appeared between his eyebrows. "Hey. Seriously. Are you okay?"

But she didn't want him to be concerned. If he dared to be nice to her, she'd probably start bawling like a baby. She slammed shut her door and gunned the engine.

"I will be as soon as I get out of this narrow-minded, ass-backward, super-hick town," she said, and peeled away with real style, though by the time she got out of the parking lot she could hardly see the road through her tears.

CHAPTER SIX

IT WAS ENTERTAINING, really, watching Natalie tame the two old men.

It took three omelettes, six blueberry muffins and a leaning tower of pancakes, but she did it. She chattered, flattered and teased, and by the time the coffee was cold, the irascible old buzzards were eating out of her hand like parakeets.

However, that didn't stop Granville Frome from giving Matthew a cold blue glare as he finally stood up and brushed muffin crumbs from his straining shirtfront.

"Now. How about you walk us out to the car, son."

Matthew agreed without protest—it obviously was nonnegotiable anyhow. As the two men marched him out, one in front and one in back, he caught a glimpse of Natalie's laughing face.

Sorry, she mouthed, wrinkling her nose in a way he was already beginning to feel absurdly personal about.

He had just enough time to toss her a wink to show that he didn't mind. After an hour in the company of these men, he knew they were all noise and thunder.

Crusty and sarcastic on the outside, but on the inside as soft as warm taffy, especially where Natalie was concerned.

On the way down to the car, the two men talked mostly to each other. "Damn," Granville said, "would you look at that oak tree! I thought that died years ago. Remember the time you tried to hang yourself from it?"

"I did *not* try to hang myself, you liar," Ward Winters said loudly. "It was a dare. A trick Bourke said he'd learned at college."

Granville chortled. "Some trick. You damn near killed yourself."

They exchanged insults comfortably until finally they reached the car, a fifty-year-old neon blue Cadillac convertible that was as long, sleek and shiny as the day it rolled off the assembly line.

Matthew had to work to keep from laughing out loud. How perfect! He could just see the two dapper devils streaking through the streets of Firefly Glen, the wind in their silver hair, the sun baking their weathered faces.

Ward Winters grinned at Matthew's expression. "You like cars?"

Matthew thought of the parade of clichéd silver sedans he'd owned, a new model every year, each one more ridiculously expensive than the one before. What a waste of money! If he had felt obligated to overspend on a car, he should have bought one like this. One with fun and flair.

Matthew smiled appreciatively. "It's hard not to like *this* car. This car has some serious style."

Apparently that was the right thing to say. Granville Frome, who was using his sleeve to rub extra shine into a spot on the front fender, looked up and, for the first time all morning, he grinned, too. "Damn straight it does," he said. "The ladies love it, don't they, Ward?"

The other man nodded. "Yep. Of course I don't really need a car to attract the ladies, but, as you may have noticed, Granville here has a face like a dachshund, so he—"

"Shut up, you jealous old fool. We can compare the notches on our bedposts later. Right now I need to talk to Quinn."

"Then get to it, for God's sake. I swear, Frome, you're as slow as—"

"Shut up." Rising to his full height, Granville Frome faced Matthew and gave him a hard stare. For just a minute Matthew could see the imposing powerhouse he once had been. Probably everyone in Firefly Glen had been terrified of him.

"I want you to tell me about yourself. I want to know where you come from, why you're here. That's my favorite cousin you're living with. She's book smart, but about people— Well, let's just say she's too nice. If termites came knocking on her door, she'd make up the guest bed for them to sleep in."

Matthew nodded. "I noticed that. She obviously doesn't have a cynical bone in her body."

That might not have been the happiest choice of images. Granville went back to scowling, obviously disliking the idea of Matthew becoming too well acquainted with Natalie's bones.

"Yeah, well, *I* do," the old man said firmly. "And seeing a guy like you working as a handyman? It makes all my suspicious bones ache, you know what I mean? I haven't got a damn thing against handymen. But you aren't one."

"God, Granville," Ward Winters broke in, "you've got about as much tact as a—"

"No time for tact. Listen, Quinn, here's how I see it. You're used to giving orders, not taking them, that's obvious. You talk fancy. I'd be willing to bet you've got a college degree or two in your pocket. A pretty expensive pocket, too, if you don't mind my saying so. You're clearly used to having money. So, bottom line. Where did the money go?"

Matthew had to appreciate the dazzling display of deductive reasoning. It deserved a straight answer, so he took a deep breath and gave him one.

"My partner lost most of it in bad investments, and then he absconded with the rest." He told the tale quickly and steadily, no frills. "The authorities think he might be in South America, but no one can prove it. He and I had a financial consulting company together for about eight years. When he turned up missing, all our transactions were investigated, and I was convicted of securities fraud. I spent the past three years in prison. I just got out a month ago."

Both Granville and Ward were silent for a minute, but Matthew couldn't tell if they were surprised, furious or just intensely interested. Granville's shaggy eyebrows were pulled together hard.

"Natalie know about this?"

"Yes."

"Damn. Lot of people lose their money?"

"About a hundred and fifty million was lost altogether." Matthew would never forget the rage, the desperate disappointment, even fear that those defrauded clients had felt. He could see their faces still, and he knew he always would. But it wasn't something he talked about. So what if he felt haunted? That didn't put money back in anyone's bank account.

"Hmm." Granville chewed on the inside of his lip for a minute, then squinted at Matthew. "Why didn't you go to South America, too?"

Matthew took a minute to phrase his answer. He wanted to filter out any hint of pathos. He'd rather leave Summer House this minute than ask for anyone's pity.

"I didn't know I needed to," he said simply. "I didn't know what he'd been doing."

"You didn't know he'd been cheating your clients?"

"No."

"You trusted this guy so much you didn't even keep tabs on him?" Granville still hadn't broken eye contact. "That was stupid, wasn't it?"

"Yes. It was."

Another silence stretched out, and finally Granville began to chuckle. "Damn, son, you may be pretty nearly as naive as Natalie."

"No," Matthew said quietly. "Not anymore."

From the car, Ward Winters cleared his throat loudly. "Okay, then, that's settled, right? The kid's paid his dues, he's told it straight, Natalie's okay with it, it's none of our business, life goes on. Let's go, dammit. I've got a date."

Granville looked at his friend irritably. "You haven't got a date. You think you got a hot tip at Theo's this morning, and you're just dying to go make another million dollars. Like you need it, you greedy bas—"

"Well, what if I am?" Ward glanced at Matthew speculatively. "So you were an expert, huh? Know anything about a company named Richbern Corp.?"

For a split second, Matthew debated with himself. He had been out of the business for more than three years. A lot could have happened in that time. Even a rotten company like Richbern could have improved. Besides, he'd sworn he was going to stay out of the financial advising business—even casually, even with family and friends. He hated to let Ward Winters, who seemed like a decent guy, take a bath on this company, but—

"No," he said evenly. "Nothing."

Ward grinned triumphantly. "Oh, but your face says something else, my friend. The minute I said

Richbern, you looked as if you'd just spotted a snake in the grass.''

Matthew almost laughed. These old guys were regular Sherlock Holmes types, sniffing out truths however well you tried to hide them.

"Honestly," he said, shaking his head. "I've been out of the loop too long for my word to be worth much. I'm sorry."

"Besides," Granville put in tartly, "his last clients all ended up broke, remember? We're done here. Let's go."

Both men climbed into the Caddy, Granville behind the wheel. He checked his thick mane of silver waves in the rearview mirror, then started the engine, which turned over with a perfect purr. His grin was pure possessive pride.

At the last minute he stuck out his hand.

Matthew walked over and took it. Coming from an eighty-year-old man, the handshake was amazingly solid.

"You seem like a straight-up guy, Quinn," Granville said loudly, over the hum of the engine. "I actually kind of like you. But don't forget one thing. I will chop you up into bite-sized pieces and feed you to the termites if you make that cousin of mine unhappy."

SUZIE STRICKLAND was ecstatic. She wished Natalie were in the room, just so she could give her a great big hug. Natalie was *the best*. Being allowed to paint a trompe l'oeil here in the Summer House library was the most fantastic thing that had ever happened to her.

She'd been at it for a week, doing all the preparatory, drudge work. She'd chosen a picture, a distant, sunny vista of a hillside Tuscan village that seemed to be viewed through an imaginary window. Then she had drawn it in a 1:20 scale, which was much harder than it looked. She had prepped the wall, familiarizing herself with its rough texture, applying a solid base coat. She had transferred her picture in chalk and finally, yesterday, she had begun the fun part. She had begun to create.

She'd been painting since sunup today, and now, at almost six o'clock, she was tired to the aching point, and already late for dinner. But the clouds in her painting's sky had been driving her crazy. She simply had not been able to get the color right.

It had been a messy war. Slashes of blue, white, phthalo green, cadmium orange and burnt sienna covered her, from her sweaty hair, down her oversize black shirt and leggings, all the way to her dirty bare toes.

But she didn't care about any of that now. After two hours of trying one mix after another, she had finally got the clouds right. It was the phthalo green that cinched it. She'd been hung up on blue, or maybe gray, but now the answer seemed obvious. Of course the clouds would pick up the green of the hills beneath them.

Yes, yes, yes. It was perfect. She dabbed at the last

cloud with a damp cloth, softening the edges. Maybe she should kiss the clouds. She was so damn happy she just *had* to kiss somebody.

She flicked a glance out the real window. Hmm... If that sexy handyman of Natalie's should happen by, maybe he would do in a pinch.

Suzie giggled, imagining the guy's shock. And she had an idea Natalie wouldn't like it much, either. But *darn,* he sure was great to look at.

She had a little paint left on her palette, so she started dotting in some of the trees closer to the faux window, humming as she worked.

''O Sole Mio'' was the only Italian song she knew. She didn't know all the words, but she filled in the blanks with robust ''lah, lah, lah-lahs.'' In an Italian villa, painting a landscape of an Italian countryside, you should definitely sing an Italian song.

''What's going on in here? Oh, it's just you.'' Mike Frome's grinning face popped around the library door. ''Man, I thought somebody was beheading a hyena.''

Amazing. Her mood was so good even Mike couldn't spoil it.

She took a deep breath. ''Get lost, you loser,'' she sang heartily, pleased with how nicely it fit the tune to ''O Sole Mio.'' ''You make me puke.''

Apparently he didn't speak Italian. Chuckling comfortably, he came strutting into the room as if she'd just issued him an engraved invitation. He must have been mowing the yard. He smelled kind of sweaty, but nice, like summer grass and sunshine.

"So, what's up? I heard you were painting something."

He propped his leg on the stepladder she'd been using and wiped his face with his T-shirt before he gave the wall a serious look.

Suzie realized she was holding her breath, which was ridiculous. She didn't need this Neanderthal's approval of anything she did.

"Hey." He looked at Suzie briefly, then turned back to the painting. He seemed gratifyingly stunned. "This is nice. I didn't know you could paint like this. I mean, it's going to be good. *Really* good."

She concentrated on wiping her brush against her cloth. It would be moronic to care what he thought.

"Yeah, like you'd know anything." She dunked the brush in her jelly jar of murky water. "The only pictures you hang on your walls have staple holes in the center."

"Aw, now that's not fair." But he was laughing, so she knew it was true. "I almost bought a velvet Elvis once from a guy on the highway."

"Sorry," she said wryly. "My mistake."

She glanced up then, and saw that he was looking at her. He had the same old cocky expression. He'd had it launching spitballs in kindergarten, and he'd probably have it throwing horseshoes in retirement. But something new touched the edges of his laughing blue eyes. Something less sarcastic. Something more real.

Whatever it was, it made her uncomfortable. She searched for a cutting put-down, but the ordinarily reliable computer in her mind wasn't cooperating. *Searching, searching,* the screen said, but nothing clever came through.

"Hey, Suzie," he said in a funny voice. "Why don't you come here a minute?"

She wiped her fingers compulsively on the towel. "What for? I'm busy, moron."

"Just come here."

She twiddled her brushes in the water and bent over her toolbox, counting her tubes of paint.

"Hey." He chuckled. "You're not afraid to, are you?"

"As if." He knew that would get her, didn't he? But she couldn't help it. She cocked her head, lifted her chin and took the four long steps to the ladder.

She stopped beside him. She was so close she could see tiny little rectangles of grass stuck to his neck, his wrists, his sneakers. So close she could see where the bronze of his summer tan paled behind his ear. "Well? What?"

He reached up slowly and touched one finger to her nose. She remembered smearing paint there, hours ago. "You're a mess," he said softly.

"Yeah, well, you should talk," she countered, wishing she could breathe better. He must be giving off pheromones or something. He was clogging up the air with all that sexy self-confidence. She wished she could just kick him, the way she used to when he bothered her in kindergarten.

"I wanted to tell you…you look kind of cute in blue," he said. He touched her cheek. "And green." He ran his forefinger across her collarbone, raising goose bumps that she knew he could see, damn him. "And white and yellow and red."

"Oh, yeah?" Brother, *that* was clever. Maybe this was why all the popular girls were stupid. The boys got you so tense you could hardly breathe, and not enough oxygen could reach your brain cells.

Maybe, she thought disjointedly as his finger trailed down her arm, maybe sex fogged up your brain the same way it fogged up your windshield.

Maybe she was finally going to find out.

"Hey, Frome, how about it, man?" The voice belonged to Rutledge Coffee, one of Mike's best friends, one of those lazy, preppy, superior jocks that Suzie particularly hated. He stood at the library door, looking from Mike to Suzie curiously. "Sorry, man. But do you think we could do this *today?*"

Suzie and Mike stepped back simultaneously. She busied herself arranging the paints, trying to hide her stupidly flushed cheeks.

She didn't look at Mike, but she knew what she would have seen if she had. He would have been puffing out his chest, running his hand through his hair, refusing to make eye contact with her. Maybe he was even now giving his Neanderthal buddy a knowing grin. *Well, sure, she's a freak, but I thought I'd give her a thrill.*

Egotistical dumb-ass. *Give* her *a thrill?* Like hell.

But the hardest part to swallow, the part that just wouldn't go down, was that it was true. Being touched by Mike Frome was definitely the biggest thrill she'd ever had.

And for that she could cheerfully have killed him.

FOR A RARE MOMENT of pure self-indulgence, Matthew stood on the patio and watched Natalie as she worked on the pool.

She obviously was enjoying herself, though he knew from personal experience that it was rough, hot work. That was one of her specialties—making labor seem like fun. This past week had been one of the most pleasant weeks of his life, though he had worked harder than he ever remembered working before, even in prison.

Natalie was down in the deep end today, sitting cross-legged by the drain, pounding out bad spots in the finish with a hammer. The loose marcite went flying everywhere, and the acoustics down there were terrific. Every whack reverberated off the tall, empty walls, so one hammer sounded like an army.

She must be exhausted. The empty pool collected heat like a solar bowl. He came to the edge of the coping and raised his voice over the din. ''How about if I take over?''

She looked up, wiping grains of marcite from her face, and smiled.

"I thought you decided the staircase was more important."

"It's done. It wasn't as serious as I thought. I just had to replace a few boards, a few nails. I can take over here."

"Oh, well, if you *insist…*" She stood eagerly, wiping debris from the seat of her blue polka-dotted bikini. "I sure could use a break. I've been pounding so hard I think I dislocated my shoulder."

He climbed quickly down the small staircase and walked the steep slope to the deep end.

"Thanks." She held out the hammer, grinning. "It's actually kind of fun, in a destructive, preschool kind of way. You can work out a lot of your frustrations with this thing."

Frustrations. Yeah, he had his share of those. Spending eighteen hours a day shoulder to shoulder with a gorgeous woman whose wardrobe seemed to consist entirely of skimpy shorts, cutoff T-shirts, and bikinis—but not allowing yourself to notice how sexy she was—could definitely give a man a few frustrations. Eventually, he figured, it could make you rubber-room crazy.

Not that Natalie ever consciously worked at driving him nuts. He knew all the tricks—the sidelong glances from under heavy eyes, the "unintentional" flash of cleavage, the slow crossing and uncrossing of long legs. He knew women who could turn anything into an advertisement for sex—smiling, blinking, putting on a glove, peeling an orange, caressing the stem of a wineglass, applying lipstick, *anything*.

Natalie either didn't know those tricks or didn't like them. Maybe, he thought, looking at her now, she knew she didn't need them.

She almost never wore makeup—unless the white triangle of zinc on the tip of her nose counted. Right now her cheeks were bronze and glowing, just another hour or two from serious sunburn. She had clipped her hair carelessly on top of her head in a crazed tumble of curls. Even her bikinis and short shorts were for comfort, not flirtation.

And yet she hit him like an eclipse. If he allowed himself to look straight at her for more than about ten seconds, he was a goner.

"Why don't you go in and take a long, cool shower?" He took the hammer. "I'll handle this for a while."

"Oh, no, a shower would be way too much work." She yawned. "The sun's made me sleepy. I think I'll just catnap out here on the lounger and watch you pound rocks." She raised her eyebrows. "Hey, did you really do that? In prison, I mean. Did they make you pound rocks?"

He smiled, shaking his head. He was getting used to her casual references to prison. She made it sound interesting, exotic, as if he'd gone there to do research for a novel, or to win a bet. Amazing how much of the sting it removed from the topic.

"No," he said. "They made us build houses for people who had nowhere to live."

"Oh, what a great thing to do! And the perfect apprenticeship for coming here!" She wrinkled her nose. "Although building a new house from scratch is probably easier than trying to fix this old mausoleum, isn't it?"

"A lot easier," he admitted. "But not nearly as exciting."

She brightened. "Right. I mean, I bet you never found a secret room."

"Never," he agreed. They had done that yesterday, when he was repairing a light switch. Pressing on the wood-paneled walls to balance himself, he had opened a secret door into a small, empty, closetlike space. Natalie had loved it, though she'd expressed disappointment that it wasn't full of stolen treasure.

"Or a hidden mural under a mural?"

"Nope, never." Two days ago, Natalie had been cleaning the dining room mural, an awful thing with cattle and wagons, and she had realized that, under one of the cow's heads, you could just barely make out the head of a woman. She'd brought in an art expert, who seemed quite excited about the find.

"Or a Chinese vase that just might be worth ten thousand dollars?"

"Hey, now. Don't get your hopes up," he said. He had been looking through the toolshed last Wednesday, and there among the empty terra-cotta flowerpots and coiled garden hoses—don't ask him why—had been a four-foot-tall Oriental vase that might, just might, be a Ming. She had danced with glee and shipped it off immediately, via Stuart, to her favorite antique dealer in town. They were still awaiting the verdict.

"I always get my hopes up," she said, laughing. "I can't help it. Granville genes are incurably optimistic."

For an hour or so after that she seemed to doze, stretched out on a lounger at the far end of the pool. The noise he made pounding weak spots didn't seem to bother her. Every now and then he'd glance up, but she was always limp and peaceful. Her blond curls sparkled in the light. She lay on her back, one graceful arm thrown over her face to block out the sun, the other hand resting on her bare, golden midriff.

He was careful not to exceed his ten seconds. He just kept pounding rocks, draining tension as best he could.

Once, though, when he looked up, he was surprised to see that she was sitting up, talking to some man who was perched on the foot of the lounger. He squinted against the bright sunlight, wondering who it was. Granville, maybe?

No. It was Stuart. Natalie was facing him, laughing merrily while they talked, allowing him to apply sunscreen to her shoulders. After a minute, she swiveled on the lounger, presenting her back, and Stuart began rubbing lotion there, too.

Matthew's reaction was immediate and visceral. It was so definite he couldn't even pretend he didn't recognize it. Insane as it might be, the feeling was jealousy.

Oh, brother. He was an even bigger fool than he'd realized.

During this week of living at Summer House, he had kept a straitjacket on his conscious thoughts. *It's a job. She's your boss, nothing else. Don't notice, don't want, don't feel and, for God's sake, don't touch. Don't start thinking it's a partnership, don't start letting it get all cozy, domestic and personal.*

He thought he'd managed pretty well.

But apparently while his conscious mind had been trussed up, his unconscious mind had been having a field day, romping about with all kinds of reckless ideas.

Apparently his subconscious had built this ridiculous daydream in which her crooked smiles, her sweet, wrinkling nose, her sunny laughter, her infectious enthusiasm, all existed just for him.

He almost laughed out loud. What a moron he was. He'd have to work a lot harder at keeping this impersonal, or he'd have to pack up and move on.

He forced his attention back to the pool, pounding a bubbled spot with so much force the marcite sprayed up around him like a geyser of pebbles.

His arm burned, but he kept at it. This was his job. This was what she paid him for.

A few minutes later, cool fingertips rested against

his shoulder. He looked up, and Natalie was standing next to him, her oiled shoulders glistening in the sunlight.

"Guess what?" She grinned. "You're all finished for today!"

He couldn't help smiling back. "I am?"

"Yep." She patted the waistband of her bikini bottoms. "I've got a little something here I need your help with."

He looked down. A small piece of blue paper stuck up above the polka-dotted fabric, tickling her hipbone. "What is it?"

She pulled the paper out with a flourish, opened it up and waved it in front of his face. "It's the check for the vase, my doubting friend. It's a check for ten thousand wonderful American dollars!"

She took the hammer from his hand. "And now I need you to come inside and tell me how to invest it. I want to turn it into *twenty* thousand wonderful dollars. And then forty! Eighty! A million!"

Enthusiasm radiated out from her in palpable waves. Its touch was warm and vital and exciting. It wasn't easy to resist. But he had to.

"I can't do that, Natalie," he said calmly. "You know I can't."

She waved the check dismissively. "Of course you can. It'll be fun. You found the vase, after all. It's practically your own money."

"No," he said. "It isn't."

She frowned, but he could tell she wasn't taking

his refusal seriously. "Oh, Matthew, don't be like that. I'm not talking about anything formal, anything you'd need a license for. Surely they can't stop you from offering a little advice to a friend?"

"I can't do it, Natalie. You need a professional."

She tsked. "You are a professional."

"Not anymore."

"But—" For the first time she looked uncertain. "Am I imposing? I honestly thought it would be fun." She hesitated. "Do you feel that I'm trying to take advantage, trying to get something for free?"

He made a small noise. "Of course not. But being a good investment advisor is a full-time job. You have to follow the companies, chart the stock movement, study financial publications and profit statements. You have to know the executives, understand the market, talk to thousands of people. I don't have the tools or the time for all that anymore. I'm out of it, Natalie. Get a professional."

She smiled. "Granville says you don't seem to need all that. He says you're the kind of guy whose gut tells you if a company is bad."

Matthew tilted his head, surprised. Though everything he'd said to Natalie was true, he had used a lot of gut instinct. And his instincts had rarely been wrong, at least about stocks. "And how would Granville know that?"

She laughed. "Apparently he and Ward were going to invest in something called Richbern Corp. Ward said you made a face when he mentioned the company, so Ward held back. Granville, who is the stubbornest man on the planet, refused to listen. He invested about fifty grand in Richbern, and apparently their profits are down, they fired their CEO or something, and the stock sank like a stone. Granville pretends to be mad at Ward, but he's really just mad at himself.''

"CFO," Matthew corrected automatically. So Richbern finally unloaded that crook? It was about time. The guy had been rotten for years. The company would be better off in the long run. If Granville could sit tight, he might make some money on this stock after all.

"Whatever. So, see?" She waved the check again. "You don't need the *Wall Street Journal* and all that stuff. You just *know*."

He wanted so much to say yes. How wonderful it would be to help her make extra money, to lighten this burden she carried. But what if his instincts failed him? What if, instead of lightening her load, he added to it? What if he lost that ten thousand dollars with one bad decision?

"Natalie," he said softly. "I'm sorry. I can't do it."

She studied his face for a long, quiet moment. He braced himself for her disappointment, perhaps even resentment. After all, she had taken a big chance by hiring him. Maybe she thought he owed her something.

But, as always, she surprised him.

"Oh, well, that's okay," she said pleasantly, tucking the check back into her bikini pants. She picked a fleck of marcite from his thumb, took his hand in hers and started pulling him up to the shallow end.

"Still, no more work today," she said. "Let's take a shower and do something wild."

He laughed in spite of himself. "In the shower?"

She shook her head and kept pulling. "Of course not. I'm talking about *really* wild. You think I'm just this boring young innocent, but you don't know the real me. Having too much money in my pants always makes me feel reckless."

CHAPTER SEVEN

"A MOTORCYCLE?" Matthew's face was strangely
blank. "That's your wild idea? You want to ride a
motorcycle?"

Natalie shoved the garage door the rest of the way
open, so that the sun winked on the shiny silver
chrome. A very expensive, huge piece of machinery,
it had belonged to her grandfather, who had always
kept it in tip-top condition. Even after he got too sick
to ride it, he'd taken it out of the garage every Sunday
and run the engine for an hour or so, just for the joy
of hearing it rumble.

"It was my grandfather's favorite toy. He prowled
the mountainside on it every weekend until he was
almost ninety. But he refused to let me ride it. He
said it wasn't for girls."

Matthew clearly still couldn't believe it. "This is
your wild idea?" he repeated.

The implication that it wasn't wild enough annoyed
her. "Look," she said, "do you know how to drive
one of these or not?"

He seemed to be smothering a laugh. "I think I
could manage. Why? Don't you?"

"Not really," she admitted. "I tried a couple of

times, after I put a new battery in and everything, but I keep falling over. But I'm dying to go out on it. I've wanted to ride it ever since I was fifteen years old. It looks like so much fun.'' Her heart was racing just thinking about it. "I've got this fantasy of going really, really fast on the edge of the mountain.''

The fantasy had a second act, too. She secretly wanted to make love on the back of a motorcycle. She'd read it in a book once, and it had sounded absolutely thrilling, all that vibration, all that danger...

That would scare him off for sure, so she didn't mention that part.

He wasn't even trying to hold back his laughter anymore. "When you said reckless, I wasn't sure what to expect, but never in a million years—''

She lifted her chin. "I'm sorry I can't come up with anything more exotic. Not all of us have the advantage of doing hard time with ax murderers to give us truly creative ideas.''

He chuckled, which pleased her. Thank goodness he'd gotten over being so stiff and monosyllabic about the topic of prison. Maybe it was like a wound that had started to heal and wasn't so tender to the touch anymore.

"I hate to disillusion you,'' he said, "but ax murderers are among the least creative people you'll ever meet.''

"Whatever. Come on, Matthew, please. We've worked hard all week. I feel as if I do nothing but work. If I'm not at the nursery, then I'm chained to the house. Let's have some fun.''

He looked at the motorcycle dubiously. "I really should get to work on the roof. Couldn't someone else take you? What about Bart? Or Stuart?''

"I want you." She folded her arms. "Look, you turned me down about the investments, and I didn't give you a hard time. You owe me this.''

"Natalie, it's not that I wouldn't enjoy it—"

"Grrr." She tapped her foot. "Do you want me to have a Granville moment?''

He grinned. "I thought you already were.''

She shook her head ominously. "Not even close.''

He sighed and held out his hands for the keys. "All right, then. Let's go.''

The minute he started the engine she knew it would be everything she had dreamed—and more. The seat felt thick and sensual between her legs, and when it began to vibrate she got an adrenaline rush so strong it took her breath away.

She wrapped her arms around his waist, something she'd been fantasizing about for a whole week now. He had an extraordinary body—lean and muscular and perfectly proportioned, with the hardest, flattest belly and angular hipbones she could feel right through his jeans.

She wriggled up close behind him shamelessly. He cocked his head slightly, curious. "I just don't want to fall off," she explained innocently, and he laughed softly in response.

But when she tightened her knees around him and let her hands fall right to his belt line, she thought she felt him inhale sharply. She might have imagined that, though, because suddenly they were on the move.

They cruised through Vanity Gap sedately, but when, after a very few minutes, they reached the unpopulated, curving mountain roads, he gave it more gas, and the bike began to fly.

She laughed out loud as the wind tore at her hair and tried to rip the helmet from her head. But the wind took the laughter, too, and flung it out like a colored scarf in the air behind them.

It was wild and wonderful and easily the sexiest experience she'd ever had outside a bedroom. Their bodies were connected through the growling, powerful machine, and they dipped and tilted together, riding the curves. They strained up the inclines, the big bike panting. They plunged as one when the road dipped, their hearts in their throats as the bike fell and fell, and finally leveled out again.

She could have gone on forever. The late-afternoon sunlight was soft and the air was thick with peonies and roses from unseen gardens hidden behind the curtain of leafy green trees.

But several miles out of town, they saw a roadside farm stand, and Natalie was suddenly overcome with an intense desire for some warm, sweet, wet watermelon. She pointed eagerly, and Matthew let the motorcycle glide to a halt.

The stand was untended and simple, just a long wooden table heaped with fresh produce, and several bunches of daisies and marigold. Dozens of watermelons lay off to the side, huge ones, as big as small children.

A rusty tin cash box sat on one edge of the table, with a hand-blocked sign that merely read "Honor System."

Natalie's mouth began to water. She slipped off the bike, unhooked her helmet and dropped it on the ground. Digging in her pocket, she found a five and slipped it into the cash box. Then she picked the biggest, ripest watermelon of all, lifting it with a groan.

"I don't guess you have a knife," she said without much hope.

He had taken off his helmet, and she could see that his brown eyes were shining, his thick hair tousled and blown. He must have felt the adrenaline pumping, too.

"Sorry," he said. "Not unless it came with my Hell's Angels introductory kit."

"Well, darn," she said, eyeing the watermelon with frustrated desire. "I'm starving." And it was true, even though she had fixed them a large lunch before they'd left. Excitement burned up a lot of calories.

He climbed off the bike and took the giant melon from her hands. "No problem," he said. He walked over to a granite outcropping and, before she could call out in protest, he slammed the watermelon hard against the stone.

With a rather unpleasant thud, it broke into half-a-dozen large, glistening red pieces. "My lady," Matthew said with a smile, "dinner is served."

They sat there together, their backs against the rocks, until the shadows were long, and their hands and faces were messy with watermelon. It was the most delicious food she had ever tasted, and she ate it all the way down to the pale green rind.

"You mention your grandfather a lot, but you don't say much about your father," Matthew said when most of the eating was over. "What was he like?"

She looked out over the empty road. "I don't really remember much," she said. "He and my mother died abroad when I was only about eight. I have a few memories. Mostly I just remember being loved very much. And, of course, that my father was a true Granville. His contribution to our crazy house was to try to build a small planetarium on the roof."

"Try to?"

She laughed. "Apparently it was done on the cheap, and it didn't seal properly. And the weight of the room, and the huge telescope, was too much for the existing supports, so the whole roof practically collapsed. They had to dismantle it. You'll find pieces of it in the garage to this day."

He laughed, too. She liked that his laughter didn't sound scornful. He seemed to think it was rather charming to do such wacky, Granville things.

And then, for a long while, they talked of little things—and sometimes they were comfortably silent.

Eventually, though, the sky turned as pink as the watermelon. Matthew scanned the sky, as if gauging how much daylight was left. "Ready to go back?"

She shook her head. "Never. A woman can live on watermelon and string beans, can't she? I don't ever want to go back."

He added one last seed to the small pile they had built between them. He hesitated a moment, and then he spoke.

"It's probably none of my business, but why do you stay there? This is the second time this week you've said how much you'd like to get away and never go back. Obviously you hate the hassle and the worry and the expense of that house. Anybody would. So why don't you just sell it and be free?"

She looked at him, wishing she could make him understand. Sometimes, though, she wasn't sure she understood herself.

"I don't hate Summer House," she said. "I love it. It's my legacy. In a way, it's my life. I want more than anything in the world to make it right again, to make it the beautiful, glamorous showplace it was meant to be. Maybe someday I'll break down and apply for the historical preservation designation."

"I thought your grandfather had pretty much outlawed that."

"He did." She sighed heavily. "I hate to let him down. But the only thing I hate worse is feeling that

I'm failing, that I'm letting down the whole scowling gallery of ancestral Granvilles.''

She sighed and looked toward the road that would lead them back home. That wasn't quite true, was it? That wasn't the thing she hated *most*. Worst of all, she hated the hollow, empty darkness of those big rooms late at night. She hated how lonely it was to face the morning, and the endless struggle, with no one at her side.

''And—'' But she stopped. She couldn't say all that. It would sound like maudlin self-pity, which would embarrass him to death.

''And what?''

''Nothing. It's just that—'' Impulsively, she turned to face him, not caring that her mouth was probably sticky and red. ''I just wanted to thank you for taking me out on the bike today. It was absolutely perfect.''

''My pleasure,'' he said, smiling. He rubbed his thumb at the edge of her mouth, removing a small red remnant of watermelon. ''Tell you what, I'll teach you to ride, so you can go out anytime you want. That way, after I'm gone—''

''Don't say it,'' she broke in, reaching out and grabbing his arm, as if she could physically restrain the words. ''Don't talk about leaving. Not today.''

His eyes looked grave. ''But I will go, Natalie. You know that. When the summer's over, I'll have to—''

''Don't,'' she said, and then, without thinking it through at all, she moved closer. ''I know it's true,'' she whispered. ''Just don't say it today.''

And then she kissed him.

He tasted sweet, like watermelon and sunshine. His lips were hard and warm but utterly still, and at first she thought he was going to let her do all the work. But she didn't give up. She probed lightly with the tip of her tongue. She touched his cheeks with her hands, and she let her upper body sink softly against his.

He groaned as her breasts met his chest, and then suddenly he was kissing her back. He moved over her mouth with such a driving expertise that her head began to feel light and whirly. She ran her hands through his hair, glorying in the knowledge that he had been ready for this, too.

It lasted almost forever. But finally, slowly, he pulled back. His dark eyes were soft on her, and she thought she could see in their depths both intense desire and confused regret.

"Natalie—"

But she wouldn't allow it. She stood with a smile, then held out her hand to pull him to his feet, as well. "Come on," she said. "I'm ready to go back now."

"Natalie." His gaze was still troubled. "I didn't mean to let that—"

"Don't you dare apologize," she said, pointing her watermelon-red finger at him fiercely. "I know it was just an afternoon fantasy, but it was a great one. I'll be darned if I'm going to let you mess it up now."

TWO DAYS LATER, Matthew made his first trip into town to buy supplies.

Big Mountain Hardware on Main Street certainly

lived up to its name. It was the largest retail store in Firefly Glen and, as Natalie had described it to Matthew, the unofficial meeting place for the town's male population. They could trade bits of personal news in comfort there, secure that the presence of so many chain saws and drill bits and backhoes would prevent anyone from calling it "gossip."

He was looking for a sturdy wrecking bar or cat's-paw to remove the tiles on the Summer House roof. He had ordered a couple of four-foot rolls of roofing felt paper, too, and he planned to check on their status while he was there.

The owner seemed busy—a crowd of men gathered at the main counter, admiring a 120-horsepower slab saw someone was buying—so Matthew wandered over to the wall of assorted fasteners. He could use some more ten-penny nails. He'd never seen a house eat nails the way Summer House did.

"You've got to be kidding," a man's voice was saying from the other side of the tall wall. "You can't put in your new carpet because Fred decided not to put in his new pool because Tim couldn't go through with the landscaping because he lost the job of re-roofing Summer House? Man, it's a mess. It's like watching a line of dominos fall down."

Another man laughed. "Yeah, that's life in a small town for you. The whole damn city may grind to a halt just because Natalie Granville called off her wedding."

Matthew squeezed the plastic packet of nails he'd just picked up and listened hard. Eavesdropping rubbed him the wrong way, but this time...

From the start, he had suspected that Natalie had been the one to back out of that wedding. Except for the first drunken Saturday, she certainly couldn't have acted less like a jilted bride. But she hadn't ever volunteered any information, and he wasn't about to ask.

"Heck," another man said firmly, "I say anyone who really believed those two were going to get married was a fool to start with. Old friends like that don't just suddenly fall madly in love."

"Love had nothing to do with it. Bart was on the rebound from that other woman, and Natalie was looking for the money to fix up her granddaddy's crazy old haunted house. If ever a match *wasn't* made in heaven..."

"*I* thought she'd marry him," a younger voice piped in. "She loves that house. I honestly thought she'd do whatever it took."

"Oh, she'll find herself another millionaire," the first man said with an air of authority. "Half the men under forty in this town are in love with her, and quite a few of the old geezers, too."

Laughter rumbled through the crowd.

"Yeah," someone said, chuckling, "but now they've got to get past the handyman, who I hear is really good with his hands, if you know what I—"

That was enough. Matthew made his way around the wall, where he could be seen.

"Hi," he said casually. "Sorry to interrupt. I just wondered where you keep the wrecking bars."

A sea of red faces stared at him uncomfortably. The gossip bouncing around town must have included photos, because obviously every man knew exactly who Matthew was.

"I—I don't think we have any in stock right now," the owner said, struggling for a normal tone. "But how about a cat's paw? I'm pretty sure we've got those."

The front door buzzed as someone else entered, and every face at the desk looked over, desperately hoping for a distraction.

"Parker!" Half-a-dozen voices said his name at once, and the newcomer looked up with surprise.

"Hello, gentlemen," he said with a quizzical smile. He put his hand over his heart humbly. "I'm touched. Are you the official hardware store welcoming committee?"

The owner recovered first. "We're just eager for news about Sarah. How's she doing? When does Heather say that baby's going to make an appearance?"

"Sarah's fine. Heather says maybe a week. Maybe ten days." Parker turned to Matthew. "Hi," he said pleasantly, holding out his hand. "I'm Parker Tremaine. I think we met outside the sheriff's office the first day you arrived in town. I was escorting one of my clients home to bed."

Matthew shook hands. "Yes, I remember," he

said. And he did. The town lawyer, buddies with Harry, the town sheriff. "Good to see you again."

"So you're working for Natalie now?" When Matthew nodded, Parker smiled. "Brave man. Summer House is quite a challenge."

"I'm just tackling the small stuff," Matthew explained. "Loose stairs and broken windows, things like that. I'm only here for the summer."

"Really?" Parker looked curious, but when Matthew didn't go on he politely let the subject drop. He unfurled a set of floor plans he had rolled up under his arm and spread them out on the main counter.

"Well, my wife's Uncle Ward reports that you're excellent," Parker said, glancing at Matthew. "Apparently he's seen your work. So, anyhow, what do you say, men? I need some advice on these. As you know, we're putting in a nursery, and we've hit a snag."

Matthew knew that Parker Tremaine hadn't come in here expecting to consult the Summer House handyman about his private business. But it would have been awkward to walk away, so he glanced down at the floor plans, just as everyone else did, prepared to give them a cursory look for courtesy's sake.

"See, the architect decided to put the nursery in here, using part of the office connected to the master bedroom. But Sarah thinks it destroys the view of the lake, and I have to agree with her."

"Damn right you do," one of the men around them

said, laughing. "No one disagrees with a pregnant woman unless they have a death wish."

Parker chuckled and went back to tracing the area with his forefinger. "But what else can we do? With only a week before the baby comes, it hardly makes sense to start over."

Several suggestions were put forth, and Parker considered them all politely, though Matthew could tell they wouldn't work. He actually had an idea—a simple reapportionment of space—but he disliked the idea of butting in. Gradually he weaned himself from the crowd and went over to pick out a cat's paw. He didn't belong here, pretending to be one of the Firefly Glen good old boys.

Besides, it was time to get back to Summer House.

As it turned out, after he made his purchase, he and Parker were exiting at the same time. Parker stopped him on the sidewalk.

"It was good to see you. I've been hoping we'd run into each other again sometime."

Matthew could almost believe he meant it. This was one millionaire who didn't seem to have any status issues about handymen.

On an impulse, perhaps to thank him indirectly for treating him as an equal, Matthew mentioned the easy fix he'd spotted for Parker's nursery dilemma.

"You know, I was thinking maybe you could switch your spaces. Turn the nursery into the bedroom, and vice versa. You'll need to move that one wall back a few feet to correct your proportions. But that shouldn't take long. From the blueprints, I'd say it isn't a load-bearing wall. After that, it's just a matter of shifting furniture."

Even without looking at the plans, Parker obviously saw immediately that it would work. His whole face lit up, and he shook Matthew's hand with a gratitude that was almost embarrassing.

"I love it," he said. "And Sarah will, too. God, what luck to run into a man with common sense!"

Matthew was a little embarrassed. It had been such an insignificant fix, but apparently to Parker nothing that made Sarah happy was insignificant.

"Oh, and by the way," Parker added, "when you get back to Summer House, would you give Natalie a message for me?"

"Sure."

"Tell her I said I was disappointed to hear she'd called off the wedding."

"Really?" Matthew paused, not sure what he should say. He wasn't even sure what he was supposed to know. But he found it hard to believe that Parker thought Natalie should have married Bart Beswick for his money. "You were?"

Parker lifted one eyebrow and smiled. "You bet. I had planned to make a fortune representing her in the divorce."

"AHH-CHOO!"

"Bless you again," Suzie said, laughing. "For the

millionth time. Can't I just say one 'bless you' now and let it cover all sneezes to come?''

"Sorry." Natalie looked over at Suzie and grinned helplessly. The air in the attic was dancing with dust, and she'd started sneezing about every three minutes. She ought to get out of here, but she was having too much fun.

"Look!" She held up a beautiful green beaded gown. "Can you imagine wearing this one?"

Suzie wasn't listening. She had discovered a trunk of her own, and was absorbed in pulling out the lovely old fabrics. "Oh, man," she said as she unearthed a sleek bloodred satin evening dress. "This is so amazing."

Natalie looked up and groaned appreciatively. The red dress was fantastic, so exquisitely cut it didn't need a single bit of ornamentation. "You know, that would look great on you."

Suzie snorted. "Right."

"I mean it. With your dark hair and your fair skin, you can carry off jewel tones." Natalie sighed enviously, thinking of her own tawny monochromatic coloring. The only color she looked really good in was white, and how boring was that?

"Why don't you try it on? Just for fun." Natalie was careful not to push. She knew that Suzie probably took a lot of criticism about her minimalist Gothic black wardrobe, and she didn't want to add her voice to the din. Besides, Suzie looked wonderful in black, too. With that coloring, and that slim, gamine elegance, the kid could wear a garbage sack and look gorgeous.

Natalie kept searching her own trunk. They were supposed to be hunting for old papers about Summer House. She needed to find one last detail about the original mosaic design on the pool, and Suzie had volunteered to he!p while she waited for her latest painting to dry.

But these vintage clothes were just so beautiful, neither of them could quite resist.

Out of the corner of her eye, Natalie saw Suzie stand up, the red dress draped over her arm, and amble with a deliberately casual air over toward the full-length mirror propped against the front wall.

With movements so small they attracted no attention, the younger girl lifted the bodice of the dress up to her breast. Natalie, who shouldn't have been watching, caught her breath. The transformation was instantaneous and magical. Suddenly Suzie, the irritable teenage witch, became Audrey Hepburn at her most deliciously glamorous.

Suzie's mouth hung open, and her shining black eyes were as round as two dark moons. Obviously she couldn't believe what she saw in the mirror.

"Wow," Natalie said succinctly.

Suzie angled a glance at her in the mirror. Realizing she was being watched, she immediately donned her air of bored cool and let the gown drop.

"Yeah, so what? I guess anybody could look good in a dress that costs about a million dollars."

Natalie chuckled. "Not that good."

"Besides, I'm not planning to start dressing up like Barbie just to impress anybody." Suzie came back over to the trunk and draped the red satin over the open lid. "If they don't like Suzie Strickland the way she is, to hell with them."

Natalie was quiet a moment, trying to decide what her best response would be. She sympathized with Suzie's position and yet...

Suzie obviously interpreted her silence as disapproval. "What? You think I'm wrong? I just want to be myself, darn it. Why can't everyone just deal with that?"

"I don't think you're wrong." Natalie shrugged. "I guess I just think maybe there's more than one 'real' Suzie. I know I have a lot of different moods and they're all equally real."

She grinned over at the scowling teen. "You know how it is. Sometimes I feel gorgeous and to-die-for, just like that red dress. Sometimes I feel bored, like torn jeans and a stinky sweatshirt." She lowered her voice and wiggled her eyebrows suggestively. "Sometimes I feel buck naked and bad to the bone."

As Natalie had hoped she would, Suzie laughed. Then she sighed, letting her hand stroke wistfully across the satin.

"Yeah, but when everybody is bugging you to change your style, backing you into a corner, then you can't change even if you want to. It would be like letting them win."

She looked up at Natalie, and her dark eyes were shining suspiciously. "You should have heard that witch Mrs. Putnam when I asked her for a recommendation. She as good as told me she wouldn't write me one unless I started acting more girly and sweet. She told me to try wearing some pretty dresses, like that has anything to do with whether I can paint."

She scowled even harder, but her eyes caught the sunlight, and Natalie could see that she was an inch away from shedding an actual tear. Natalie was shocked. She didn't think she'd ever seen Suzie cry before.

But now that she'd started talking, Suzie didn't seem to be able to stop.

"And that moron Mike Frome," she said harshly. "He acts like I don't exist, which is fine with me, don't get me wrong. But I know darn well that if I showed up in tight sweaters and short skirts, he'd notice me big time. Not that I give a damn."

Oh, dear. Suddenly it all made sense. Suzie, who came from a perfectly respectable middle-class family, which in Firefly Glen practically qualified as the wrong side of the tracks, had a crush on Mike Frome, who came from zillionaire row.

Hmm. On the face of it, it seemed hopeless. The artsy outcast had foolishly let herself fall for the king of the in crowd.

But Natalie knew Mike Frome pretty well, being his cousin as well as his summer employer. And she knew that Mike was a lot smarter and more sensitive than he let on. Also, now that she thought about it, once or twice she'd seen Mike watching Suzie from across the lawn, and frankly she had to disagree with Suzie's assessment. Mike Frome had definitely noticed Suzie Strickland.

She gave Suzie a frank look. "So. Does he know you like him?"

"I don't— I hate—" Suzie started to work up another head of steam, but she subsided under Natalie's unflinching stare. She sighed heavily and ran her hand through her short black hair. "No. He doesn't know. At least I hope he doesn't."

"Maybe you should tell him."

Suzie made a rude sound. "Like hell."

"I'm serious." Natalie smiled. "I don't think you'd need to change your wardrobe to get his attention. Maybe you just need to let him know the door's open."

"Right. And how exactly would you suggest I do that?" Suzie sounded irritably skeptical, but she also sounded curious.

"Oh, I don't know." Chewing her bottom lip, Natalie considered possibilities. Only one truly good idea came to mind. "Maybe sometime when the two of you are alone, you should just lean over, take his head in your hands and kiss him."

"*What?*" Suzie was clearly too stunned to snort or roll her eyes, or toss back any of her usual sarcastic responses. "You have *got* to be kidding."

Natalie smiled, thinking of watermelon-scented lips and red summer sunsets. "Do I?"

"Yes. Either kidding or *crazy.*"

Natalie flipped the lid of her trunk shut. She'd said enough for today.

"I'm a Granville," she said, grinning. "So I'd put my money on crazy." She stood, brushing dust from her skirt, which of course made her sneeze again.

"On the other hand, you'll never know till you try."

CHAPTER EIGHT

FIREFLY GLEN WAS HAVING a mild summer, and the nights were as cool and clean as black glass. In the pool house, Matthew slept with the windows open, enjoying the watery trickle of the wind moving through the treetops and, most of all, the absence of any remotely human noise.

But Wednesday night he awoke to a different sound. Voices carried across the clear air, hushed but definite, and not far away. He looked at his watch—3:00 a.m. Through the trees he could see lights, probably, judging from the position, in Natalie's greenhouse.

What could she be doing out there in the middle of the night? She usually spent only the morning hours working on her nursery business, devoting the afternoon to the house, and then going to sleep early, exhausted.

Could anything be wrong? He pulled on jeans, T-shirt and tennis shoes, knowing he wouldn't sleep until he was certain she was okay.

Once he passed the stand of oaks between the pool house and the nursery, he saw that the large glass greenhouse glowed like a fire opal against the black night. At least, he thought with relief, there was nothing surreptitious about whatever was going on in there.

When he opened the door, he found a bustling scene. Natalie and all three of her part-time employees were rushing around creating dozens of flower arrangements, just as if it were noon instead of the middle of the night.

When she saw Matthew, Natalie looked distressed. "Oh, darn. Are we making such a racket you can't sleep?"

Matthew shook his head. "No, I just saw the lights and wondered if everything was all right."

She smiled. "Fine. It's just that Sarah Tremaine went into labor a few hours ago. A whole week early. By morning we'll be swamped with orders for flowers, and we're not ready."

Her main nursery assistant, an elderly man named Thomas, came by holding out an armful of flowers. Natalie scanned them quickly. "Save the lilacs for Jocelyn—she insists on having the most expensive arrangement in the room. Give the peonies to Harry and Emma, and a few of the roses." Thomas nodded and moved on, nodding again as Natalie called after him, "But don't use any of the long-stem reds. Parker will want everything we've got."

"I really am sorry we woke you," she said, turning to Matthew. She looked tired. He knew she had been working after dinner on stripping old wallpaper from the Blue Bedroom. He wondered if she'd slept at all.

"Go back to bed if you can," she said, smiling. "We'll try to keep it down, although—" But then Natalie noticed Mike Frome at the far table, adding ferns to an arrangement of daisies. "No, no ferns on that one," she called out. "We might risk some snapdragons—just don't mix orange and red."

Matthew watched her, amazed at her military command of the room.

He hadn't spent much time in Natalie's small nursery, just a few odd jobs—reglazing a couple of panes in the roof, steadying a wobbly potting bench. He knew she had three regular helpers. Thomas came in four afternoons a week, and a middle-aged woman named Blanche managed the books and was always tut-tutting about Natalie's refusal to dun her slow-paying clients.

Then a couple of hours a week Mike Frome pitched in. The boy mowed Natalie's lawn for pay, but worked in the greenhouse as some kind of community service. Matthew gathered Mike must have stumbled into some mischief a while back and was paying off his debt to Firefly Glen society in man-hours.

Matthew didn't know much about nurseries, but he could tell Natalie was good. She had a light touch with the plants. She complimented the ones that flourished and coaxed the stragglers along like a mother encouraging a timid child. She handled her crew lightly, too. He suspected that all of them felt more like friends than paid employees and would, if necessary, have worked for free.

But the surprising part was the lack of Granville chaos. In the greenhouse, Natalie was organized, energetic and creative, still charmingly quirky but always in complete control. People who called her "too naive to live" must never have seen her scanning a delivery for errors. She knew her inventory to the last leaf, and she could calculate a five-digit receipt to the penny in her head.

Even so, the radar intensity of her focus tonight was amazing.

"Put me to work," he said. "I'd like to help."

She tilted her head and smiled. "I don't know, Mr. Quinn. You don't strike me as having much florist potential." She picked up a feathery pink stalk lined with flowers. "Foxglove or poppy?"

He squinted at it. "My first guess would have been 'pink thing.'"

"Nattie, dear, we're falling behind," Blanche reminded her from behind a gigantic concoction of white things. "In three hours that telephone is going to be ringing off the hook."

Natalie sighed. "Okay," she said to Matthew with a small smile. "You're hired." She pointed toward a pile of cardboard boxes in the corner. "That is about a million vases and baskets. If you'd cut the boxes open and get the containers out, it would be a big help."

After that, they didn't have a minute to talk about anything but color and size and price, baskets and bows and greenery. As the minutes ticked by, and the eastern sky grew gradually lighter, the rows of her unbelievably beautiful creations began to fill the tables and benches.

It was as exhausting as running a marathon, but by the time the telephone rang, they were finished. The water-filled cans where hundreds of cut blossoms and stalks of greenery had once stood were nearly empty. The floor was scattered with broken ferns, bits of ribbon, lost snowflakes of baby's breath, extraneous leaves and the odd blossom that Natalie had deemed inferior.

Thomas was standing closest to the greenhouse phone, and he answered it with a stately demeanor quite unlike the frenetic energy he'd been using for the past three hours. He listened a moment, thanked the caller, hung up the telephone, and then turned to the rest of them with a grin.

"It's a girl!"

After he disclosed the details, a tired cheer went up. It was then that Matthew realized Natalie was missing. He looked behind the flowery mountains of arrangements, but she wasn't there. He checked around the greenhouse benches, under the confusing wall of hanging plants.

"I think she said she was going to get the enclosure cards ready," Mike said, washing his hands at the big central sink. He nodded toward the small office at the back, where Natalie had a desk and a file cabinet for keeping germination records.

"Thanks." Matthew walked back quickly, and sure

enough there she was. She was resting her head on the heel of her hand, staring into space, the enclosure cards fanned out on the desk in front of her.

She looked up with a smile as he entered. "Was that the hospital? Any news?"

He nodded. "Cordelia Lee Tremaine was born exactly forty-five minutes ago. Six pounds and, I think, three ounces of healthy baby girl."

Natalie clapped her hands. "Oh, how perfect! Parker's mother's name was Cordelia. He must be so excited." She yawned broadly, remembering at the last minute to try to cover it with her hand. "Wow. What a night." She touched his arm. "You must be tired. Thanks for helping."

"I enjoyed it. Besides, I learned a lot."

She grinned, obviously skeptical. "Yeah? Like what?"

He held out a small, single pink flower he'd saved from extinction on the greenhouse floor. "Snapdragon," he announced smugly.

"Sorry." She shook her head. "Dianthus."

"Oh, well. I tried." He tucked the little flower into her hair, then stood back to survey his work. "Pretty. Actually, I think that's the botanical name. Pretty little pink thing."

Her cheeks turned as pink as the flower, and when she reached up to touch it he could see that her fingers were trembling slightly.

Oh, hell. He shouldn't have done that. He'd spent the past three days—ever since that shockingly sexy watermelon kiss—trying to cool things off between them. But it wasn't easy. Every time she looked at him like that, he could hardly remember his name, much less his irritating vow that he would never take advantage of her innocence, even if she wanted him to.

"Maybe you should take a nap," he said. "You look exhausted."

She tugged at her blouse self-consciously and smoothed a hand over her curls, which were almost bronze in the dawn's colored light.

"I must look a wreck." She cleared her throat. "We should both get some sleep. But how about if I make you breakfast first?"

He shook his head. "Thanks, but I'd better not."

"I've got fresh muffins, and I could make an omelette. It wouldn't take long."

"I can't," he said. "We agreed that I'd have Thursday and Friday off this week. I have to go to the city, remember? I ought to get going right away, actually."

Her eyes looked disappointed, though she smiled valiantly. "Oh, that's right. I'd forgotten. I'll miss you, but of course I wouldn't want to interfere with your trip. I know you must be eager to visit your old friends—"

"I'm not going to visit old friends," he interrupted sharply. Actually, maybe it was the perfect time to talk about this. Maybe they both needed to be reminded of who he really was. "People who embezzle millions of dollars don't have many friends. I have enemies, but they aren't exactly planning a welcome-back lunch at the country club, either.''

She frowned. ''Then don't go,'' she said impulsively. ''Stay here. You have friends here.''

''I can't,'' he said without inflection, without mercy on himself or on her. ''I have to go. I have to check in with my parole officer. If I don't show up, they'll come here to find me. And then they'll put me back in prison.''

SHE COULD HARDLY BELIEVE how much she missed him. How could she so quickly have come to rely on any man's presence?

She had lived here alone for five years, ever since her grandfather died. She'd been lonely, of course, maybe more than she had ever admitted to herself. That had probably played a part in her foolish acceptance of Bart's proposal. She'd found the money tempting, naturally. Summer House devoured money. More than that, though, maybe she'd been looking for someone to bring warmth and companionship to these big, empty rooms.

But, just in the nick of time, thank God, she had realized that living with a man she didn't love would be worse than living alone. Though they were good friends, and they respected each other tremendously, it could never be passionate, as a marriage should be. Eventually, their longing for more would come between them. And the house would seem bigger, colder and lonelier than ever.

Horrible. She would much rather turn the whole house over to the city, assuming they'd take the moldering old money pit.

And she'd definitely rather live alone.

But then came Matthew. From the first moment she saw him, her feelings had been completely inexplicable and yet somehow sublimely simple. She liked him. She trusted him. She enjoyed his company, respected his opinion, relied on his support.

And she wanted to have sex with him so badly it nearly drove her mad.

When he was out there, just yards away, lying in that wild, wonderful bed in the pool house, she found herself watching from the window, a pathetic Juliet whose Romeo had already gone to sleep.

But clearly the feeling wasn't exactly mutual. She'd pretty much offered herself to him on a tray with the watermelon, and he had responded by pretending it hadn't ever happened.

In fact, she'd noticed that, since then, he spent a lot of time working wherever she *wasn't*.

Darn. Maybe she'd better talk to Suzie. That advice she'd given her had a flaw. In theory, giving your man an unexpected kiss could be good, fiery fun that got things cooking. Sometimes, though, if you'd misread the guy's signals, if he wasn't really interested, you just ended up looking dumb and desperate.

Even so, she found herself counting the hours until

Matthew returned from New York. He'd said he'd be back early Friday evening. On Thursday she was busy. She delivered flower arrangements from sun up to sun down, which was at least distracting. Friday morning, she moped over a bowl of cold cereal, deciding it was too much trouble to cook.

By Friday afternoon, though, she had a roast beef, potatoes, carrots, onions and tomatoes in the slow cooker. Maybe he'd be home in time for dinner, which was less than five hours away. She began to hum as she put the finishing touches on her own bouquet for Sarah Tremaine.

Dumb and desperate, maybe. But also determined.

She arrived at Firefly Glen's very small community hospital in midafternoon, and she stopped by the nursery to peek at the sleeping bundle marked ''Tremaine, Cordelia.''

She couldn't see much. Just a soft pink blanket wrapped around a tiny pink face and a tiny pink fist. And yet somehow the sight nearly moved her to tears.

As she might have predicted, Parker was sitting on the edge of Sarah's bed, holding his wife's hand, looking down at her as if adoring this woman was his full-time job.

It was very sweet. Ever since their wedding last winter, you hardly ever saw Sarah and Parker apart. Firefly Glen loved a love story, and this was one of the best. Parker wasn't the biological father of Sarah's baby, but no one doubted that, in every way that really mattered, this newborn little girl was his.

Sarah looked up as Natalie entered. "Oh, how beautiful," she breathed, extricating her hand from Parker's to accept the arrangement of miniature pink roses and baby's breath. "You're so talented, Natalie. Just look at all the lovely flowers!"

Natalie surveyed the room with a modest pride. The space was wall-to-wall color, and some of the bouquets really were pretty special, though she probably shouldn't brag. Parker had asked for five dozen roses in every imaginable color, and that had turned out nicely. It looked as if someone had caught a rainbow and tied it up in pink velvet ribbon. Which, Natalie thought, watching him with Sarah now, was probably how he felt.

"Hi, Nattie," Parker said easily, leaning over to kiss her cheek. They were such old friends that he didn't bother to compliment her work. He hadn't bought a single plant or flower anywhere else since the day she opened up shop. That was compliment enough for her. "Pull up a chair."

She nudged a few arrangements closer together, trying to make room for her own, and then she plopped onto the extra armchair. One good thing about living in a posh town like Firefly Glen—hospital rooms were more like four-star hotels.

"So," she said, assessing Sarah's pretty, pale face and honey-colored hair hanging loose around her shoulders. "How was it? You look okay."

"She looks gorgeous," Parker put in emphatically.

He took Sarah's hand again. "But I don't know how she got through it. She was unbelievably brave."

Sarah laughed. "It was pretty easy, really. I was only in labor for ten hours, which is nothing for a first baby."

"Nothing?" Parker looked a little pale himself. "Good God."

"You should have seen him, Natalie." Sarah shook her head. "He was insufferable. He kept ordering Heather to give me pain pills, to put me under, to make it go faster, to make it stop. We had to get quite firm with him, actually, and finally he quieted down."

Parker's blue eyes crinkled at the corners. "That was probably about the time I fainted."

"You know I'm just teasing." Sarah squeezed his hand. "I couldn't have done it without you. You were wonderful."

"No, sweetheart. *You* were wonderful."

Natalie cleared her throat loudly. "In case you hadn't noticed," she said tartly, "there *are* other people in this room."

"Oh." Parker looked up, grinning. "You still here?"

"Yes," she said. "And if you had an ounce of sense, you might realize that you ought to go check on Cordelia. If you had any subtlety at all, it might occur to you that Sarah and I had some girl talking to do."

Parker shrugged. "Too bad I don't."

"He'll go if you really want him to," Sarah said,

casting a meaningful look at her husband. "Why? What's up? Have you made a pass at the handyman? Everybody's talking about how yummy he is."

Parker raised one eyebrow. "She'd better *not* have."

"And why not?" Natalie felt herself bristling. Parker was several years older than she was, and when they were children he'd always been protective, like the big brother she'd never had. It had been nice at the time, but right now it was extremely annoying.

She glared at him. "What would be wrong with making a pass at him? Because he's a handyman? He's not, really, and besides, I never thought you were that kind of snob, Parker. And if you think he's after my money, forget it. He knows I haven't got any, and besides, I'm the one who is doing the pursuing, not him."

"Oh, sweetheart, one thing I forgot to tell you about Granvilles," Parker said to Sarah conversationally. "They fly off the handle with no provocation at all. They're like mosquitoes, buzzing around in a blind fury."

Sarah smiled. "Is that so?"

"Sadly, yes. It's something in their DNA, I'm afraid." He turned to Natalie calmly. "Settle down, Nat. Did I say anything about Matthew Quinn's social status? I'm not talking as a snob here. I'm talking as a lawyer."

That was a surprise. She wrinkled her nose. "As a lawyer? What's that go to do with anything?"

"Everything," Parker said flatly. "He works for you, doesn't he? If you even come close to making a pass at him, officially that's sexual harassment. Creating a hostile work environment. It's not fair to him. And, by the way, it's also against the law."

Natalie just sat there, her mouth slightly open. She couldn't think of anything to say. She had never, ever looked at it that way. She never really even thought of Matthew as her employee. Which just showed, she supposed, how far gone she was. She'd been imagining that they were friends. Partners. That he was helping her out because he liked her.

"That's ridiculous," she said finally. But it sounded weak.

"Is it?" Parker didn't sound weak. He sounded serious. He even looked serious.

"Yes, of course it is. Matthew knows I'd never— I mean, he doesn't for one minute think that just because I kissed him, he has to—"

"Good grief, Nat. You kissed him?"

"Just once. I didn't mean to. It was kind of an impulse thing." She felt herself flushing. "You know, Parker, this is why I wanted you to leave the room."

"Well, don't do it again. For God's sake, Natalie. Think about it from his perspective. We've all heard about his prison record. He probably needs this job pretty bad. And now you're hinting that the paycheck might come with strings attached."

It was an ugly picture. But it was false. It wasn't like that. The attraction had been mutual. She was *not* forcing herself on anybody. Frankly, though Parker might not think so, she'd never found it necessary to force herself on men.

Comfortably indignant, she straightened. "And you're hinting that he might find the idea of kissing me so unpleasant that he'd quit his job to avoid it. Thanks a lot."

Parker sighed and held out his hands, giving up.

He turned to Sarah. "Another thing you should know about the Granvilles, sweetheart. They're genetically incapable of having a logical discussion, so don't even bother trying."

CHAPTER NINE

MATTHEW CAME BACK EARLY. The sun was still high and yellow over Firefly Glen when he passed through Vanity Gap and made his way up the side of the mountain to Summer House.

The first thing he noticed was how sweet the air was compared to the hot, thick fumes of the city. Once he had believed he couldn't thrive without the adrenaline rush of crowded urban life. But now, as he parked in his car around the back of the quiet old estate, in the shade of a two-hundred-year-old sugar maple, he felt himself relaxing, clenched muscles easing, his psyche smoothing out into a comfortably peaceful state.

He liked it here. He felt sane here.

If he didn't mistrust the word, he would have said he felt happy here.

The second thing he noticed, as he walked toward his quarters with duffel in hand, was that a half dozen men were collected in and around the pool, working on it with an unmistakable sense of masterful, controlled urgency.

Matthew paused and looked into the empty pit,

which, when he'd left just forty hours ago, had been a rubble of pitted concrete and debris.

A miraculous transformation had taken place. All the pounded-out weak spots had been expertly filled in with concrete. New pieces of colored tile had been applied to complete the deteriorated mosaic. For the first time, Matthew could make out the distinctive hind part of a lion, head and wings of an eagle. It was a griffin—and, he realized, a very beautiful piece of art.

In fact, right now the men were in the process of masking the mosaic so that they could safely apply the new finish to the pool. It was a job that required patience and precision, and Matthew hadn't been looking forward to it.

But what had happened? When had Natalie decided to get the work done professionally instead of struggling through it herself? Matthew approached one of the men who was working at deck level, masking off the rim tile.

"Looks good," Matthew observed casually.

The man looked up and nodded. "Pretty amazing, huh? She's had about six of us working around the clock. Once we get the tiles covered, we'll spray on the finish. Should be done by dark."

"You made great time," Matthew said. "How did you manage? I'd have thought it could take weeks just finding the right tiles to fix up that mosaic."

"Oh, we've been working on it for a couple of months, researching and hunting down the right materials. Then, just when we were ready to roll, there was a hitch. No big wedding, no expensive pool restoration.''

The man shrugged. ''It was a blow, I'll tell you that. Lots of companies in town hated to see that love affair go sour.''

''So?'' Matthew looked down at the elaborate design. He knew that if he and Natalie had attempted to do this, it would have taken months and still it would never have been quite right. ''What changed?''

The man chewed thoughtfully on his gum. ''Don't know for sure. We got the call a few days ago, job's back on, hold everything else, big rush. Guess she decided to spring for it herself.'' He pointed down at the mosaic. ''A job like this isn't cheap, either. Gotta be at least ten grand.''

Ten grand. And suddenly it made sense. The lucky Ming vase, discovered in the garden shed in true Granville chaos, had become a brand-new, historically accurate swimming pool.

He deposited his duffel in the pool house, where he saw that Natalie had filled his refrigerator with new drinks and snacks and had left another fresh vase of flowers—was it snapdragons? Something pretty and pink. He touched one of the soft petals and couldn't help smiling.

He placed a quick call to his sister, just to touch base so she wouldn't get into a lather worrying about him. Maggie needed kids of her own, he thought as she rambled on, mother-henning him nearly to death. Then maybe she'd stop worrying about him.

Finally, though, he got Maggie to hang up.

And then he went looking for Natalie, to tell her he was back and let her know he was going to spend a couple of hours working on the Blue Room wiring before it got dark.

Something smelled delicious in the kitchen, but it was simmering away all by itself in a large pot, untended. Natalie didn't answer his call.

He had fixed the doorknob of the green playroom, so he assumed she wasn't stuck in there. And he hadn't noticed anyone scampering around on the roof.

Maybe the library? Sometimes she'd spend hours in there, researching dusty papers for new tidbits about the house. Occasionally he'd find her at the desk after midnight, asleep hunched over old journals.

When he touched her shoulder, she'd wake up bubbling with enthusiasm, eager to tell him of some fascinating historical Granville anecdote she'd just discovered.

And so they'd sit there together, in dark-honey lamplight, while she spun wonderful stories of her family and their years of wild adventures in this house. He loved to hear her talk. Her reverence for this old pile of stones was unwavering—and sometimes almost contagious—no matter how expensive, frustrating or depressing it got.

He opened the library door now.

"Oh. Hello, Mr. Quinn." Suzie Strickland, who

was at work on her trompe l'oeil, looked over at him. He got the feeling she was disappointed that he wasn't someone else. "Natalie's not here. I think she went to the hospital to see Sarah's baby."

"Okay," Matthew said. "Thanks." He started to back out. Suzie was notorious for preferring to work in private.

But she surprised him. "Mr. Quinn? Are you busy? Any chance you could help me with something?"

He came back in. "Sure," he said comfortably. Though they hadn't spent a lot of time together, he and Suzie had hit it off from the start. That seemed to surprise Natalie. Apparently Suzie didn't warm to many people.

But it didn't surprise Matthew. Suzie was starving for someone to recognize her talent, and Matthew did. He knew art. Everyone in New York City snob circles had to know art or risk being branded a philistine. So it didn't take him two seconds to realize that this grouchy little black-clad girl was going to be an artist someday. A damn fine one.

"What's up?" He stood back to better view the painting. "Yes," he said thoughtfully. "You've got the perspective just right now, don't you?"

Suzie blinked and squinted. She had recently moved from heavy black glasses to contact lenses, and she was still getting used to them. "I don't know. Do I? That's what I wanted to ask you. The dog." She scowled at the animal. "I don't know. I still think he looks goofy."

Matthew studied it. "Maybe it's the shadow," he suggested. "I'm not sure that's where it would fall, given where you've got the sun."

She tilted her head. "Yes!" She made a fist of triumph. "Yes! That's it." She smiled at him. "Thanks."

He wondered if she knew how lovely she was when she smiled. But of course he would never mention it. It would have been completely inappropriate, and besides, it was obvious that she was trying to persuade herself that artists didn't give a damn how they looked. Although he did wonder about the contacts, which had just appeared.

And now that he noticed it, she was wearing a little black skirt and a gray sweater instead of her usual uniform of black jeans or leggings and plain black T-shirt. His curiosity was piqued. Wonder what this was all about?

The smile didn't last long, anyhow. In seconds, she was scowling again. "Um, actually, Mr. Quinn, there was something else I wanted to ask you. It might make you mad, and I don't want to do that because you've been really nice to me, but—I mean, I can't help it. I just have to."

She looked pretty worked up. "Don't worry about it," he said evenly. "If it's not okay, I'll tell you."

She sighed and twisted her paintbrush nervously.

"Thanks. I wouldn't bother you, except that I'm desperate. You see, I have some money saved for college. An art college. I've been saving for years. I work all the time, and a few months ago I bred some golden retriever puppies, and I made quite a bit then. But it isn't enough. I was thinking I could get a scholarship or something, you know, to fill in. But no way that's going to happen now.''

He raised his eyebrows. ''Why not? Surely an art school can tell you have talent.''

''Talent!'' Suzie snorted. ''That's not what counts around here. You have to look and act like a cheesy bimbo to get recommendations from anyone in this dumb town. I'm not going to put on pink lipstick just so I can kiss somebody's rear end, not even for an art scholarship.''

Her voice was harsh and determined. He had to listen hard to hear the small crack of pain behind the words.

''Okay,'' he said. ''I get it. So what are you going to do?''

''I was hoping you'd give me some ideas about investing. To make the rest of what I need. I've got a whole year to make it grow, so it doesn't have to be like overnight or anything.''

Oh, man. He looked into her smart, bright, hungry brown eyes and wished like hell he had about a million dollars. If he did, he'd put a new roof on Summer House, send this talented kid to the best art school in the country, and then he'd move to a deserted island, or the North Pole, or anywhere that he wouldn't get dragged into all these heartbreaking little personal dramas.

''Actually, Suzie, I'm kind of out of that business,''

he said through clenched teeth. Somehow saying no to Suzie was even harder than saying no to Natalie. Because while Natalie was naturally cheerful and buoyant, this kid was dark and desperate. If she didn't get to develop this extraordinary talent, it really could end up destroying her life.

"I know." Suzie faced him squarely, and her hunger was written all over her pale, unhappy face. "I know all about the trouble you had. I don't care. I trust you."

"It's not just that. Investing is risky. You could lose every penny."

"I don't care," she repeated tightly. "Look, I have five thousand dollars. I need ten thousand by next summer, or I might as well have nothing." Her hands were squeezed into fists at her side, and the paint-splattered knuckles were pale with desperation. "No one else will help me. My parents don't even want me to go to art school. They just want me to marry some rich jock in Firefly Glen so they can finally get accepted to the goddamn country club."

Matthew felt a pulse of frustration jerk in his shoulder. God, were her parents insane? This girl wasn't just artistic. She was an *artist*. She wasn't ever, ever going to be happy as a trophy wife, swanning around the country club while mom and dad played golf with the snooty in-laws.

The North Pole was looking more attractive than ever.

"Suzie, it would be way out of line for me to get

involved in this. I don't have a license. I don't have any current expertise. And I certainly don't have any right to drive a wedge between you and your parents.''

''You could drive a Mack truck between me and my parents,'' she said roughly. Her brown eyes were shining dangerously. ''Please. I am going to invest. You can't stop me. All you can do is keep me from making a bad mistake. I've got friends who will actually make the investment. Just tell me what company to pick.''

''I can't.'' The words tasted like ground glass.

She didn't seem to be listening. ''I was thinking maybe that big chain of drugstores. You know, the one with the dog on the commercial.''

No, no, no, he thought inside. That one was going nowhere. Inventories had fallen in that company for three straight years. But he didn't say a word, though he damn near choked on the silence.

She was smart as a whip, though, and she knew what ''no comment'' really meant. ''Okay, then, something else. What about the computer companies?''

He shook his head slowly. Too unpredictable. Oh, God, he was going to hate himself in the morning.

''The utilities?''

''You know,'' he said tensely, still trying to stop himself with every word, ''if I had money to invest— which I do not, and that ought to tell you what my advice is worth—I'd probably invest in something I liked personally. Something that consistently offered a good product. Better than its competitors. Like— well, do you go to the movies?''

She chewed on her lip, which had a splash of brown paint from the tree trunks she'd been painting. ''You're talking about investing in a movie company? One that makes movies I like?''

''Maybe. What movies do you like?''

She named the ones he'd been hoping—artsy, independent, classy movies, most of which were made by the production company he'd been considering. When he'd been in the city, he'd heard a lot of buzz— he couldn't help it, he was still conditioned to listen, though he couldn't do anything with the information—and experts seemed to think that company was poised for a stock split.

''Yeah. Something like that,'' he said carefully. ''That's what *I'd* do, anyhow. But no matter what I picked, I'd be very, very restrained. I wouldn't even consider risking more than one fifth of my capital to begin with. Just in case.''

''Okay,'' she said, and her voice was new. She sounded almost happy. ''Okay. I understand.'' She pressed her fists to her chest, apparently not caring that they were covered in paint, as if she needed to contain a heart that was swelling with emotion. ''Thank you so much, Mr. Quinn. I'll never forget this. Never.''

He shook his head. ''Maybe you'd better not thank

me yet. If you lose your money, you may not feel quite so grateful.''

"Yes, I will," she said thickly. "Because it's not just the advice. It's that you believe in me. You're the first person ever to really believe in my work."

He looked at the painting on the wall and smiled.

"Don't worry," he said. "I won't be the last."

THOUGH NATALIE TOLD HERSELF Parker's comments about sexual harassment were ridiculous, they bothered her anyhow.

And so, for a while, she played it safe. When Matthew returned from the city, she kept herself busy outside the house, in the greenhouse potting and pruning, down at the hardware store picking out supplies, over at the historical society looking through old documents, visiting Granville or Theo or Sarah or Stuart or anyone who would put up with her.

The result was that, except at breakfast, she hadn't spent more than ten minutes with Matthew in the past week. But it had been hell. And frankly she was scraping the bottom of the old willpower barrel.

By the next Friday evening, when her technician announced that the restored pool was completely refinished, cured, filled and balanced, Natalie couldn't wait any longer. She wanted to christen the pool, and she wanted Matthew to help her do it. She liked him, darn it. She had fun with him. It wasn't *all* sexual. Not quite all, anyhow.

She put on her most demure one-piece bathing suit,

though it was old and shapeless and didn't flatter her a bit. Then she added a threadbare terry cover-up and cheap flip-flops, washed off all makeup and tied her curls back in a plain red rubber band.

She checked the mirror. Perfect. She definitely did not look like a woman intent on sexual harassment. She didn't quite look like a woman at all.

She waited until dark, when she could be sure he was finished with whatever chores he'd been tackling that day. Then she gathered up her towel and her courage and knocked on the pool house door.

Matthew took a while answering it, and she wondered if he'd been asleep. But when he opened the door, he was pulling down the last couple of inches on a shirt he obviously had hastily tossed over his jeans.

"Hi," he said. And then he waited, smiling politely.

"Hi," she echoed brilliantly. Dumb pause. She should have rehearsed an opening line. "Want to go for a swim? They tell me the pool is good to go, and I was hoping maybe you'd help me celebrate."

He hesitated, and, suddenly self-conscious, she hurried to overexplain. "It's just that, well, it's a pretty darned expensive pool, and it is summer, and it's been kind of hot today. And honestly, I'm just talking about a swim, I'm not feeling reckless or anything, in case you were worried about that."

Oh, God, Natalie, shut up. One of the least attractive of the quirky Granville traits, this foot-in-mouth problem.

Thank goodness, though, he was smiling. "Okay. It sounds like fun." He looked out toward the pool. "Actually, I've been dying to try that slide ever since it arrived this morning."

She beamed. At the last minute, she'd added a fifteen-foot-high bright blue plastic slide, the kind you usually found at hotels. It had definitely been a Granville moment. The pool restoration guy, apparently a swimming pool purist, had left no doubt about his disapproval.

"Oh, yes, me, too! Isn't it cool? I know it's kind of crazy, with this formal Italian grotto look, to add one of those tacky slides, and Elspeth Grant at the historical society would have a fit. But I've wanted one ever since I was a kid. And I had just enough money left over from the vase, so I thought, why not?"

"Exactly. Elspeth Grant has no power here." Matthew tilted his head toward the pool house interior. "So. I'll just change into a suit, and then I'll meet you out there?"

"Of course," she said quickly, backing up. "Naturally. I'll wait for you out here."

It didn't take long. She'd just barely waded in up to her thighs when he came out again. Oh, dear, she thought, watching him walking toward her and feeling a cool shiver race up her body as the water licked at her swimsuit. He must have worked out a lot in prison.

Parker just didn't get it. Surely to harass someone sexually implied a certain amount of power over that person? She didn't have any power over Matthew Quinn. When he was around, she barely had power over her own limbs. If he touched her now, with his shoulders and chest so bare and beautiful and mapped with muscles, she'd probably sink like a stone and drown.

But he didn't touch her. Instead he executed a perfect cannonball into the water, splashing her mercilessly. He came up grinning, as if he understood that the moment needed to be defused, and splashed her some more.

She retaliated, of course. And for the next few minutes, they laughed and played and dived and teased, and before long she was having so much fun she almost forgot she'd been at death's door just from laying eyes on his naked chest.

The pool lights worked perfectly—as they certainly should have, they cost a fortune—and turned the water into a glowing, swirling, magical liquid. When he swam underwater, she watched him, and he was like a graceful sea creature caught in a translucent blue sea, his arms parting the water, his strong legs kicking up bubbles that trailed out behind him like diamonds.

She swam from one end of the long pool to the other, back and forth until her heart pounded in her ears. She had forgotten how much she loved to swim. The pool had been dry for years. What a shame.

After a while, she took the rubber band from her hair, and enjoyed the cool tickle of her curls against her back, her shoulders, her collarbone. She went deep, as deep as her breath would take her, down by the mystical multicolored griffin. She imagined herself a mermaid with streaming hair and iridescent blue-green fins and siren song. But she stayed too long, and she came sputtering to the surface, choking noisily, more a sea cow than a mermaid.

Matthew laughed at her and tossed a beach ball that bounced lightly and precisely against the crown of her head. "Time to try that slide, don't you think?"

She pretended that she hadn't heard him. It wasn't worthy of a graceful mermaid such as herself, but she'd realized, over the past fifteen minutes or so, that she was just a tiny bit nervous about trying the slide.

She hadn't realized, looking at it in the catalogue, how very high it would be. Fifteen feet didn't *sound* all that tall. But it was.

"Hey." He caught her foot as she paddled by. "Aren't you going to christen your new slide?"

"Soon." She smiled graciously. "You can go first, if you want to."

"I wouldn't dream of it. It's your slide, the one you've wanted since you were a child. Of course you'll go first."

Did he suspect? The pool lights threw strange shadows on their faces, so it was hard to be sure. But still, it was ridiculous to be nervous. She was the one, after all, who climbed around on the roof and in the trees.

So she hoisted herself out of the water and, feet slapping against the newly finished pool deck, she made her way to the slide. She wished her bathing suit looked a little better. It was so old it was kind of saggy, and she kept adjusting the neckline, making sure it covered everything.

Okay. Up. Three, four, five steps. Six, seven, eight. It took nineteen steps to reach the top. And from way up here the slide itself seemed to disappear into the darkness, leaving only a black void between her and the pool, which glowed below her like a large vat of something hot and blue and strange. The mosaic griffin at the bottom looked like the Loch Ness Monster.

This wasn't a very good idea. It was cold up here. The water had felt warm, like bathing in the tub, but the night air was chilly, and she was suddenly awash with goose bumps.

"You know," she called down airily, "I don't think I'll—"

But as she tried to turn around, she bumped into the warm, solid wall of Matthew's chest. He had come up the ladder, too, obviously expecting her to plunge down with easy enthusiasm.

"I'm sorry. I've…I've changed my mind." She couldn't think straight. She was shivering, and he was so close, and suddenly the whole potent sexuality of his marvelous male body was right there, in her face. "I—I'll just go around you and—"

But she couldn't get around him. They were both on the platform now, and it was only about two feet wide, so, though she fought it for all of three or four seconds, there was nowhere else to go but into his arms.

"Oh, Natalie," he said softly. His hands were warm, and they felt so good against her wet skin. She moved closer. He made a low sound and tightened his hands. "Oh, God. Natalie."

She looked up at him, her lips asking, her eyes asking, her whole body telling him what she wanted. But he had to make the first move. She shut her eyes, her heart thumping, please, please...

And then, thank goodness, he kissed her. Slowly, not grasping or demanding, but hard and sure, with all the easy confidence of a man who knew how to kiss. He moved over her lips, tasting of chlorine and night roses and something sweetly masculine that was all his own.

She felt her legs giving way, and she leaned against him, which drove the kiss deeper. She felt the white edges of his teeth, then the sensual intrusion of his tongue.

She opened, asking for more, growing dizzy. But all too soon he stopped. He pulled away, and the night air was cold on her wet lips.

"Natalie," he said again, thickly, and then he kissed her neck.

She put her face into his shoulder and breathed, aware that his heart was going very fast, as if he'd been swimming a long, long way. His whole body said how much he wanted her.

"Let's take the plunge together," he whispered against her hair. "Would you like that?"

Together. She nodded slowly, even though she wasn't sure it was true. Something tight and thrilling, something that was half sharp, sexual desire and half dull, throbbing fear, was rising up from the bottom of her spine and taking her breath away.

"Do you trust me?"

She nodded again. He turned her carefully, so that she stood with her back molded against the front of him. Then he eased her down to a sitting position. He was right behind her, his legs on either side of her hips, his arms wrapped around her, his fingers just under her breasts.

And then, holding her tight, he slowly pushed forward.

She resisted, frightened, and he pushed a little harder. And then harder still. Never so hard that she didn't have time to say no, but hard enough that the thrill caught her by the throat, and she thought she might scream into the night from the sheer wonderful terror of it all.

And then, as if he knew the time was right, he pushed one more time, and it was done. They plunged down the long, curving tunnel of black night air and sank together, body against body, into the glowing blue pool of light.

CHAPTER TEN

BECAUSE HE WAS A FOOL and a coward, Matthew ate breakfast the next morning at Theo's Candlelight Café.

Just after dawn, he had smelled the coffee brewing, wafting from the open window of the Summer House kitchen. And suddenly he'd realized he simply couldn't sit there, across the table from Natalie, all alone with her. He couldn't make small talk, couldn't sink his teeth into sweet strawberries and press his sterling silver fork into soft, warm pancakes, without going completely mad.

Not after last night.

He hated to think how close he had come to making love to her. Against every ounce of better judgment, he had nearly taken her right there in the cool summer moonlight, right there in the open, for anyone to see. Right there on the pool steps, with the rippling phosphorescence of the blue water lapping at their shoulders and the ancestral Granville griffin watching silently from below.

Somehow he had controlled himself, although her delicate golden body, wet and shivering and poised on the knifepoint of need, had nearly undone him.

Somehow, when they climbed out of the pool after their breathtaking plunge from the slide, he had forced himself to say good-night, with just one last, selfish, lingering kiss.

And, thank God, she hadn't tried to stop him. Perhaps she, too, knew it would have been insanity to stay any longer.

He took a punishing gulp of Theo's extra-strong black coffee. Sooner or later he'd have to go back to Summer House. But not yet. It would take more than eight sleepless hours to get the memory out of his system.

But if he'd come here to be alone with his thoughts, he'd picked the wrong place. So far he'd seen half-a-dozen people he knew, including Sheriff Harry Dunbar and his pretty wife, and Parker Tremaine, who had been handing out pink bubble-gum cigars since he'd brought his new family home. And the eggs hadn't even arrived yet.

He saw Theo heading toward him with a steaming plate of food and the coffeepot, so he turned a page of the newspaper blindly, aware that he'd been staring at the same spot for far too long.

"Tough night?" Theo topped off his coffee and watched him curiously. "You look all done in."

"I'm fine," he said. He lifted his cup. "Nothing this good coffee can't handle, anyhow."

She fiddled with the flowers on the table, but he could tell she was glancing at him from the corners of her eyes. "I guess trying to keep up with Summer House could wear anyone out."

He smiled. "It's a challenge, that's for sure."

"And of course the Granville style takes a little getting used to."

Having grown up with a nosy younger sister, Matthew easily recognized the classic female fishing expedition. Theo was hoping to catch a nice, juicy romantic rumor.

"Oh, I don't know," he said lightly, refusing to bite the hook. "I can't say I have any complaints."

With a small cryptic grunt, Theo moved on. Taking care of her customers was even more important, apparently, than trying to force the truth out of him.

But, as usual, he wasn't alone for long. To his surprise, the minute Theo returned to the kitchen, one of the young, well-trained waiters appeared at Matthew's elbow.

"Hi," the young man—he couldn't have been more than twenty-two, though he wore a wedding ring—said nervously. "Are you Mr. Quinn? You work up at Summer House?"

Matthew nodded.

"I'm sorry to bother you, but I've heard that you give advice. You know, financial advice." He sighed. "And I sure need some."

Matthew put down his coffee cup slowly. "Where did you hear that?"

The young man looked anxious. "I don't remember. One of the other waiters here, maybe? Lots of people are talking about it. I'm sorry. I didn't know it was supposed to be a secret.''

"It's not.'' Matthew controlled a sigh. "It's just not true. I used to be in that business, but I'm not anymore.''

"Oh, I didn't mean like a business. I meant like tips and stuff. I really just need a pointer. See, my wife really wants to have a baby, but right now we can't even think about it. We've only got about five hundred dollars saved up. They probably don't even let you invest little bits like that, do they?''

"Sure they do,'' Matthew said politely. "Why don't you talk to a financial advisor about a game plan? Surely a town like this has one or two of those.''

The young man rolled his eyes. "That's the problem. Financial advisors in a town *like this* don't want to bother with you unless you've got a couple mill to invest. They'd laugh me right out of their offices.''

Matthew wanted to contradict him. Anything to make the kid go away before he got hooked by another sob story. But he couldn't. He remembered too well how bored he'd been, back in his high-flying days, by the earnest little clerks who had expected him to take their hundred-dollar deals seriously. He had instructed his secretary to pass them down the line to some other, less prestigious, advisor. Like trash sliding down a chute.

God, what a bastard he'd been!

He looked at the waiter's name tag. *David.* David,

who had saved five hundred dollars the hard way. David, with a restless wife, a tough job and a man's responsibilities, even though he still had acne on his chin.

"Maybe something safe, like a short-term CD, is your best bet right now, David," Matthew heard himself saying. "Then maybe you could earmark the *next* hundred for the stock market. It's not easy to wait, but you're young. You've got more time than money. Buy something solid and steady."

David was clearly dubious. "Won't it take forever?"

Matthew nodded. This was the essence of being a good financial advisor. You didn't tell people what they wanted to hear. You told them the truth.

"Yes," he said. "But it's the only safe way. And, like it or not, babies are a long-term investment."

"David!" Theo's voice whipped out from the other side of the café. "May I see you over here for a minute, please?"

"Oh, gosh, I'm in trouble now." David looked stricken. "I'm sorry, Mr. Quinn. I didn't mean to keep you from eating. It's just that everyone says you really know what's what, and I really needed the advice."

Matthew raised his eyebrows. "Everyone?"

"David Andrew McKuen." Theo's tone was polite but glacial. "Now, please."

The young man ducked his head, murmured a thank-you to Matthew and rushed over to his angry boss, apologizing all the way. Matthew didn't have the heart to delay him, though he would very much have liked to know who "everyone" was.

He got his answer soon enough, anyhow. The café door tinkled merrily, and Suzie Strickland came breezing in, looking positively feminine in a silver shirt and short gray skirt. She hadn't quite found her way to rainbow colors yet, but she was clearly moving in that direction.

She grinned when she spotted Matthew and made a beeline for his table. He set down his coffee cup again, resigning himself to doing without breakfast this morning.

"Hi," she said. "Don't stop eating. I can't stay long. I just came by to tell you that I love you. And that you're the most fantastic financial advisor in this entire solar system."

He grinned back. "I take it the stock split."

"You bet that baby split! One day after I bought it!" She clapped her hands and squealed softly. "*And* it went up three whole dollars a share! In one week I made three hundred dollars!"

Matthew did the numbers. That company had been selling at around fifty. "Wait a minute. That means your original investment was—"

She sat back, stretching her arms wide with an intense, physical satisfaction with herself, her bank account and probably her whole world. "Yep. Five thousand dollars. I bought a hundred shares."

"Suzie," he said. "I told you to start small. I said

no more than one thousand at first, until you could see how the stock performed, and—"

"I know," she said, blinking innocently over a shameless Cheshire-cat grin. "But you also told me your advice was worthless. So, as you can see, I decided not to take it."

WHEN MATTHEW GOT BACK to Summer House, Stuart's car was in the driveway. Good, he thought. With Stuart hovering around, trying to impress Natalie, there would be no awkward intimacies, no chance just yet for heart-to-heart talks about last night's insanity.

But he was only halfway to the pool house when she called out to him.

"Matthew," she cried happily. "Oh, Matthew, come! Guess what I found!"

He turned, arranging his face in a neutral smile. "Good morning," he said, politely including both Stuart and Natalie in the greeting. "What did you find?"

Stuart was standing beside Natalie in the kitchen doorway, smiling down at her with a kind of amused tolerance. And in Natalie's arms something black and white was squirming.

It was a dog. A wiry dog with perky ears, a quizzical expression and a tail that wagged ceaselessly and apparently effortlessly, as if someone had tied a metronome to his backside and he didn't even know it.

"Well, hi, there," Matthew said, coming over and

giving the dog's nose a soft pinch. The animal wriggled more energetically than ever. Natalie had to work to hold on to him. "Who are you?"

"It's Rob Roy," Natalie said, smiling broadly. "Theo's dog. I found him on the property behind the house, right up at the foot of the mountain. Isn't it wonderful?"

"Absolutely," Matthew agreed. He and Natalie had talked about Theo's missing dog several times. Natalie had always refused to accept what seemed obvious to Matthew—that a dog missing for that many weeks probably had met a bad end. But the little rascal seemed blissfully unaware of having scared anyone. He was dirty and matted, but he looked frisky and completely undaunted by his adventures.

"Have you told Theo?"

"We just called her," Natalie said. "She's thrilled. She can't leave the café, of course, so Stuart is going to take Rob Roy to her right away."

Stuart didn't look terribly enthusiastic. "You know," he said optimistically, eyeing Matthew. "I have to get to a city council meeting. And now that Quinn is here, maybe he could—"

Natalie shot him a look of shocked indignation. "Absolutely not," she said, holding Rob Roy out firmly for transfer. "You know I need Matthew here. He has a million things to do. Do you want this place to fall down around my ears?"

Stuart looked chastened, and he accepted the dog

meekly, though Matthew noticed he didn't cuddle the dirty animal as Natalie had. And he kept the questing pink tongue facing out, where it couldn't reach his chin.

"Oh, come on, Stuart," Natalie complained, laughing. "He wants to kiss you."

"Tough," Stuart said, finally showing some spine, and he and Matthew shared their first completely harmonious glance. Rob Roy was cute, but he was the kind of squirmy, high-strung dog only a female could truly love.

Natalie blew kisses to the dog as long as he was in view, but the minute Stuart's sports car disappeared down the driveway, she stopped abruptly, turning to Matthew with a conspiratorial grin of barely contained excitement.

"Thank goodness he's gone," she said. She took Matthew's hand and tugged. "Come with me. I've got something completely amazing to show you."

Matthew hesitated. Natalie was so unpredictable he never could be sure what he'd encounter. He'd been expecting an earnest, perhaps painful, analysis of where their relationship might be going. Instead, he found this laughing, playful woman-child who was bubbling over with the excitement of sharing a secret.

"Come *on*," she said impatiently, looking over her shoulder. "It's so cool, Matthew! Rob Roy wasn't the only thing I found this morning."

He followed—how could he resist? They hurried past the western gardens, with their headless statues, and on toward the rear of the property, where the house came within a few yards of bumping its backside against the mountain.

He hadn't spent much time back here. It was particularly overgrown and unwelcoming, and here in the mountain's shadow even summer days were a little too cold for comfort.

But someone had loved it once, a long time ago. He could see the rough outlines of a forgotten garden, and the remains of a neglected grape arbor traced a weather-beaten roof, connecting house to mountain.

Natalie led him under the arbor, chattering every step of the way.

"I was standing in the back parlor, and I looked out the window, and I saw something moving, and when I came out I could see that it was Rob Roy. I chased him all over the place. I was *not* going to let him get lost again. But he was determined not to let me catch him, so we went around and around, and a couple of times I tripped on some of these old gnarly roots, and I almost fell slap on my face. But one time, I caught myself by putting my hand here—"

She paused dramatically, leaning against a small copper plaque set into the wall of the mountain. It depicted Bacchus, or some equally fat, hedonistic old god, turned green with time and neglect.

"And I pressed." She raised her eyebrows dramatically. "Like this."

She lowered her voice to a hushed reverence. "And then *this* happened."

He hadn't really counted on anything spectacular. Natalie's enthusiasms were easily excited, and he knew she might well have reached this pitch over nothing more surprising than a nest of baby sparrows or a secret patch of wood sorrel.

But what happened stunned even him. As she pressed, a small crack appeared in the granite, then widened, then slowly shifted out like the door of a bank vault. He stared, disbelieving, as the fake granite slab came fully open, revealing a large, dark room that had been hidden inside the mountain, probably for decades.

"So!" She waved her hand toward the opening dramatically. "Wasn't I right? Isn't this the most amazing thing we've found in Summer House yet?"

He looked at her, still dumbfounded. "What is it? Had you ever heard of its existence before?"

"Not really," she said. "I mean, Granvilles have always hinted about secret rooms in Summer House, but I thought they meant those little cupboard spaces for hiding bootleg liquor. You know, like the one we found that day."

"Have you gone in yet?"

She stuck her face into the opening, peered into the darkness, then pulled it back out and wrinkled her nose. "Well, no." She smiled sheepishly. "I wanted to wait for you. Not because I'm nervous, you understand. I just thought you'd enjoy discovering it with me."

"Is there electricity?"

"I don't know." She dug in her pocket and pulled out two candles and a pack of matches. "But I came prepared." She lit them both, then handed one to him. "Wow. Don't you just feel like Nancy Drew?"

He laughed. "Actually, I feel like Nancy Drew's faithful sidekick, the one who's probably going to take a nasty spider web in the face, or fall and break his leg, just so spunky Nancy can rescue him."

She took his hand and held it hard. "I have to be honest with you," she said as they carefully eased around the fake granite door. "Nancy isn't feeling all that spunky right now, so be careful."

It was very dark, but the air smelled clean, as if fresh air might have been making its way into the secret room even while the door was shut. He felt along the wall carefully, hoping he wouldn't encounter anything with a lot of legs.

What he encountered was a light switch. He flicked it without expecting much, but suddenly the room was flooded with light from a dusty but clearly expensive crystal chandelier.

"Oh." Natalie's voice was small and breathless. "Oh, my goodness."

The room, which was about as big as one of the Summer House parlors, held half a dozen long tables, a small dance floor, and a long mahogany bar. Each of the tables was clearly outfitted for playing one of the classic gambling games—roulette, poker, black-jack, baccarat, craps.

The bar, which ran the length of the room, fronted

shelves laden with hundreds of drinking glasses—
highball tumblers, champagne flutes, brandy snifters,
and special shapes for drinks Matthew couldn't name.

Liquor and gambling in a luxurious secret hide-
away carved in the side of the mountain. It had *Prohibition* written all over it.

"Oh, my goodness," she said again, her shock obviously beyond words.

Matthew laughed. "I don't think goodness had
anything to do with it."

Blowing out his candle, he moved to the roulette
table and twisted the wheel, which spun as easily as
if thousands of dollars had been won and lost here
yesterday—instead of eighty years ago. Even the little
silver ball remained, spinning and spinning, and finally clattering to a stop on red.

"Miss Granville, I hate to be the one to break it to
you, but you come from a long line of shameless he-
donists. Apparently they didn't intend to let a little
thing like the Prohibition law stop them from getting
drunk and gambling away the family fortune."

She was smiling now, too, running her fingers
along the dusty green felt of the poker table. An elaborate, gilt-edged pack of cards still sat in the middle,
alongside a decorated chest filled with smooth, shining, mother-of-pearl chips.

She looked up, an arch gleam in her eye. "What
makes you think we lost? Granvilles are excellent
card players. We probably brought the suckers of

Firefly Glen in here to fleece them like so many sheep.''

She bent down and blew a layer of dust from the cards. ''Don't believe me?'' She gestured grandly toward the stack. ''Let's cut. High card wins.''

He lifted a few cards from the top, exposing a medieval queen in full-color regalia. He raised one brow. That would be hard to beat.

She shrugged extravagantly. ''No problem,'' she said, making her own cut with a flourish. Grinning, she held out the ace of spades, ornamented with so many flowers and filigrees it filled the whole oversize card.

''I can do it every time,'' she said smugly. ''It's a Granville thing.''

And looking at her now, with her wild, pre-Raphaelite curls tumbling over her little blue home-stenciled T-shirt that read Save Llewellyn's Lake, he believed her. She could do whatever she wanted. It had something to do with faith, he decided. She believed in things so completely that it made them true.

How would a man feel, he wondered, if she believed in him? Faith like that just might redeem a lot of sins.

''Aw, rats,'' she said suddenly. ''I missed my chance. I should have made you bet something on that.''

''Like what?''

''Hmm.'' She stuck her hands in the pockets of her jeans, considering. ''We haven't got much, that's true.

I could have bet three broken windowpanes and a bent door knocker.''

"I don't know," he said, laughing. "That's a little steep for me."

"Okay, then." She paused. "We could have bet a kiss."

He looked at her, glad the poker table was between them. "And how exactly," he queried lightly, "could you tell the winner from the loser?"

Her answering smile was a little too bright. "Well, see, you couldn't. That's the beauty of a bet like that." She held out the cards. "We could try again, if you like."

He held her gaze steadily. "But you already told me you never lose. So now I know better than to bet against a Granville."

Lowering the cards, she let her artificial smile drop slowly from her lips. She gave him back an unflinching, honest gaze. She looked somber and suddenly very tired.

"I see," she said softly. "Maybe we ought to just talk about this straight. Are you trying to tell me there won't be any more kisses?"

Oh, God, he hated this. *Hated* it. "I'm trying to tell you there shouldn't have been any kisses in the first place."

"Why not? And don't give me that predictable *I'm not worthy, I'm just an ex-con* script. We both know you're not really a criminal. And we both know that isn't why."

"All right." It was part of the reason, of course, but he would humor her. He had reasons to spare. "Because I'm leaving in a few weeks. Because it couldn't ever amount to more than a fling, and I know enough about women to know that you're not the fling type."

She lifted her chin. "Maybe you don't know as much about women as you think you do."

"I know," he said soberly. "I know more than I should."

"Well, then, maybe you don't know as much about yourself as you think you do."

Though she might not realize it, that was a direct hit.

"Maybe. But I'm learning more all the time. A lot of it I don't like." He gripped the edge of the table with his fingers. "I may not have been a criminal, Natalie, but I wasn't exactly a great guy. I spent far too many selfish, greedy years thinking only about myself."

"I don't believe it."

"You should." He closed his eyes. "I cared more about money than anything else in the world. I valued people according to how big their bank accounts were, or how much they could add to mine. I liked my women rich. Usually I preferred them jaded and great in bed. But sometimes I thought innocent and naive was entertaining. Whatever I wanted, I took."

"You are just trying to paint yourself as black as

possible," she said with heat. "You're just trying to scare me off."

"I'm being honest." He looked beyond her to the dingy walls of this homemade casino. Probably the flocked paper had once been creamy white. Now it was as gray as old snow.

"In a way, I'm glad it all fell to pieces, because it was seductive and addictive, and I don't think I would have had the courage to walk away from it on my own. But fate gave me this chance. This chance for a new life, a chance to remake myself into someone better."

He took a deep breath. "Surely you can see that I'll have no hope for a new life, if I begin it by committing the same selfish sins that poisoned the old one."

She didn't say a word for a long time. She just looked at him, a dozen different emotions playing across her beautiful, expressive face. He tried not to think how exciting it would be to see her sexual passions displayed there with that same unguarded honesty.

Finally he saw the expression he'd been waiting for. Resignation.

She sighed once, heavily. Then she summoned up a smile and held out the cards one more time. "Cut?"

He reached out blindly and picked a card. The king of clubs, smiling cruelly from under his jeweled crown.

She cut then, too, and held out the two of hearts.

"Oh, well," she said, still smiling a brave smile that obviously was intended to make him feel better but somehow did anything but. "I guess you're right. Even Granvilles can't win all the time."

CHAPTER ELEVEN

SUZIE'S TROMPE L'OEIL was almost finished. Actually, she had worked on it a day or two longer than absolutely necessary, just because she liked being at Summer House.

The mansion was a goofy old run-down mess, but at least it had atmosphere. It had personality. Suzie's own house, which her mom kept obsessively tidy in an irritatingly bourgeois way, had zero personality.

And Natalie had a way of making everybody comfortable. It was as if she had some sixth sense. If you wanted to be alone, she ignored you. But if you were getting bored or lonely or hungry, suddenly she appeared in the doorway with sandwiches and a funny story.

Best of all, she let everybody around her be natural, too. She didn't have any stuffy ideas about how people *ought* to act. She seemed to chill fine with everyone—crusty old coots like Granville Frome, hot hunks like Matthew Quinn, boring sticks like Stuart Leith, and even grumpy, confused teenagers who hadn't quite decided who they were yet.

Truth was, Suzie didn't want to leave. She dabbed at one last leaf, which didn't need it, and chewed on her lip, thinking. She wondered if Natalie would let her help the art expert who was coming next week to work on the newly discovered dining room mural.

Through the open window she saw Mike Frome loping toward the house. She felt a wriggle of excitement but squashed it immediately. Mike was *not* the reason she wanted to stay at Summer House.

To her surprise, he didn't head for the front door. He headed straight for the library window. When he got there, hardly even breathing fast, he looked kind of worried.

"Hey, Suzie," he said. "I just got a call on my cell phone. One of your weirdo art friends is trying to find you. I don't know how she got my number, but she said no one is answering the phone in the main house."

Suzie tried not to look as confused as she felt. She'd heard the Summer House phone ringing, but no one had answered it, and she didn't think it was her place. She didn't know where Natalie and Matthew were.

"Yeah? Well, what did she want?"

"She said she saw one of your puppies locked in a green Mercedes on Main Street. She said the windows were all shut, and it seemed pretty hot."

"What?" Suzie dropped her brush into her paint box in horror. "It must be ninety degrees today."

Mike frowned. "I know. Who would do such a dumb thing?"

"I have to get out there," she said. She wiped her

hands on her shirt, hardly thinking. "He could die." But then she stopped. "Damn! I don't have my car today. My mom dropped me off."

Mike tilted his head cautiously. "Wait a minute—"

"You have to." She glared at him furiously. "You just have to. Natalie isn't here, and neither is Mr. Quinn." She went over to the window and grabbed him by his sweaty T-shirt. "The lawn can wait, dammit. You *have* to help me."

"Okay!" Mike put his hands up. "*Chill*, for God's sake. My car's out front."

All the way into town, Suzie could hardly breathe, thinking of that poor little puppy. She knew who had done it, too. She knew all the people who had bought her puppies. And she knew which one drove that car.

"A green Mercedes," Mike said slowly as they hit the edge of town, his thoughts obviously mirroring hers. "Isn't that what Mayor Millner drives?"

"Yes," she answered tersely. "Can't you go any faster?"

"I can't see Mayor Millner leaving a dog cooped up like that," Mike said, his voice troubled. "Can you?"

Suzie didn't answer. The Millners were a sore topic between them. Mike had been fooling around with that tramp Justine Millner last year, and now she had been shipped out of the city. Rumor said she was pregnant, and once, when Suzie had stumbled over Mike's body and nine empty beer cans out behind the high school stadium, he had admitted that he was afraid the baby was his.

They hadn't ever mentioned the bizarre confession again. Mike was probably hoping it had been a bad dream. But Suzie remembered, and she'd hated the Millners even more ever since. So what if they were big-shot, good-looking millionaires? The Millners were trash.

And she should never have sold them one of her puppies.

The green Mercedes was parked in front of Duck-puddle Diner. Thank goodness, one of the leafy green maples that lined the town square extended its shadow just far enough to touch the car.

Still, Suzie thought desperately, if the driver of the car was having lunch in the diner, it hadn't been just a quick stop. It would be long enough for a young dog, not even a year old yet, to die of heat and thirst and...

But the dog was still alive. His tongue was hanging out, but he was standing on his hind legs, scrabbling weakly at the front window, begging to be released.

Mike whipped his Jeep into the adjoining space, which luckily was free. Suzie didn't even wait for him to come to a complete stop. She jumped out and raced to the Mercedes. "I need something heavy. I need to break the window."

Mike was beside her, his hand on her arm. "No, you dope. Do you know what a new Mercedes window costs? Besides, you don't even know if it's locked.''

She pointed to the bags and purchases mounded up in the back seat. ''Who would be dumb enough to leave a Mercedes unlocked with all that stuff in it?''

Mike grinned wryly. ''Who would be dumb enough to leave a dog in the car without opening the windows?''

He had a point. And so she let him try the door. To her immense relief, it opened easily. The dog practically fell into her arms, panting.

''Oh, you poor thing.'' She cooed soothing noises and patted his damp head. ''It's okay, sweetie. You're okay now.''

Mike loped away, into the diner. After a very short absence, he returned with a soup bowl full of water. ''Take him to my car and give him this,'' he said.

Suzie sat in the front, with the dog draped heavily across her thighs and the bowl on the seat beside her. He hardly raised his head, just lapped and lapped and lapped at the water. She began to wonder if he might make himself sick.

Suddenly she heard a strident, high-pitched female voice.

''Hey. What do you think you're doing with my dog?''

Suzie looked up, fury in her eyes. It was that stupid Mina Millner, Justine's younger sister who had just turned sixteen and obviously was out in daddy's car blowing daddy's money. She was almost as pretty as

Justine, but dumber and meaner, if you could imagine such a thing.

"I'm saving his life," Suzie said fiercely. "You practically killed him, you moron. You can't leave a dog in a closed car like that."

Mina narrowed her beautiful blue eyes. "Listen, Suzie. My father paid you a whole lot of money for that dog. It's mine, and I can do whatever I want with it."

"Actually, that's not true," Mike said quietly. Suzie looked around, surprised. She hadn't realized he had climbed into the car beside her.

Mina aimed her icy gaze toward Mike. "You're not going to take *her* side in this, are you?"

Suzie looked at Mike, almost feeling sorry for him. Mina clearly thought the rich kids had an obligation to stick together, especially against an outsider like freaky Suzie Strickland.

Mike shrugged neutrally. "I kind of think I'm taking the dog's side, Mina. He was in pretty bad shape."

Mina flushed angrily and turned back to Suzie. "Give it to me. It's mine."

Suzie tightened her hold on the soft, warm fur. She wanted to scream at Mina to stop calling the dog an "it," but she didn't quite have the courage.

"Not anymore, he's not."

"If you think you're going to steal it from me, you've got another think coming." Mina's temper was building. She suddenly didn't look very pretty at all. "Mike, tell her to give it back right now."

Mike looked from one girl to the other. Then he looked at the dog. "Tell you what, Mina. Let's go talk to Sheriff Dunbar. The station's just down the block. Maybe he can decide what should be done in a case like this." He gave the angry blonde a straight look. "A case of animal abuse, I mean."

Shocked, Mina made an ugly, strangled sound in her throat. She glared at Mike, and though she didn't quite say "traitor," it hung in the air between them. She breathed heavily for several seconds, and then, in an impotent fury, she turned around, climbed into her daddy's car, slammed the door and peeled away.

Suzie could hardly breathe, even though the air-conditioning was going full blast. She definitely couldn't speak.

After a minute, Mike reached silently across her and pulled the passenger door shut. He patted the dog's head, and then he reached up and smoothed a strand of hair from her flushed cheek.

"Hey, Suzie," he said gently. "He's going to be all right."

"He's a boy," she said stupidly. Why say it now? Mina wasn't even there to know she was being corrected. "He's not an *it*."

And then, without any warning at all, a small choking noise escaped her trembling lips.

"Hey," he said again as the tears began to fall. "Come here."

She couldn't resist. She had used all her courage to face down Mina Millner, and she was limp with the effort. She let him press her head down against his shoulder, with the dog panting softly between them.

"I know," he whispered. "Go ahead and cry."

And so she did.

If anyone had told her, a month ago, that she'd be sitting in Mike Frome's Jeep, sobbing loud, wet tears into his grass-stained designer T-shirt, she would have said they were insane.

But here she was. And maybe she was the one who was insane. Because she didn't feel dumb, and she didn't feel embarrassed. She felt relieved.

And, weirdest of all, considering how vicious preppy kids like Mike could be when you gave them ammunition, she actually felt very, very safe.

MATTHEW MADE FANTASTIC progress on the roof repairs that week. He started work early every morning and kept at it until dusk forced him to stop.

Then he worked at indoor repairs, often not turning in until well after midnight. He realized that, subconsciously, he was racing the calendar. He would be at Summer House only a few more weeks, and he wanted to get as much done as possible. He didn't want to wake up in the middle of the night, months from now, wondering if Natalie had fallen through a bad stair, or started a fire with a rotten electrical switch.

He had a feeling he'd be waking up often enough, just thinking of the way she smelled of flowers after she'd been working in her greenhouse, or the way she wrinkled her nose when she was embarrassed. Or thinking of what a treasure she had offered him, and kicking himself for turning it down.

With her typical sweetness, Natalie accepted his decision without any fuss, and even tried to make things easier between them. She seemed to work at moving to "friend" mode, and she carefully avoided all those small touches on the hand, impulsive hugs and teasing nudges under the table that she used to sprinkle through their days like confectioner's sugar.

She didn't know, of course, that he'd been living on those tiny moments for the past several weeks. She didn't know that eliminating them left him starved almost beyond endurance.

He'd learned a lot about endurance in the past three years. Prison had taught him that a person could stand almost anything if he had to. But this wasn't prison, he thought bleakly as he lay in his sensuously carved bed at night and stared at the undulating mountains in the distance. This was almost worse. This time, the key that would open his cell was right there in his hand, and somehow he had to stop himself from using it.

If she suffered over their decision, she didn't show it. She seemed her normal cheerful self and continued to pamper him like royalty. Over her usual Sunday morning feast, which she had concocted in bare feet while singing off-key and leading an imaginary orchestra with her pancake turner, she announced excitedly that she had decided to hold a party in the newly discovered casino.

"Can you believe it?" she said, popping a grape into her mouth and munching on it happily. "Granville and Ward knew all about the casino. Apparently my grandfather had poker parties in there as recently as eight or ten years ago."

She came and sat on the edge of the table, her bare, tanned legs swinging back and forth carelessly. "I don't know how they kept it such a secret. Or why. You'd think they were a band of Al Capones, with Elliott Ness sniffing around the door."

"That was probably half the fun," he said, thinking about the irrepressible old men, instead of allowing himself to think about the particularly sensual shape of her kneecaps, which were only inches from his hand. "They probably loved that cloak-and-dagger stuff. All little boys do."

"Yep. Anyhow, the members of the historical association and I have put our heads together, and we've decided to clean up the casino and put on a wonderful Prohibition Party. We'll have dancing, and all kinds of gambling, which won't actually be illegal, because all the money is going to charity."

He smiled. "What charity? I hope it's the Save Summer House Fund, which is the neediest charity I can think of."

"No, silly." She started to kick him playfully with

her bare foot, but at the last minute she remembered, and she stopped herself. "We all decided to work together and get everything donated, so it won't cost me a cent personally. And the proceeds will go to the Save Llewellyn's Lake foundation, which Ward Winters started last year."

"Even if it doesn't take cash, it will take time," he said. "I know you. You won't do anything but get ready for this party, and all your own problems will get neglected."

She shook her head.

"That's okay," she said easily. "Everyone has problems, but if we all just lived in our own little cocoons, working on our own selfish problems, what would happen to the world? Even if my roof is leaking, I still love this town, and I still want to help."

She made a good case. People who thought only of themselves lived pretty miserable lives. He had been proof enough of that.

"So what is threatening Llewellyn's Lake, anyhow? Killer bullfrogs? Chronic beer-can poisoning?" He grimaced. "Whatever it is, it can't be as desperate as the creeping decadence and wheezing blight that are taking over this place."

She grinned. "Admit it, Matthew. You're just fussy because you lost the war with the wiring in the Blue Bedroom."

"Excuse me," he corrected her somberly. "I lost the battle. Not the war."

"Forget about all that for now. I want you to help me plan the party. It'll be fun."

"Oh, really? And while we're sending out party invitations, who's going to repair those soft spots in the roof?"

"The same person who's been fixing them for the past fifty years," she said gaily, tossing a grape into the air and catching it in her open mouth. "Nobody."

NATALIE AND SUZIE HAD BEEN in the attic for more than an hour, and they still hadn't found the right party dress for Natalie.

Suzie would wear the red satin, of course. That had been a no-brainer, considering how exquisite she looked in it. But, though Natalie had tried on a dozen lovely dresses, she couldn't settle on any of them.

"No," she said disconsolately, shrugging out of a chiffon sheath of peacock-blue. "Not good enough. It has to be absolutely perfect."

Suzie sighed. "It *was* perfect. So was the last one. What's the matter with you today?"

Natalie gritted her teeth and pulled another gown from the trunk. God, no, not orange. "*Nothing's* the matter with me. It's just extremely important that I have the perfect dress for this party."

"Why? Have you invited the fashion police?"

Natalie ignored her and burrowed deeper into the trunk. Good grief. This one was practically puce.

Arghhh. In a hundred years of Granvilles, hadn't there been a single sexy female with good taste? Of course, she had to admit that if future generations went digging through *her* wardrobe looking for fabulous getups, they'd be sorely disappointed. She had a grand total of one good dress, and it was a yawning bore. Made her look like a fusty second-assistant pencil-pusher.

"So, Natalie, I was thinking about what you said." Suzie was trying to sound casual, which piqued Natalie's interest immediately.

She looked up. "What did I say?"

"You know, about maybe finding a way to show a guy that you're interested. That you don't really hate him."

Natalie sat back on her heels. "Oh, yeah? And?"

"And…" Suzie chewed on the already-short nail of her index finger. "And I was wondering. You said to surprise him with a kiss or something. But do you think maybe crying on his shoulder kind of does the same thing?"

Natalie blinked, trying to absorb the implications of the question. "Maybe," she said carefully. "It doesn't sound like anywhere near as much fun, but I guess it might do the trick." She tilted her head. "Why? Did you do that?"

"Sort of." Suzie screwed up her mouth. "I didn't mean to. It just happened. The problem is, that was a week ago, and I haven't seen him since. I think maybe it just grossed him out."

"I doubt that," Natalie said, smiling. "But it may have confused him. Guys are pretty easily confused."

Suzie rolled her eyes. "Boy, you got that right."

Natalie pulled out a yellow sequined dress that had potential. It might look nice with her hair. She went over to the mirror and held it up. Nope. It made her skin look like the color of wet hemp.

"Well, I would suggest that you try the kiss thing next time," she said, tossing the yellow dress back into the trunk irritably. "But frankly, that one seems to have had mixed results, too."

Suzie squinted at her thoughtfully. Natalie noticed that, over the past few weeks, the teenager had toned down her makeup, and she had trimmed off the purple edges of her hair. She still looked edgy and individual, but she no longer looked scary.

In fact, she looked like a girl who knew who she was and liked it. *Good for you, Suzie,* Natalie said mentally. It was a rare seventeen-year-old who could say that.

"Ooh, I get it," Suzie said suddenly, as if her mental scanner had finally hit the right frequency. "You're interested in somebody! *That's* what all this drama is about the dress. Your little kiss trick didn't get the guy to call, so you're trying to get his attention with a hot outfit that shows him what he's missing."

Natalie wrinkled her nose. "I don't think I'd put it quite as coarsely as you did, but—" She unearthed a simple white gown with a rhinestone belt. "I guess it's something like that."

Suzie made a disgusted sound. "I hate to say this, Natalie, but I'm not sure this guy is worth it. I mean, if he knows you, and he's even kissed you, and he isn't interested yet… Maybe he's gay.''

Natalie laughed. ''He's not.''

''Then he's a superficial idiot. He ought to see how cool you are, no matter what you're wearing. Even if you're wearing those saggy, gross old shorts you love so much.'' Natalie glanced over and scowled, but Suzie just grinned and went on. ''Seriously. You don't really want a man if you have to snag him with a sexy dress, do you?''

Natalie held up the white dress. Hmm…maybe. White really was her only color.

''It's not like that,'' she said, glancing at Suzie in the mirror. ''He's already interested. I just need the dress as a kind of—kind of a battering ram. He's thrown up this wall between us. A very frustrating, very thick wall of misguided nobility.''

''Nobility?'' Suzie frowned, confused. Then her face split in another impish grin. ''Oh! You mean that hottie Mr. Quinn! Yeah, he sure can do that nobility thing to death, can't he?''

Natalie froze, staring. ''What do you know about it?''

Suzie giggled. ''No, no, nothing like that! I was just trying to squeeze some investment advice out of him. But I hit that wall you're talking about, and I've got the bruises on my head to prove it.''

Natalie sighed. ''Me, too.'' She swayed in front of the mirror, trying to get the rhinestone belt to shimmer, but the darn thing just wouldn't cooperate. Oh, hell, this one wouldn't do, either. It made her look like a vestal virgin, which pretty much defeated the purpose.

"I give up," she said wearily, tossing the dress toward the growing pile of rejects. "I'm just going to have to get him drunk."

MATTHEW KNEW Natalie expected him to go to the party.

He also knew he shouldn't. Whatever he had been in his former life, in this life he was the handyman. He was her employee—a blue-collar, down-and-dirty workman who at some estates would still be expected to use the back entrance and avoid making eye contact with his betters.

It obviously hadn't occurred to her that he might be thinking such things. She solicited his opinion on everything from the brand of gin they should stock— "How cheap can I go without shocking the snobs?"—to the music they should play—"It ought to be something sexy and reckless, so that they'll all bet like madmen."

Gradually, under her loving care, the casino began to gleam. The historical association sent in a team of people to polish all the silver and brass and gilt and crystal until the casino sparkled like the inside of a pirate's treasure chest.

They washed the walls and waxed the beautiful wood floor until you could see your reflection in it. They calibrated the roulette wheel, and they repaired the green felt tabletops so that the cards slid across them like ice.

Natalie worked harder than anyone, wearing jeans and T-shirts that were almost as old as the casino, and tying her hair back with a faded blue bandanna. For a full week, she was constantly covered in dust or furniture polish or glue, and when she wasn't working, she was buried in a library book called *Playing By the Rules: 100 Fun Casino Games.*

"Just so nobody cheats," she'd say, wrinkling her nose playfully.

Two days before the party, he found a tuxedo hanging in his room, crisp and elegant, still enclosed in a dry cleaner's bag.

"For the party," the note pinned to it had read. He smiled at her silly calligraphy, remembering when he had thought it meant she was old, instead of merely eccentric. "It belonged to my great-great-uncle Theodore, who they say was a lady-killer. It may have been a figure of speech."

He went looking for her then, to explain to her why he couldn't wear it. Why, though he hoped for her sake the party was a success, he didn't plan to attend.

He tried the casino first. That's where she always was these days.

The secret door stood open, letting the flower-scented summer air make its way inside and chase away the musty smells. He looked in, and there she was, kneeling in a shaft of sunlight, her golden curls bouncing as she scrubbed the floor and laughed with the ladies from Happy Housekeepers Inc., who worked alongside her.

He stood in the doorway and watched her for a long moment, just for the pleasure of drinking in her unadorned vitality and enthusiasm, her vibrant energy and utter lack of affectation.

God, she was beautiful. He couldn't take his gaze away, though it made the pit of his stomach ache with needs he'd been trying to ignore.

He knew that, no matter how many years away he traveled from this moment, he'd see her like this in his mind. He'd see her glimmering gold, laughing in the sunlight.

And suddenly, rashly, he decided that he would attend the party.

He wouldn't even argue with her. If the Granville heiress could scrub floors joyously, then surely, if it would please her, the handyman could put on a borrowed tux and dance under the rich, rainbowed light of a Waterford crystal chandelier.

At least until the stroke of midnight.

CHAPTER TWELVE

THE NIGHT OF THE PARTY WAS as lovely as anything the Adirondacks had to offer.

A white moon rode the sky in a carriage of silver clouds. Fireflies twinkled like fairies in the distance. Warm, perfumed breezes whispered past you so subtly you might turn, believing a woman had brushed your shoulder.

On such a night, Summer House was once again the queen of Firefly Glen. Summer moonlight hid a multitude of sins and, her imperfections masked, she rose from the mountainside with her old, regal confidence.

Matthew, standing at the foot of the driveway looking back, felt as if he were seeing Summer House for the first time. As the floodlights came on, and the noble facade glowed golden against the night, he suddenly understood why a person would do anything to save her.

"Matthew?" Natalie's voice drifted toward him. She had sent him down to open the wrought-iron gates while she dashed up to put on her party clothes. He'd been gone quite a while, lost in the beauty of the night. She probably wondered what was keeping him.

"Down here," he called. "I'm on my way up."

But as he walked up to the house he heard light footsteps running toward him, and he smiled to himself. It simply wasn't in Natalie's nature to wait.

He thought of something teasing to say, something about her chronic impatience, but when he saw her the words disappeared, suddenly completely irrelevant.

She was the most beautiful thing he'd ever seen. She wore a dress of something soft that was shot through with metallic threads of yellow, bronze and gold. It clung to her breast, traced her waist, then fell lush and wanton to her feet in candlelight flickers of topaz.

Her hair was loose—not lacquered and brittle in the classic dress-up mode, a dreadful look, he'd always thought, an effect created purely for viewing. Hers was soft and flowing and begging to be touched. When she moved it shimmered, flashing first white-gold, then a burnished copper.

She looked like a small, dancing flame.

But, God help him, he was the one who was on fire.

She twirled for him, a tiny firecracker sparkling in the moonlight. "Well? What do you think? Do you like it?"

"It's beautiful. You look…" It wasn't the kind of thing he could describe with words. If only he could take her in his arms, he could show her. He clenched his teeth and settled for understatement. "You look wonderful."

She smiled up at him. "You do, too." She ran her hands appraisingly over the shoulders of the tuxedo. "It fits perfectly, doesn't it? You know, Mr. Quinn, I believe you could have given Great-Uncle Theodore a run for his money."

He didn't answer. If she didn't stop touching him, he was going to lose what little control he had left.

"Okay, well, I guess we'd better hurry," she said, taking the hint. "People will be showing up any minute, and I can't find my shoes." She lifted her skirt and held out her bare foot. "See?"

He had to laugh. "I may have seen them," he said. "Are they soft leather slippers? Kind of butter colored?"

She nodded eagerly. "They're kid. They cost a fortune, but they were the only things I could find that didn't hurt my feet." She wrinkled her nose. "You know I actually hate shoes."

"Yes, I know," he said. He hoped she hadn't spent too much. She'd kick them off by midnight anyhow. "I'm pretty sure the garden gnome just outside the kitchen door is wearing them. You know, the one who's standing on his head?"

She clapped her hands happily, not at all embarrassed. "Oh, that's right. I had too many packages to hold, and I needed somewhere to set the shoes while

I opened the door. And there were these two feet just looking up at me. It was obviously the perfect place.''

"Of course," he murmured politely.

She caught his gaze and began to laugh, clearly aware of his amusement and not minding it a bit.

She slipped her arm through his companionably. "It's not nice to make fun of the afflicted," she scolded as they began to walk. "I can't help being a Granville. Which reminds me, if you see me gloating in an obnoxious way about beating the pants off all my neighbors tonight, take me outside and walk me around in the fresh air till I snap out of it. Granvilles are notoriously tacky winners, and it would be nice to have a few friends left when this party is over."

He chuckled. "I thought you'd accepted the fact that Granvilles don't always win."

She glanced up at him once, then looked away, smiling serenely into the middle distance.

"Oh, that," she said equably. "Well, tonight's different. Tonight we Granvilles plan to win big."

EVERYTHING WAS PERFECT. Absolutely one hundred percent perfect. Natalie wanted to shout out her happiness, or kick off her silly shoes and dance her delight on the shiny mahogany bar. She couldn't have dreamed a party more perfect than this.

Helium balloons in every color of the rainbow clustered on the ceiling, tendrils of ribbon dangling down to tickle noses, creating silliness and laughter. The jukebox played classic hits from the twenties, everything from Tommy Dorsey to Eddie Cantor, Rudy Vallee to Marlene Dietrich.

Everyone had come. Saving Llewellyn's Lake from the rape-and-pillage developers was a popular cause, and of course lots of people were dying to see the secret casino.

The city council had given her permission to hold the charity ''gambling'' event, and to thank them she had let them each run their own gaming table.

Mayor Millner, the only one who had refused to wear a costume, presided over roulette. Playboy Griffin Cahill, looking dashing in a striped blazer only he could pull off, was also the only one who actually understood baccarat, so he got that table. Stuart, wearing a raccoon coat that looked great but would very soon be much too hot, took blackjack. Crusty Hickory Baxter claimed poker because, he said, it was the only game that wasn't reserved for sissies and James Bond.

At the moment, it seemed to be reserved for drunks. Boxer Barnes, who had a few dozen too many every Friday night, had homesteaded one of the chairs at the poker table, though he was losing every hand. Boxer would have to be driven home, but he'd always been such a good friend to her grandfather that Natalie wouldn't have thought of leaving him out.

Granville and Ward Winters manned the bar, and it was quite a show-stopping performance. They were tossing glasses and bottles around like vaudeville jugglers, and the ladies in little fringed flapper dresses were lining up, ready to pay anything for a drink and some attention.

Suzie had arrived a little late, looking fetchingly nervous and exactly like a princess in simple red satin. Natalie laughed out loud when she saw Mike Frome notice her. The poor kid almost ran into a wall. He clearly was at the mercy of his hormones, and Suzie had triggered a serious attack.

Natalie and Suzie had exchanged knowing smiles before Suzie glided on to stand with some of the other high school kids. When Natalie had decided which of the Glen's teens to invite, she'd decided to bring more of the artsy group than the jocks. Might as well let Mike see what it was like to be the underdog for a change.

Best of all, though, was that Matthew seemed to be having a good time. He wasn't gambling, of course. She'd racked her brain, but she hadn't been able to think of a way to get some chips to him without insulting him, so ultimately she'd just decided to let well enough alone.

But she had introduced him to Parker and Sarah, and Griffin and Heather, and Mary Brady and a dozen other people who all looked so lighthearted and friendly in their Roaring Twenties costumes. She was proud of her neighbors, and glad that he seemed to enjoy their company.

Right now he was talking comfortably to several of the other men, and he didn't seem to feel at all ill at ease. Thank goodness there weren't a lot of snobs in Firefly Glen. She was a little worried about Mayor Millner, but the roulette table kept him pretty busy. Witchy Elspeth Grant was too excited about the historical find to be much trouble.

And Bourke Waitely, another little pocket of boorish snobbery, wasn't here yet. With any kind of luck, maybe Bourke would decide to stay home and play with his money.

And besides, she thought, watching Matthew as he traded football stories with Parker and Reed Fairmont, the Glen veterinarian, why should anyone treat Matthew badly, anyhow?

Without a doubt he was the best-looking, classiest guy in the room. And it wasn't just the lady-killer tux. Matthew always looked classy, whether he was wearing jeans or shorts or, she suspected, nothing at all.

With that thought, she decided it was time he danced with her. She went over to the men and tapped Matthew on the arm.

"This," she said politely, "is my favorite song. I really think someone should ask me to dance, don't you?"

"'Bye Bye Blackbird'?" Parker made a skeptical noise. "That song was written before your grandparents were born, Nattie. How could it possibly be—"

"Why, my dear Mr. Tremaine," she interrupted sweetly. "Would you please be so kind as to *shut up?*"

All three men grinned, but Matthew took her hand and led her to the dance floor.

Parker didn't know everything. Natalie did love this song. It was slow and poignant, with a lot of saxophone. She only hoped it was the longest song in the world.

Matthew held her softly but very close. She sighed and shut her eyes, feeling his body move against her, hearing the safe, steady beat of his heart. She rubbed her cheek against the cool fabric of her great-uncle Theodore's jacket.

"So tell me the truth," he said. His chin was warm against her hair, and his voice was deep and quiet. "Is this really your favorite song?"

"Yes, sir." She looked up at him and smiled. "It is now."

SUZIE SWALLOWED HARD, wondering if she'd heard Mike Frome correctly. She thought he had just asked her to go outside with him. But the music was pretty loud, something weird and bouncy about the Sheik of Araby, and she was having trouble hearing.

"What did you say?" She made an extra effort not to sound annoyed or sarcastic. He had danced with her three times already, and the last time it had been kind of hot and flirty. So maybe she really had heard him right after all.

He smiled in a cocky, sexy way that used to irritate her. Now it just gave her rubber legs.

"I said, let's go outside and get some fresh air."

Her stomach began to churn. She had wanted this so long she was afraid to believe it had finally arrived. What if she was reading too much into it? What if he really did just want some fresh air?

But she saw that look in his eye, and she knew she was right. That *you turn me on and if I don't kiss you I'll die* look. The kind of look boys always gave to the Justine Millners of the world, but never to the Suzie Stricklands who stood silently by, just watching and wanting.

''Okay,'' she said, and she let him take her hand. She hoped her palms weren't sweating. She wiped her other one against the red satin, just in case.

His weren't a bit damp, naturally. He was good at this. He was probably the Olympic gold medalist of ducking out into the dark with girls.

They eased past the grown-ups, and she could tell he especially didn't want his grandfather to notice him. They were lucky. Granville and Ward Winters were busy competing for the funky bartender award, singing along to the new song, which was about having no bananas. They couldn't have cared less what the kids were doing.

In fact, from the way Madeline Alexander was drooling over Ward Winters, Suzie had an idea that those two might be doing some ducking out themselves before the night was over.

They made it to the door without being stopped. As the cool night air hit her cheeks, Suzie realized how hotly she was flushing.

"Come on," Mike said, pulling her hand. "I know a place we can go."

They walked so far she almost said, *No, wait, I've changed my mind, I want to go back.* But she didn't, and finally he took one last turn and Natalie's greenhouse was right in front of them. It was very big, completely dark and slightly frightening.

"Here?" She was embarrassed at the way her voice cracked.

"It's open," he said.

"Yeah, but I don't think we should—"

"It's okay. We won't hurt anything. It's just a place where we can be alone. Where we can talk."

Talk, she thought, trying to be cynical. Did he think she really believed he wanted to talk?

All around them fireflies were blinking, hundreds of tiny golden lights that sent signals only they could understand. She'd read once that the female firefly blinks in a certain rhythmic pattern, which attracts the right kind of male to be her mate. If she flashes the wrong pattern, he isn't interested. He'll know they aren't the same kind, and he'll keep looking for the female that's his true match.

Was that what she had done, she wondered? Had she changed her looks, her way of dressing, her entire pattern of flashing so that this boy would fly her way? So that he would think they were two of a kind?

It was too late to start second-guessing herself now. Mike had opened the greenhouse door and was tugging her inside.

It was cooler in here. The air smelled alive and green and earthy. It was sensual in a primitive way she only half understood.

Mike led her to a long wooden table and lifted her onto it. Then he stood in front of her, parting her legs just a little to let him come in closer.

That part she understood perfectly.

He touched her face. "You look gorgeous tonight," he said.

She shook her head. "Don't be silly."

"It's true." He played with her hair, running his fingers over the shining black curve she had carefully moussed to that it would tuck attractively behind her ear. "Why haven't I ever noticed how fantastic you are?"

It's the dress, dummy, she wanted to say. *It's still just me inside this red satin. I'm still the same geek you won't talk to in class.* But she couldn't say it. She was shivering inside. She was alive with a twisting excitement, and she wanted him to go on touching her.

There was something special about him, she'd always felt that. Some energy, some force so compelling she couldn't even think when he was around. Every other boy she'd dated had wanted to talk to her, talk and talk and talk about art, about school, about philosophy, about how they hated the in crowd. She liked being smart. But sometimes she felt talked to death.

This elegant, muscled young jock wanted something else. He wanted something more. And so did she.

"Dammit, Suzie," he said roughly, his face strangely frustrated. "You're too much of a mystery. I don't ever know what you're thinking."

She shook her head. "Yes, you do," she said simply.

He was too smart to misread her. And he was too eager to miss his chance. Moving in, he took her head in his hands and kissed her fiercely. He kissed her so long she thought she might faint. Maybe she did faint, because the next thing she knew her arms were wrapped around his neck, and she was pulling him closer.

He groaned and kissed her again, harder and deeper. He let his hands move across her neck. He followed with his lips. He took the elastic of her gathered neckline and pulled it gently down, exposing one of her breasts.

He looked up briefly, his eyes flashing in the moonlight. And then, when she didn't stop him, he bent over her, doing things she'd only seen in the movies, or in her dreams.

Never, never had she imagined his mouth would be so hot, or that, because he was doing these things, her whole body would begin to tighten into one bright flash point of tension.

"Suzie," he said, groaning. He bared the other breast. "You're unbelievable."

She was breathing so fast she felt dizzy. She ran

her fingers through his hair, but he didn't seem aware of anything but the dazzling things he was doing to her breasts. She let her head fall back and made a soft sound of surprise and hunger. What had seemed like too much sensation just minutes ago suddenly wasn't quite enough.

He gathered the satin of her skirt in his hands, folding it between his fingers until he had found his way under it. And then he touched her between her legs. She cried aloud as a beautiful pain streaked out in all directions from his fingers.

"No," she whispered, shoving at his hand clumsily. "No."

He looked up, his eyes unfocused. He shook his head, a little boy lost. "No?"

She just stared at him, her body still pulsing from the aftershocks of his fingers.

This was it, then. This was what she had never known. This was why girls like Justine ended up in trouble. Not because some selfish boy pushed them into a dumb, humiliating mistake. But because the mistake itself was so beautiful, and so exciting, and so nearly irresistible.

"No," she said again, swallowing hard. "I'm sorry, Mike. I don't know what you thought, but I'm not ready for more than this."

He was hunched over, as if he were in pain. His head was bowed, his hands splayed out on the bench on either side of her. His breath came loud and rapid.

"Mike?" She touched his shoulder tentatively.

"Okay," he said sharply. "Just give me a minute."

She waited. Through the smoky panes of the greenhouse, she could see the blinking fireflies. There weren't as many now. Most of them had already paired off for the night.

Was he just going to leave her like this? Self-consciously, she tugged her dress up over her breasts. Why didn't he *say* something?

After a couple of minutes, he pulled back. He moved to her left, so that their bodies didn't touch at all. He still stared down at the empty bench, though she could tell his breathing was growing a little more normal.

"Mike," she said again. And when he didn't answer, she slid down from the bench. "I think I should go back to the party now."

No answer.

Suddenly his pouting silence made her furious. She hadn't promised him anything, dammit. Was he so spoiled by the girls that he thought every single one of them was just waiting for the chance to have a quickie in the moonlight?

"Come on, Mike. Don't be such a jerk."

"Yeah?" His voice was harsh. "Look who's talking. There's a name for what you just did, you know."

That was too much. She squared her shoulders for battle. "Hey, get over yourself, why don't you? I'm only seventeen. I have plans for my life, and frankly, they don't include spending the next year in Timbuktu having your illegitimate baby.''

His head whipped around, and his face was a mask of misery. Oh, God, she shouldn't have said that. No wonder the boys didn't like her. She always let embarrassment make her cruel.

"Oh, darn. Mike, I'm sorry. Look, just talk to me, would you?"

"Why should I, Suzie-freaka?" His voice was suddenly scalding, the voice of the prom king tired of slumming with the geek. "Since when have you and I had anything to *talk* about?"

THE LAST TIME MATTHEW HAD BEEN this happy was right before the cops came and arrested him. And that's how he knew something terrible was probably going to happen tonight.

He was, quite simply, tempting fate. What right did he have to hold her like this? What right to feel such idiotic pride that she, who could have any man in the room, from the oldest to the youngest, had chosen him? What right did he have to know this mindless contentment, as if she belonged here, against his heart?

Already people were watching. They stood around in their Roaring Twenties costumes, gambling and drinking and singing along to ''Bye Bye Blackbird,'' which they all seemed to know. But occasionally they'd look over at him and Natalie, and then at each other, their eyebrows raised in silent speculation.

The only one oblivious to the minidrama was Boxer Barnes. Matthew remembered the morning he'd arrived in Firefly Glen. Parker Tremaine had been escorting Boxer home from a night spent sleeping it off at the city jail.

Apparently Boxer still had a weakness for booze, because he'd arrived at tonight's party in a genuine 1920s tux with the tie already loose, already staggering. Now he was so plastered he kept dropping his hand, revealing his cards. Needless to say, he was losing.

So Boxer didn't care who was dancing with Natalie. But from the rest of her guests, Matthew could feel the curiosity building behind their avid eyes until it was almost palpable.

Look at the way they're dancing. Why is the handyman monopolizing the hostess?

Matthew decided to disregard them, even though he knew it was this kind of blind stupidity that had led him into trouble before. It was never wise to ignore the ugly realities for long. They had clever ways of forcing themselves back into the spotlight.

But he closed his eyes willfully and pushed away his premonitions. He needed to be blind a little longer.

When "Bye Bye Blackbird" ended and the next song began, he looked down at her, a question in his gaze.

"Can you believe it? This is my favorite song,

too.'' Her butterscotch eyes twinkled. "And the one after that. And the one after that.''

He took a breath. "People will talk," he said.

"Yes.'' She smiled at him. "But we won't listen.''

God, she was one in a million. How could he possibly let her go before he had to? He gathered her in again and told fate to do what it must.

Fate gave them three songs. Just three.

The first sign of trouble started over by the bar, one voice that rose a little above the others. It built slowly. A woman's strident tones, and then other voices, urging her to keep her voice down, to be calm.

And then a flurry, a shuffle of angry movement. More strident tones competing with the music.

Eventually the guests began to transfer their curiosity to this new, interesting commotion. They looked, and then in ripples of awareness that spread out from the bar to the dance floor to the tables, they stopped everything else and watched.

Matthew watched, too, every nerve on alert. The woman was probably seventy, but decades of cosmetic surgery had left her face sharp and shiny and not quite normal. She wore a blue sequined flapper costume that might have looked great on a woman half her age. But on her it was awful, exposing her painfully thin arms and legs, which had spent so many years in tanning beds that they had the texture of old leather.

She certainly dispelled the myth that you could never be too rich or too thin.

Though he racked his memory, Matthew didn't recognize her. But she recognized him.

Someone held her elbow, obviously counseling caution, but the woman was beyond caring. She stared at Matthew, her eyes so engorged with fury they seemed to bulge out of their sockets.

"Yes, I'm sure, you fool," she said shrilly, trying to tug her arm free. "That's Matthew Quinn. That's the son of a bitch who ruined my sister's life."

CHAPTER THIRTEEN

MATTHEW FELT STRANGELY clear-headed, but numb. He let his arms fall away from Natalie, and he stepped back a pace, instinctively trying to put distance between her and the ugliness that was rushing inexorably toward them.

She'd heard it, of course. Everyone had. She stood so rigid and regal that she seemed several inches taller, and she appeared to be trying to freeze the other woman in place with a fierce glare.

"Don't you dare, Jocelyn Waitely." Her murmur was not meant to be heard. It was no more than a savage underbreath. "Don't…you…*dare.*"

"It's all right, Natalie," Matthew said, touching her arm, which was flexed and stiff. He retained enough inner calm to find that amusing and very sweet. The quirky, peaceful princess of Firefly Glen was ready to punch out one of her aristocratic guests to defend the handyman's honor.

Only problem was, the handyman didn't have any. Jocelyn Waitely, whoever she was, probably was telling the truth. The collapse of his company had ruined a great many lives.

Ignoring everything, including his own common

sense, he placed one knuckle softly beneath Natalie's chin, turned her face to his and gave her one last smile.

"This isn't the time for a Granville moment, sweetheart," he said softly. "Something like this was inevitable, sooner or later. Let her get it out of her system."

Natalie shook her head minutely. "No."

But the fire-breathing dragon had broken its restraints. Jocelyn Waitely was upon them.

"How dare you show up here?" She pointed a red fingernail at his face. "You should be in prison. I thought you *were* in prison."

"I was," Matthew said evenly. "I was paroled a couple of months ago."

The woman rounded on Natalie, her oversize diamond earrings flashing like knives. "Did you know that when you hired him? When you invited him to a party with decent people? Did you know this man was a common criminal?"

"I've known about Matthew's past from the start," Natalie answered with a quiet ferocity. "But you're quite wrong, Jocelyn. There is nothing *common* about him."

Jocelyn laughed bitterly, her red lips parting to show small, sharp teeth. It was a particularly unpleasant vision

"Why? Because he's smooth? All con artists are. Because he looks attractive standing there in his fancy clothes, pretending he's one of us?"

A small, fat, balding man who seemed to have come dressed as President Warren Harding scurried up and took the woman's arm. "Jocelyn, honey, I think that's enough."

"No, it isn't, Bourke. It's not anywhere near enough." The woman shook off the little man's touch viciously. Somewhere Matthew found a sliver of pity for the man, who must be this hideous woman's husband.

Talk about living in a prison. Obviously, Matthew thought, Bourke needed to dress up as the commander in chief because he never got the chance to be the boss in real life.

Matthew wondered if he'd be a fool to apologize to Jocelyn Waitely. He didn't remember her sister—she must have a different last name—but that didn't matter. He *was* sorry, sick with an impotent regret over what had been done to each and every one of his clients.

But he had a feeling this bitter woman would spit in his face if he tried to tell her that.

"So tell me, Mr. Quinn. Whose hard-earned money are you gambling away tonight?" She cast a withering glance at Natalie. "Hers?"

Natalie's arm tightened again, but Matthew was pleased to hear that, when she answered, her voice sounded smooth and completely controlled.

"If you weren't too self-absorbed to see past your own beautifully bobbed nose, Jocelyn, perhaps you might have noticed that he isn't gambling at all."

Natalie lifted her chin high. "I don't mind telling you, though, that I would have been happy to give him anything I had. But I knew he wouldn't accept it."

"Good God, you certainly have *her* fooled, don't you?" The older woman curled her lip and made a sneering noise. "Not that you should consider that much of an accomplishment. The Granvilles have always been as gullible as newborn babies."

Matthew heard Natalie's jagged inhale, and he wondered what she'd say next. He was even starting to worry what he himself might say next. But neither of them got the chance to speak.

Through the entire scene, Boxer Barnes had been sitting foggily at the nearest poker table, his head hanging slack between his hands. But he must have suddenly tuned in, because he lifted his head and announced in adamant, if slurred, tones, "Natalie Granville is a damn sweet woman, and I'll kick the ass of anyone who says otherwise."

Jocelyn didn't even deign to look at him. "Shut up, Boxer," she said dismissively. "You're too soused to know what you're talking about. As usual."

Matthew felt Natalie's arm flex again. She even made a noise that sounded like a soft growl. He knew he'd better break in quickly.

"Mrs. Waitely," he said, keeping his voice and face courteous. "I'll be glad to answer any questions you'd like to ask me. But I think we're making Natalie's other guests uncomfortable. This is a private matter, and we probably should discuss it privately."

"You'd like that, wouldn't you? You don't want everyone else to know the truth about you. Well, I want them *all* to know. Maybe then you won't be able to pull the wool over their eyes the way you did my sister."

Heather Cahill, a lovely young obstetrician Matthew had met for the first time tonight, had moved over quietly and was standing supportively at Natalie's other elbow. She spoke up now, her voice clear and sensible.

"Jocelyn, Mr. Quinn has offered a reasonable compromise. Maybe you and he could get together tomorrow? If you'd like, maybe the two of you could meet at—"

"What I'd like," Jocelyn Waitely said, her enunciation as sharp as ice, "would be never to set eyes on that lying, thieving bastard again."

With another small, repressed noise, Natalie took a step forward, coming toe-to-toe with the older woman.

"I think that is an excellent idea." Her voice was deceptively smooth. "Obviously, Jocelyn, I should never have invited you here tonight. But don't worry, I quite understand that you will feel it necessary to leave immediately. And of course I will never put you in the uncomfortable position of receiving one of my invitations in the future."

"What?" Jocelyn looked at Natalie hard. Her blood red lips were a thin line of fury.

"You heard me."

"I have been welcome at Summer House since before you were born, you little fool." Jocelyn tilted her head, and the Waterford chandelier turned her dyed-blond hair as gray as cigarette ashes, which it probably was, underneath. "And you dare to throw me out of this party? Out of this house?"

Matthew considered intervening. The old woman looked downright dangerous in her insulted fury. But apparently Granvilles were as tough as they were eccentric. Natalie met Jocelyn's hot wrath with a cold smile.

"Absolutely, Jocelyn. With my bare hands, if necessary."

HALF AN HOUR LATER, "Someone to Watch Over Me" was playing, and Natalie watched Matthew dancing with Heather Cahill, trying not to be jealous. She really *did* love *that* song.

Since Jocelyn's departure, Matthew had been the most popular partner in the room.

He had already danced with Sarah Tremaine, and he'd even let Theo Burke give him a lesson in the Charleston. And before that he'd spent many minutes at the bar, letting the men laugh with him and make jokes and in a dozen subtle ways assure him that Jocelyn didn't speak for the whole city.

It was a spontaneous, thoughtful group effort, and Natalie appreciated her friends for trying.

But through it all, she could see that Matthew wasn't letting their warmth touch him. He had that oh-so-polite distance in his expression, that remote dignity in his bearing that told her he had put his inner self somewhere else.

He probably had learned that trick in prison. It pained her to think that here, in her home, he had found himself in need of it again.

She hoped she was wrong, but, of course, she wasn't. She knew him too well. Ten minutes later, just as she had suspected he would, he came to her to say goodbye. He had work to do, he said politely. He really should get to it.

"No, please," she said, "don't go." She did her begging with her eyes. Her lips kept smiling, because people were still watching. Still wondering.

"I have to," he said, smiling back, understanding the game. "It's the perfect time. If I stay, it will spoil the party. You know that."

She hated to hear that tone. That untouchable, implacable resolution. He didn't use it often, but when he did, it meant business. It was the tone he had used when he had refused to invest the money from the vase.

It was as if, occasionally, an issue took him down to core metal, an inner substance that couldn't be altered. Not by negotiating or wheedling or begging or threats. Not by anything.

So, though she lamented all the fun and laughter, all the dances and the drinks and the little excuses to touch each other that she had dreamed they would share tonight, she wouldn't argue. She would let him go back to the pool house now, and hold on to the hope that maybe later, when all the guests were gone...

"You know, I haven't had a chance to thank you properly," he said, his tone strangely formal, "for all you did to defend me."

"Don't be ridiculous. You have nothing to thank me for. I might as well have brought a snake in the house and let it bite you on the leg."

He looked at her from that distant place, that place she knew she could never find, not in a million years, not if he didn't want her to. His eyes looked empty.

"Granvilles are extremely loyal, aren't they?"

"Yes," she said simply. "We are."

"It may," he said with another smile, this one a little softer, "be one of your family's most charming characteristics. Though not necessarily one of the smartest, given how unpleasant the world can be."

"We don't live in the real world," she said, trying to lighten the mood. "As I'm sure many people have warned you already, we live on our own planet."

"Yes. I know." He touched her cheek briefly, then turned to go.

She followed him to the door, which stood open, allowing in the night air. At the last minute she touched his hand, wishing she could hold him, if even for another minute.

He turned, his cool gaze politely questioning why he'd been detained.

"I just wanted to...to thank you for staying as long

as you did," she said, a little stiffly. "I know you only did it for their sake. To make them feel more comfortable about what happened."

He shrugged. "It was a fairly ugly scene. Your guests needed to see that I'm fine, that no real damage has been done. Now they can relax and start to have fun again."

"But is that true?" She wanted to reach up and touch his face, to feel whether it was as tense and tightly managed as it looked. But she couldn't. Everything about him deflected intimacy.

"Is what true?"

"You seem so—far away. Is it true that no real damage was done?"

"Not tonight," he answered hollowly. "The damage you're talking about was done a very long time ago."

MATTHEW SAT on the large, comfortable armchair, Great-Uncle Theodore's shirt unbuttoned at the throat to make it easier to toss back the neat Scotch he had sitting on the end table beside him.

He'd been sitting there for an hour, trying to decide what to do. Or rather, trying to accept what he already knew he must do.

It wasn't just because one old bitch had shown up and begun tossing about a few rather clichéd insults. In the months leading up to his trial, and during the trial itself, he had survived a hundred insults more powerful, personal and ultimately painful than anything Jocelyn Waitely had been able to invent.

No, what had undone him tonight was knowing he had brought that poison, that petty ugliness and sordid disgrace, into Natalie Granville's world.

Into her home.

And, judging from the way she so fiercely defended him, into her heart.

He had seen in her anxious eyes that she sensed real trouble. He had felt it in the clinging grip of her hand at the door.

That was one of the reasons he *had* to do something drastic, whether he wanted to or not. She was starting to understand him too well. She was starting to get too close. Worst of all, he was starting to depend on it, on her amazing intuition, her profound understanding, her unflinching support.

That was complete insanity.

Because Natalie Granville could never be Matthew Quinn's life partner. *Never.* What did he have to offer her? Could he really consider asking her to marry him, to give up her ancestral home, her friends, her birthplace, so that she could come with him to Florida? So that she could cut coupons, make meat loaf, and maybe, on a very exciting day, help him scold the busboys at the newest Granny Gator's Family Restaurant?

Of course not. But what was the alternative? That he should stay here? That she should marry the handyman and spend the rest of her life banishing her friends, one by one, because they dared to insult her husband? That she should live the rest of her life in social isolation up here on this mountain with him, struggling to make ends met, praying the roof didn't collapse over her head?

Never. Never in a million years.

Or was the answer, perhaps, that he just stay another couple of weeks, romp about in bed with her a few times to slake his post-prison hunger? And then, when he'd had enough, when he'd siphoned off enough of her sweetness and optimism to put his own soul back together, he'd hit the road for Florida, leaving her here to endure the ridicule and the shame?

He cursed viciously. He swallowed the entire Scotch in one furious, burning gulp.

And then he stood up to pack.

It didn't take long. He had arrived with only enough clothes to fit in a duffel, and he would leave that way, as well.

First thing in the morning.

Then he sat back down with another Scotch and began to rehearse the words he would use to tell her goodbye.

He heard the end of the party through his open window. He heard Sarah and Parker Tremaine go home early. They couldn't bear to be parted from their newborn for long. He heard the cheers when the final tally for the Save Llewellyn's Lake foundation was announced. And behind it all he heard the music.

"Puttin' On The Ritz." More laughter, the sound

of a balloon popping, probably drifting too close to the chandelier. "Ain't We Got Fun?"

It was very late when the last of the laughing good-byes were called out, expressions of affection pealing through the summer night air with the innocence of church bells.

"Great party, Nat. Love you, kid. Sleep tight."

"Love ya, shweetie. Getchur handsh off me, Sheriff. I can walk."

"Love you, Natalie. Call me tomorrow."

"Love you, Nattie."

Love you.

Love.

So many different people. And every one of them loved Natalie Granville. Of course they did. Who could help it?

After that, as he waited to hear her footsteps, he felt a mindless, eager anticipation overtaking him. He was still sane enough, thank goodness, to appreciate how ironic that was. He could hardly wait for her to arrive so that he could tell her goodbye forever.

Almost half an hour passed.

That didn't seem right.

Could she have decided not to come?

But if she knew him—well, he knew her, too. She wasn't the type to pout, to play hard-to-get, or even to analyze logically how pointless it would be to seek him out. She was the type to leave the sticky cocktail glasses on the tables, the dirty dishes in the sink, so that she could run out here in her bare feet, still wearing her party dress, and threaten to have a whopping Granville moment if he didn't tell her what was wrong.

He went to the casino first. The door still stood open, but the room was empty. Just as he'd predicted, everything had been left in disarray. Slowly sinking balloons floated halfway between the ceiling and the floor. Half-full champagne goblets lined the bar, the bubbles still rising and popping against the glass. Unplayed poker hands still lay, facedown, on the tables.

He called her name, but he got back only an odd echo, reminding him that this peculiar room had been carved into the side of a mountain.

He checked the house next. The kitchen was empty, and so was every other room on the first floor. His stomach began to form a knot, but he refused to let his brain even give words to the thoughts that were trying to get through, trying to make him crazy with fear.

But *dammit*. Where *was* she?

Finally he noticed that the door to the basement was just barely ajar. The light down there was on, too, though nothing but a hollow silence wafted up from the depths.

A many-legged prickling sensation crawled down his spine.

When he stood at the door and looked down, he saw the broken stair rail first. It waved loose at the top end of the staircase, useless. Treacherous, even, if you had been leaning against it when it gave way.

And then, his heart taking huge, cold beats somewhere up around his throat, he saw Natalie.

She sat on the concrete floor, her legs in front of her awkwardly, as though she'd suddenly decided to plop down and take a rest. Her back was to him, so he couldn't be sure what she was doing, or if she was all right. Her beautiful topaz-and-gold party dress flickered in the overhead light as if she were gently on fire.

Beside her on the floor was a broken bottle of brandy, the kind of brandy he remembered once telling her he used to buy. Slivers of thick brown glass stuck up like jagged islands in the pooling sea of amber liquid. And next to that, just beyond her fingertips, was a large diamond bracelet.

"Natalie?" He took all those details in as he moved, without bothering to process implications. He descended the stairs two at a time, ignoring the swaying railing. He was at her side in less than a heartbeat.

She turned and gave him a wry smile. "Brilliant, huh?"

Though she looked a little disheveled and slightly irritated, there was no blood, no bruising, no tears or confusion or fear.

She was fine. Thank goodness, she was fine.

"I came down to get some of that brandy you like," she said, as if resuming a conversation they'd been having only moments ago. "And then I found Bart's diamond bracelet, which I guess I left down here the last time I was getting a bottle of wine. So

I dashed upstairs and called him to let him know I'd found it, and then I realized that I'd forgotten to bring up the brandy, so I came back down. That's when the darn rail fell apart on me.''

"The important thing is you're okay," he said, not really interested in the saga of the bracelet, but glad, so glad, that she seemed coherent enough to tell it. She mustn't have been standing very far up on the stairs. If she'd been near the top... But he put that thought away. It was, quite literally, unthinkable.

"I'm fine. My ankle is a little sore, that's all." She looked at him sadly. "But, as you can see, the brandy is a goner."

He reached out and touched her gingerly. He pulled her soft hair back from her face, ran his hands down along her arms, scanning, looking for things that might be torn or bruised or bleeding. She wasn't wincing, didn't seem to be in pain. But you never knew...

"This must get pretty monotonous for you. I'm always tumbling off something." Smiling, she reached out and touched a finger to the pool of golden liquid. "But this time I wasn't drunk, I promise. I hadn't had a drop. And now I guess I never will. This was our last bottle of the special kind, the kind you like."

"Don't worry about that now," he said. Relief was coursing through him, a far more effective high than the most expensive bottle of brandy in the world. "It doesn't matter."

"It does to me," she said.

With a heavy sigh, she stood, putting most of her weight on her left foot while she fluffed her wrinkled skirt out around her legs. "I'll have you know I had extremely important plans for that bottle of brandy."

"Oh, really?" He smiled. "And what were they?"

She looked at the mess of liquor and broken glass, and she sighed again.

"I was going to get you drunk."

CHAPTER FOURTEEN

NATALIE SAT on the edge of the pool house bed, still unable to believe Matthew had actually said yes.

He hadn't even put up a fuss. She'd been ticking through her long, logical list of arguments why she should sleep in the pool house, why she didn't want to be alone in the huge, empty bedrooms of Summer House tonight, but he had raised his hand, palm out, and smiled.

"You can stop firing your cannons, captain," he'd said, half-laughing. "The fort has already surrendered. I wanted to keep an eye on you anyhow, just in case you have any complications from the fall."

She wouldn't have complications, of course. The fall had been minor. She was far more upset about the loss of the brandy than anything else. Matthew had insisted on taking her to the Glen hospital, where they'd spent an hour waiting for someone to wake up a doctor to x-ray her ankle and peer into her pupils, though she had assured them she hadn't hit her head at all, and her ankle wasn't broken, it was just a little twisted.

Still, it was lovely to be babied, just for this one night. And it was cozy to be here, in the comfortable, human dimensions of the pool house. Though she didn't really know why, she had dreaded the thought of sleeping in that echoing house alone.

Matthew was up there now, getting something for her to sleep in. And she was here, sitting on this wonderful bed, waiting for him. She ran her hand across the smooth, carved wing of a bird, then down the long, twisting body of a snake. The king of Tahiti had been a fool to let it go.

Matthew returned in a very few minutes. He had a long blue flannel nightgown in one hand and the matching robe in the other. "I didn't bother bringing slippers," he said wryly. "I know how you—"

"Hate shoes," she finished for him with a smile. "Good decision."

The nightgown was a modest choice, but not a very practical one, not on a mild summer night like this. She'd be smothered, much too hot and clammy to sleep.

But with any kind of luck, she wouldn't be wearing it for long.

She had no intention of rushing, though. Right now it was enough to have the old Matthew back, instead of the blank-eyed stranger she'd seen at the party. It was enough to have his companionship. She didn't like to think of herself as weak, but tonight, for some reason, she felt the need of his strength.

So she just took the gown and robe and thanked him. "Okay if I use the bathroom to change?"

He nodded. As she moved across the room, careful

to minimize her limp, she noticed all the little fixes he'd accomplished. The light fixture wasn't hanging at that odd angle anymore, and the kitchenette had new stove top burners. And the sink was definitely not leaking.

He must have done all this on his own time, she realized. During the workdays, he'd been constantly absorbed in Summer House repairs.

Once in the ridiculously sumptuous Roman bath—a room that was almost as big as the rest of the pool house put together—she changed clothes as quickly as possible. She splashed her stale makeup from her face, and then ran her fingers through her hair, smoothing it as best she could.

Darn. No perfume, no silk, no music.

Even worse, in this high-necked, long-sleeved, shapeless gown her body wasn't visible at all. Still, she had faith. If Matthew hadn't already been worried about the state of his willpower, he wouldn't have needed to choose this ridiculous gown. It looked like something worn by an eleventh-century cloistered Alpine nun who had no central heating and a raging case of consumption.

When she came out, she saw that he remained fully dressed in his jeans and T-shirt. Apparently he didn't intend to change. He probably intended to sleep standing up. Or not even sleep at all.

"You know, I feel kind of selfish taking over your comfy bed," she said politely.

"No problem," he said. "The armchair is so comfortable I often fall asleep there when I'm reading at night anyhow.''

"Tell you what.'' She patted the downy quilt and arched her brows. "I'll arm-wrestle you for it, mister.''

He shook his head, but his eyes smiled just a little. "Isn't that what the king of Tahiti said, right before he lost it?''

"Yeah, but he was only twelve. He didn't have very good judgment.''

Matthew shook his head. "You're welcome to take the bed tonight, Natalie. No arm-wrestling required.''

"Well, heck. That takes all the fun out of it.'' She lay stomach-down across the quilt and propped her right elbow on the nightstand. "Admit it. You're just afraid I'll beat you.''

He looked at her, obviously trying not to smile. He had to tuck the corners of his mouth in tightly to prevent the smile from showing, and that created a pair of dimples so sexy she was glad she was already lying down.

For a minute she thought he might say no. But then, with that tucked-away smile still peeking through, he cleared the paperback mystery and tumbler of water from the nightstand. He knelt down and put his elbow next to hers.

"Okay, you're on.''

His hand was twice the size of hers, and bronze from hours working in the sun. She clamped her fingers down quickly and pushed with all her might, hoping she would have the element of surprise.

No such luck. He held her in place so easily she might have been a butterfly. For many long, serious seconds she pressed, leaning her whole body over, harder and harder, until she was breathing heavily.

Through it all, the muscles in his forearm didn't even twitch, and his arm didn't move a millimeter. And that sexy, dimpled smile never went away.

She wriggled up to her knees and inched closer to the nightstand, trying to get more leverage. It didn't help.

"Darn," she said between breaths. "Where's a big old chunk of kryptonite when you need one?"

"Give up?" He sounded bored, as if he could do this and paint the room at the same time.

"Never," she said. She wriggled even closer, struggling to get her whole body behind the effort. Soon their faces were only inches apart, with nothing but their entwined hands between them.

Which, of course, was what she'd had in mind all along. Ever since the fiasco at the party, they had been a little stiff with each other. To break the ice, they needed some foolish laughter, a little nonthreatening physical contact, a touch of comfortable intimacy.

And then maybe, if the ice broke apart, the flood would follow.

She had promised herself she wouldn't rush things. But when she got this close to him, she almost couldn't help it. Touching him always made her sizzle inside.

"Matthew." She stared at his strong arm, his tanned, elegant fingers, trying to fight off the wave of desire. It was too soon to get serious. She'd scare him back into his walled fortress.

But she could feel his breath on her fingers. She could smell his freshly laundered T-shirt, which she had washed herself. She could see the cotton resting across the tight muscles of his chest, outlining them subtly.

"Matthew," she said. Without meaning to, she began to slide her thumb slowly along the edge of his hand.

And then she looked into his eyes, which weren't smiling anymore.

"You know," she said softly, "maybe we should just declare a tie. It's a big bed. We could share."

He shut his eyes hard for one second, and she had the strange sense that he was trying to reject the vision her words had summoned up.

When he opened his eyes again, they were dark and deep and strangely unhappy. He stared at their hands, and then very slowly, very deliberately, he let his arm drop toward the table.

She ceased applying any pressure. But still his arm drifted down. And eventually it touched the tabletop with a slow, silent finality.

He looked up at her. "I'll be fine in the chair," he said. "It's better that way, Natalie. Really, it is."

She took a deep breath. She truly hadn't meant to force this issue right now, but here it was. She'd have to meet it head-on, or she would have no hope.

"I know you sincerely believe that, Matthew. What I don't understand is *why*. Why have you erected this wall between us?"

He let go of her hand and stood. "I told you why. I'm trying to start over. I can't begin by exploiting someone I care for. I can't begin by hurting you."

She knelt on the bed, her hands making frustrated fists in her lap. "But that's what I don't understand. Why are you so sure making love to me would hurt me? I'm not made of glass, you know, physically or emotionally."

He hesitated a moment, as if debating something. Then, with firm, determined gestures, he moved to the other side of the bed and picked up his black duffel bag.

He tossed it onto the bed, and it landed with a soft leather sigh at her knees.

"That's why I'm sure, Natalie. When I left the party tonight, I came here and did some serious thinking. I should never have put you in that position, and I'm not going to let it happen again. I can't stay at Summer House anymore. I'm leaving in the morning."

She looked at the duffel. Its black bulk stained the pure white quilt. "Is this because of Jocelyn?"

"Not totally." He went to the open window and stared out at the dark mountains, as if he couldn't look at her. "It's also because of me. And us. You know things are getting out of hand. And considering there's absolutely no future possible between people like us—"

She tried not to panic. "Matthew, I—"

He interrupted her immediately, as if he feared what she might say.

"Please don't ask me to stay, Natalie. I *need* to go. I have things to sort out about myself. About my life. In a way, I've been hiding out here, avoiding making those decisions. I can't avoid them forever, and the longer I stay, the harder it will be to go."

She wanted to go up to him, to put her arms around him and take away the pain. But she couldn't. Not unless he wanted her to.

"All right," she said, trying hard to sound rational and completely under control. "I accept that. You told me from the beginning that you were only passing through. I won't deny that I hate it, or that I'll miss you terribly. But I would never ask you to make a decision that was wrong for your life just because it might be right for mine."

"It wouldn't be right for yours, either." He spoke tightly, as if his jaw was clenched. "You can take my word for that."

She started to cry out a protest. What did he know about it? Obviously he didn't understand what he h come to mean to her.

She could hardly bring herself to think ab it would be like without him. When she self to contemplate it, even for a split second, it nearly took her breath away. No wise partner in the struggle, no laughing friend to share the jokes, no comforting light in the pool house, shining like a beacon she could watch from her lonely window.

But she couldn't think about that now. If he meant this, if he really intended to leave in the morning, she refused to waste their last few hours staging a melodramatic scene.

She walked over to the window, limping just a little. She touched his upper arm.

"Matthew," she asked with all the simple honesty she could muster, "why won't you make love to me? If this is our last night together, why don't we spend it in each other's arms? Don't you want me?"

"Dammit, Natalie," he said tightly. "You know I want you. I want you like a hungry man wants to eat. But I can't do that to you."

She laughed softly and ran her hand lightly down to his elbow. "I'm *asking* you to do it," she said. "I'm practically begging you to."

He shook his head, still not turning to look at her. "You're the most generous and loving and innocent woman I've ever known. Too generous. Too loving." He closed his eyes. "Too innocent."

She hesitated a moment, wondering what she could possibly say to break through to him. He obviously had repeated these same things to himself a million times, until they had become a holy mantra of resistance.

"Matthew," she said. "Please look at me. I want to tell you something complicated. Something very important."

Slowly, as if it might be dangerous even to set eyes on her, he turned his head.

"I know I seem small and fragile and wide-eyed, like a child," she said simply. "But I'm not a child. I'm not even as naive as you might think. There are a few sweet old men in this town who like to fuss over me, and I'm sure they told you I'm too naive to cross the street by myself, but they are quite wrong."

He tilted his head sadly. "Are they? I'm not sure. Think of the way you took me in, Natalie. If that wasn't naive—"

"It *wasn't*. Acting on instincts isn't always foolish, Matthew. Not if your instincts are good. And I have excellent instincts about people. You do, too, I think."

His gaze remained dark and without hope. So she tried again. This part was more complex. She prayed she could say it right.

"You know, I think the problem is that you misunderstand the Granville personality." She smiled. "Yes, it's in our nature to be irrationally optimistic, and it's in our blood to be unconventional. We don't particularly like to march in lockstep with everyone else. We build our houses on mountainsides so that we can breathe a little freer. We build planetariums on the roof so we can be one with the stars."

She let her hand fall to his. His fingers remained

still, but she held on to them, hoping sooner or later he would respond.

"But we don't do those things because we're too naive to know any better. We *choose* that kind of life, Matthew. We choose to live impulsively, to laugh often, to dream wildly and to love fiercely."

Love. Oh, dear. She had promised herself she wouldn't say "love" in any way that could become a trap. He had come to Firefly Glen crippled, but if he was healed, if he was ready to move on, she had to let him go.

She wouldn't speak of love. She had no interest in catching him, in caging him here at Summer House like a bird with a forever-broken wing. No Granville could live that way, and no Granville would ever ask anyone else to, either.

So no...no talk of love. She refused to force his surrender at emotional gunpoint. She wanted him to come to her freely, because he wanted it, because he needed it, because he believed it could be right and beautiful.

She forced herself to go on logically. "Granvilles have always known that living this way comes at a rather high price. It's just that, unlike other people, we are perfectly willing to pay it."

"No." His hand caught hers suddenly, wrapping tightly around her fingers. "That's just it. I don't want you to pay any price at all. But if we make love tonight—"

"What?" She squeezed his hand, wishing she

could make him see reason. "If we make love, then what? Will I be 'ruined'? That's a little archaic, don't you think? Will I have an emotional breakdown, mourning the loss of my virginity? I'm sorry, but Donny Fragonard took care of that one afternoon about eight years ago, when we should have been in college algebra class. Will I end up pregnant? I doubt it. I put some condoms in your first-aid kit in the bathroom, one of which is in my pocket now."

He frowned.

"And that's because," she finished, smiling, "as I pointed out, Granvilles are not really so terribly naive after all."

"You joke," he said roughly, "but—"

"All right, then, I'll be serious." She took a deep breath. "I know what you really think. You think it will grieve me even more when you leave tomorrow if we make love tonight."

He didn't even blink. "Yes," he said. "I do think that."

"Well, you're wrong," she said, a touch of anger surging to the fore. This was so blind, so willfully, infuriatingly blind. And they were wasting precious minutes.

"It's exactly the opposite. I care about you, Matthew. When you leave tomorrow, I will suffer greatly. But if you leave tomorrow, and I have never touched your body in the darkness…if I've never known how it feels to have you moving deep inside me, if I've never heard you call my name—"

She swallowed, hoping her voice would not betray how desperately she needed those things.

"If you leave without all that, then I will suffer twice. Once for what I'm losing, and once for what I never had."

CHAPTER FIFTEEN

FOR A MINUTE, she was afraid he would turn away from her, not caring that she was desperate, hungry, helpless.

But he was hungry, too. Watching her with dark eyes, he put his hands softly on her face.

"Is that true, Natalie?"

She nodded slowly. She could hardly think, or even breathe, now that he was touching her. But she knew it was true. If he left without making love to her, she would have a hole inside forever.

"Then come to me, sweetheart." He eased her body toward him. "Love me. And we will make it a night we will never forget."

He reached down, then, and with a tormentingly slow pace, he pulled the heavy gown up over her head. As it slid across her skin, exposing her, she felt her breath catch, as if on some gossamer strand of need.

For a long minute he looked at her without speaking, and somehow she found the courage to let him. She stood before him, spotlighted by a shaft of moonlight, her curls touching the swollen tips of her breasts.

"You are very beautiful," he said, and the reverent timbre of his voice made the words sound brand-new. It made them sound true.

"Oh, Matthew. Please hurry," she said, choking on the tightness that was spiraling up through her body, as if it came up through the earth and wrapped her in golden threads of desire, all the way to her aching throat.

He shed his own clothes, then, and the naked hunger she saw took her breath away. She couldn't say anything, couldn't offer him even one reverent line of simple praise. He was so much more than beautiful. He was all beauty, all power, all love, in one magnificent body.

Her heart began to beat quickly. She had talked so brashly. She had spoken of all this as if she were the kind of practiced, well-trained partner he would be used to.

But suddenly, before the incredible, self-confident power of that body, rippling with muscles and potent desire, perfect and unashamed, she felt like a fraud. In the end, she knew nothing, nothing of the intensity, the pure sensual sophistication she saw now in his eyes.

She had promised she was not naive, not easily hurt, and remembering that, she suddenly felt frightened. What if he found her inadequate? What if all her foolish, lightweight charms were not enough at a time like this?

For the first time in her life, she wished she were

not a silly, cheerful Granville. She would far rather, at such a moment, be dark and devastating...a Cleopatra, or Helen of Troy.

He picked her up, his hands warm against her skin, and carried her to the bed. He placed her there gently, then lay beside her, cradling her head in his arm.

She looked over at him, not knowing what to do, or even what to say. He hadn't touched her yet, not in the golden places that were so warm and ready.

"Are you absolutely sure, Natalie?" His head was bent over her, and she could just barely see the hungry gleam of his eyes in the moonlight. "It isn't too late, even now."

"Yes, it is," she said breathlessly. "It is for me."

He kissed her then, his mouth exploring softly. He put his hands behind the small of her back and arched her just a little, just enough to let her sense the waiting power of his body.

She moaned and, taking the moment, he deepened his kiss, so that he claimed the small noise as his own.

She shifted, her body filled with strange, twisting pains. He obviously knew the signs, because in answer his hands began to move over her, touching each aching place, not seeking to soothe, but to intensify the mysterious, beautiful agony.

She cried his name out softly, moving restlessly against the shining white quilt. She wanted more. She wanted it now.

But he knew so much more than she did. He knew that stretching out the torment would take her higher, would help her find the special place he already knew so well.

A place where experience was an irrelevant concept.

A place made entirely of instinct and raw sensation.

He stroked her, kissed her, loved her toward that place. And finally she found it. She reached out and, with hungry, questing hands, she claimed his body, too. She began to love it without thoughts, without words, with only lips and skin, with only sweat and silence and sheer pounding need.

She was unable to go slowly, to wait or ask or wonder. Perhaps later, she thought helplessly. Sometime in this long, wonderful night, there would be time for exploring, for teasing, for taking turns and taking their time. Time for laughter and maybe even for tears.

But right now there was only the desperate need to break the barriers between them. To own and be owned. To plunge together into that place where loneliness, too, would finally cease to exist.

He was the kind of lover she'd never dreamed existed. He knew every color, every shape, every sound of her thoughts. When her thoughts said *more,* his fingers probed hard, and his mouth closed over her breast, shooting a white light between the two places that nearly left her blind.

And the minute her mind said *hurry,* he rose above her. Then, when without words she began to toss her head and beg *now, please now,* he heard that, too.

He opened her and thrust deep, a claiming driven by tenderness and fire.

She cried out, then, but it wasn't really a word. It was a sweet, answering syllable of flame.

As if he had touched match to tinder, the fire licked, sparked and instantly began to blaze. And in the wild, consuming inferno of it, everything changed. Walls fell, towers tumbled, fear vanished.

And finally, with a cry that might have belonged to him, or maybe to her, two aching, lonely bodies finally melted into one.

SHE LET HIM SLEEP, though she'd been awake for hours, and the clock on the sun-washed wall said noon.

He needed to rest. They had been up until dawn, touching and talking, laughing and drinking Scotch, then eating peanut butter from each other's fingers, and then, drawn over and over again by a hunger as great as when they had first begun, they had melted back into each other's arms.

She'd lost count of the times—and the ways—he had set her body on fire. She had never in her life known the shocking pleasure he brought her. He did whatever she wanted, and when she ran out of ideas he started on his own.

She felt a dull ache of excitement, remembering how wild she had been. Maybe she had been more naive than she realized. Compared to this, her silly motorcycle fantasy seemed ridiculously tame.

Certainly nothing in her life had prepared her for such a night. Matthew was creative and masterful and completely uninhibited, and he demanded no less of her. It was as if he had wanted to give her a lifetime of sensual experience in one night.

Eventually, though, their bodies were spent. Twisted together in a damp, naked exhaustion, they slept.

He was sleeping still.

She gazed at him, her heart aching as much as the tender, overused places of her body. It didn't seem possible that he would leave her today. And yet, never once during the long, sensual odyssey of the night had he ever said he'd stay.

She forced herself to leave the pool house. She showered and dressed and began, as always, to make him breakfast.

When the kitchen door opened, she flushed automatically. It was one thing to be wild in the strange, dim unreality of night. It was another to face him in the morning sun, realizing how many secrets he had learned that no one else would ever, ever know.

But it wasn't Matthew. It was Bart. Thank goodness she had put his bracelet somewhere safe.

"Hi," she said, hoping her flush would look like sunburn. "It's right over there, on top of the refrigerator. Sorry it took so long to unearth it. Want some breakfast?"

"Breakfast? At this hour?" Then he caught himself, obviously remembering that it was none of his business.

"A cup of coffee would be nice, thanks." He got one for himself, then sat on one of the bar stools at the central island. "I wanted to talk to you anyhow. Where's Matthew?"

"I'm not sure," she said, working hard at controlling her color. "I guess he's repairing something somewhere."

"Well, good," Bart said. "Because I really wanted to talk to you alone. It's about the bracelet."

She turned. "What? Is anything wrong with it? Did one of the diamonds fall out? Don't worry. I'll find a way to replace it."

"No, nothing like that," he said. "It's just that I wanted to say I'm sorry I made such a fuss over it. You didn't keep a single one of the presents I gave you. I want you to keep this one."

She laughed. "Don't be silly."

"It's not silly. It's sensible. You need it, Natalie, if only so that you can sell it someday when the roof caves in. I want you to have it."

She smiled. "That's very sweet, Bart, but you know I'm not going to accept it. And I would never sell it, anyhow. It was your mother's. It should belong someday to the woman you marry."

"Yeah, well, I don't think that's going to be a problem." He shook his head with a small laugh. "If all my money can't even buy a lady as desperate for cash as you are, what are the odds I'll get anyone else?''

Poor Bart. She put down the spoon she'd been using to mix the pancake batter and went over to him.

If only he knew how wrong it would have been for them to marry. She could never, never have done with Bart those amazing, terrifying things she had just done with Matthew.

And what a loss that would have been for both of them! He deserved a woman who went wild just because he touched her, whose blood sped in her veins whenever she looked at his mouth and remembered.

She put her hand on his shoulder. ''You'll find someone,'' she said. ''It just has to be the right someone.''

He nodded without much conviction. ''Speaking of the right someone—or at least the woman I used to think of that way—guess who called me?''

She looked down at him hopefully. ''Was it Terri?''

Bart had come to Natalie on the rebound from the real love of his life, an elementary schoolteacher named Terri, who had decided at the last minute she didn't love Firefly Glen, or Bart, quite enough to stay with them forever.

He'd been delighted to offer Natalie buckets of money in return for repairing his ego, showing the other woman that her rejection hadn't completely broken his heart.

''Yeah. Terri.'' Bart sipped his coffee, then sighed.

"Get this. She said she'd been thinking a lot about me lately."

Natalie grinned. "Well. That's *good* news, sad sack. It means she never really got over you, either. Why do you look so glum?"

"I don't know. Maybe I just don't want to go through it all again. I'm a little sick of being dumped at the altar, if you must know."

"Nonsense." Natalie ruffled his hair playfully, though she knew it would drive him nuts. "Take a chance, Bart! Live dangerously. That's what life is all about, you know."

He scowled and started smoothing his hair irritably. "That's what it's all about on the Planet Granville, maybe. But here on earth—"

"Am I interrupting?"

Bart looked over to the doorway, where Matthew stood, fully dressed and looking very handsome. Very somber. She looked at his firm, sad mouth, and her heart began to race all over again.

"Heck, no," Bart said. "Natalie's just trying to talk me into plopping my heart down on the floor so someone can do the Mexican hat dance on it. Interrupt away."

Natalie smiled at Matthew. "I was just telling Bart that sometimes you have to take a chance. Isn't that right?"

She begged him with her eyes to say yes. To say, if only in code, that he didn't regret what had happened last night. "If you don't take some risks, just think what you might miss."

He looked at her steadily. "I think," he said, "that it's probably a question every man has to decide for himself."

"Ha! Thank you, sir!" Bart looked smug. "I raise my coffee cup to your common sense."

Feeling slightly slapped, Natalie took a deep breath and turned back to the pancake batter. This was so much harder than she had imagined it would be. But then apparently her imagination wasn't as great as she used to think. She could never have imagined, for instance, the fun and fire and freedom of last night.

And she could never have imagined that she could love a man as much as she loved Matthew Quinn.

She knew he was leaving. It was like watching something precious fall from the table in slow motion. You knew you were about to lose it forever, and yet you could do nothing to stop it. You could only stand there, frozen with the pain of it, and watch.

She tried to make her voice normal. "Are you hungry, Matthew? I've got some eggs and muffins and—"

"No, thanks," he said flatly. "I really should be leaving."

She turned then and saw that his duffel was in his hand. She made a small sound, in spite of her resolve not to make a scene.

"Now?" She shook her head slowly. "Surely you don't have to go right now?"

He nodded. "I think I should."

Bart looked confused. "You don't mean you're leaving for good?"

Matthew looked at him politely. "Yes, I am."

"Well, God...did you know this, Natalie?"

She couldn't find her voice, so Matthew answered for her. "Natalie and I came to an agreement about it last night. We both decided it was time."

Bart cleared his throat nervously. "Look, Matthew—"

He seemed not to know where to go from there. He slicked his hair down one more time and began again. "I didn't go to Natalie's party last night, so I don't really know exactly what happened. But I've heard stories. And if you're leaving because of Jocelyn Waitely, I think you should know she represents the minority in this town. I'm not saying Firefly Glen doesn't have our share of nasty old bats, but most of us don't listen to a word they say. I hope you wouldn't let it bother you, either."

Matthew smiled. "That's generous of you," he said with deliberate warmth, as if he appreciated the effort Bart was making. "But actually my leaving has very little to do with Jocelyn Waitely. It's really more a personal decision."

He looked over at Natalie with dark, shadowed eyes. His sleep obviously hadn't restored him much.

"Anyhow," he said. "I just came up to say good-bye. And to thank you. For the job. And for keeping all your promises. And, of course, for—'' He paused. ''For everything.''

Keeping her promises. She remembered that she had, indeed, quite foolishly promised not to try to make him stay.

She smiled at him, a forced thing. She couldn't see him clearly anymore, because her eyes were rapidly filling with tears.

''Goodbye, Matthew,'' she echoed hollowly. Is this how normal people sounded? People whose hearts were not breaking? ''I hope you find what you're looking for. But there's no need to thank me for anything. As you well know, and I hope you never forget, the pleasure was all mine.''

For a split second, she thought she saw the fire behind his eyes. But before she could be sure, he doused it. He didn't say a word to show that he'd understood what she was trying to tell him. He just smiled politely, shifted his duffel to the other hand and nodded once to Bart.

And then he was gone.

IT WAS LATE AFTERNOON. The sun was bronzing the treetops of Firefly Glen, and the roses in the Strickland's front yard had overbloomed, filling the air with so much perfume it was almost something you tasted.

Suzie was standing out in front of her house, saying a slow, chatty goodbye to a couple of her friends, when Mike Frome's shiny red Jeep drove past.

He didn't stop. He didn't even look at them. Cassie

and Louisa made a rude face at the retreating car, then grinned over at her.

"Look, Suzie, it's your boyfriend," they said, giggling sophomorically. Honestly, sometimes her supposedly intellectual crowd acted every bit as asinine as the jocks-and-rocks crowd, as they liked to call the athletes and their girlfriends, who always wore diamond studs in their ears, just like their moms.

Cassie and Louisa, who had not been at Natalie's party last night, already knew that Suzie had left briefly, going outside alone with Mike Frome. They had come over here this afternoon purely to pump her for details, which she had refused to give.

Add that to the list of seven thousand million things Suzie hated about small towns. There was no such thing as a secret.

"He's not my boyfriend," she insisted heatedly, though she knew it was the kind of thing people always said when they were lying.

"Oh, yeah?" Louisa, who was about six feet tall and a genius on the saxophone, looked down the street with wide eyes. "Well, then how come he's coming back again?"

Suzie scoffed, certain that Louisa was just trying to get a rise out of her. Boys like Mike Frome hardly ever came over here, to the middle-class side of town.

Why would they? Everything they cared about, the expensive shops and the expensive restaurants and the expensive girls, were all back in the downtown strip and its nearby neighborhoods of elite historic mansions. The area Suzie and her friends called La-La Land.

It suddenly crossed her mind that they spent a lot of time thinking of snarky put-downs about the rich kids. Once it had seemed like an important element of self-defense. Now, strangely, it just seemed like a waste of time.

To be honest, she couldn't even remember for sure which had come first, the rich kids making fun of them, or the other way around.

But when she looked down the street, she saw that Louisa wasn't kidding. Mike Frome really had circled around the block and cruised right back to her house. This time he stopped. He pulled his car several feet in front of Louisa's mom's station wagon and cut the engine.

"Ooh, Suzie, look," Louisa whispered. "Mikey is coming back for another helping."

Cassie grinned, too. "I guess he liked it enough to ask for seconds." Cassie was a math whiz, and not terribly creative. So she was usually reduced to repeating whatever Louisa said.

"God," Suzie said disgustedly, "you two are such losers."

But out of the corner of her eye, she watched the Jeep. Why was he here? What exactly did he want?

He sat in the car a couple of minutes, as if he needed to psyche himself into getting out. But finally, with an abrupt jerk of one arm, he shoved open the door.

He locked the car with a *chirp* and began walking back toward the three of them. He was dressed in his typical preppy outfit, right down to the little polo-player guy. They had no imagination at all, did they?

But he had an expression on his face that looked a lot like a gladiator marching to certain death in the Coliseum.

When he got close enough, he smiled. It was the lamest smile Suzie had ever seen, but at least he tried.

"Hi," he said to her. Then, with a clear effort, he turned to Cassie and Louisa. "Hey."

"Hi," Suzie answered coolly. She was still furious about last night. And he was on her territory now. She was the one who got to cop an attitude. "What's up? You lost? Did you make a wrong turn at the Gucci store?"

Louisa and Cassie snickered softly. Mike didn't even look at them. He kept his eyes on Suzie, though she noticed he wasn't quite one-hundred-percent cocky confidence. He toed the ground with his two-hundred-dollar sneakers.

"No," he said calmly. "I don't get lost."

Okay, so he was ninety-nine percent cocky. He had more than his share of guts, she had to give him that.

He gave her a weird look. "Any chance I can see you for a minute?"

Louisa laughed out loud. "Unless you're blind, Mike, you ought to be able to see her right now. She's not invisible or anything."

He flicked Louisa a glance that could have peeled

paint. Then he looked back at Suzie. "Alone, I mean."

Louisa and Cassie exchanged knowing grins, which irritated the hell out of Suzie. Because, when you got right down to it, they didn't know much of anything.

"I guess so," she said to Mike casually. She looked at the other girls. "You guys were leaving anyhow, right?"

"Sure," they said. They didn't like it. They got all huffy and icy eyed, but they piled into the station wagon and left, which was all that really mattered.

Suzie turned to Mike, fairly icy eyed herself. "Just for the record, we're not completely alone. My mom's inside."

And Suzie hoped to God she'd stay there. If her mother knew Mike Frome was here, she'd go into a mortifying transport of joy and come flying out to shower him in welcomes.

This had for years been her mother's fondest dream, that someday a rich young social lion would discover how *special* poor Suzie Strickland was underneath the purple hair and the black eye shadow and the grungy clothes. That he'd marry her, buy her designer clothes, and open to the whole Strickland family the doors of paradise, which to Mrs. Strickland was synonymous with the Firefly Glen Yacht Club.

Oh, God, Suzie thought fervently. *Whatever bad I've done in my life, don't punish me by letting my mother look out that window right now.*

"That's okay," Mike said. "I just came over because I wanted to tell you I'm sorry about last night. I was a jerk.''

She eyed him coldly. ''I hope you're not expecting me to disagree.''

He flushed. ''No, I'm not. I just wanted to tell you that I didn't mean what I said. I—'' He took a deep breath. ''I didn't mean to hurt your feelings.''

''Don't flatter yourself,'' she said acidly. ''You didn't.''

''Good.'' He looked miserable, as if this kind of thing didn't come naturally to him. But he also looked kind of human. Kind of nice. And of course he was just as sexy as ever.

She found herself forgiving him a little.

''So. You apologized, and I accept. Was that all you wanted?''

''No.'' He looked at her. ''No, it isn't. I also thought maybe we could go for a ride in my car and—'' He exhaled hard. ''Talk.''

Was he making fun of her? She scowled at him, trying to figure him out.

''What do you mean, talk? Like you meant last night? Like you *call* it talk, but actually your tongue's in my throat and you're tearing off my clothes?''

''No, dammit.'' He was mad now. Being humble obviously disagreed with him. ''That's *not* what I mean. I mean just talk. You know, tell each other things. Get to know each other. *Talk.*''

She still felt skeptical. However she might try to spin it to her friends, or to him, last night had been embarrassing and painful. It had hurt a lot, and she had no interest in letting him humiliate her like that again.

"Really." She glared at him. "Talk about *what?*"

"Hell, Suzie, I don't know." His eyebrows went up. "No, wait. How about your painting? Yeah, you can tell me about your painting. And I can tell you about—"

He shoved one fist into the other and shifted his weight on his feet uncomfortably. He narrowed his eyes.

"Dammit, I don't know! You can't plan out a conversation like this, deciding ahead of time how it's going to go. It just has to flow, you know? Don't you know how talking works?"

"Yeah, Frome, I know," she said, smiling at his frustration. She walked to his car and put her fingers on the handle, waiting for him to *chirp* open the locks. "I just wanted to see if you did."

CHAPTER SIXTEEN

SOMEHOW, IN SPITE of the way her thoughts kept trying to turn back to Matthew—to last night, to the look on his face as he stood in the doorway this morning—Natalie managed to have a fairly productive day.

As soon as Bart went back to work, leaving her alone in the kitchen, feeling a bit numb and stunned, she forced herself to face her dilemma.

As she saw it, she had two choices. She could either get busy right now, do something productive and distracting, or she could slump to the kitchen floor, put her aching head in her hands and cry for a week.

But what good would crying do? She couldn't cry hard enough to bring Matthew back. She'd just end up soggy and exhausted, and she would have wasted a week.

So she decided on action.

She whisked the uneaten breakfast into the trash, jumped in the car and drove to the library, where she pored over historical documents, gathering a couple of excellent new details about the history of Summer House. She scribbled copious notes, adding them to the many notebooks she'd already filled with similar information.

Then, when she got home, she put in a dozen calls to various antique dealers, setting up appointments to show them the vintage dresses, and the 1920s-era glassware, and the one-of-a-kind decks of playing cards.

All in all, she thought she might be able to raise a tidy little sum. Enough to take care of the wiring in the bedrooms, probably. The roof might have to wait until she discovered another hidden room.

By sunset, she realized that throwing herself into work—particularly into work that would benefit Summer House—had made her feel a little better. If nothing else, it had kept her from sitting around thinking about Matthew.

She wasn't going to fall apart. She wasn't some impotent teenager who had no idea how to put her life back together after being dumped by her boyfriend. She was a grown woman with obligations, friends, courage, resources.

And she had Summer House to consider. Saving this place was the most important thing right now, and she was by God going to find a way, even if she did shed a few foolish tears while she was at it.

She wasn't a quitter, darn it. She was a Granville.

However, when the lovely bronze and copper sunset faded away, the house took on deep shadows and a cold, cryptlike silence. And she realized that even her tough Granville genes might not be enough.

She thought about grabbing a frozen dinner and a paperback novel and spending the night out in the much cozier pool house, but that seemed a little too passive. Too pathetic.

What was she going to do? Moon around, kissing the pillow where Matthew had laid his head? Sniffing the T-shirt he'd left behind? Reliving last night in her mind, detail by erotic detail, until she went mad with wanting him, missing him, needing him?

No.

She picked up the kitchen phone and called Stuart, who sounded surprised to hear from her so soon. He accepted her dinner invitation happily, though, and she went upstairs to get dressed, her spirits much improved.

It would be fun. He wasn't Matthew, but he was good company.

And besides, he was a very important part of her multidimensional recovery plan, which she didn't intend to waste a single moment implementing.

Action. That was the Granville way.

THE NEXT MORNING, Matthew sat in Theo's café, having breakfast across the table from a scowling Granville Frome.

"I don't like it," Granville was saying grumpily. "I'm not sure what's going on here, but I'm pretty damn sure I don't like it. I told you not to hurt that girl. I like you, Quinn, but I hope I'm not going to have to kick your ass."

Matthew smiled a little over the rim of his coffee cup.

"I think you should trust that Natalie and I are making the right decision," he said. "After what happened at the party—"

"You mean after Nattie kicked Jocelyn Waitley's ass?" Granville slapped the tabletop, which set the flower vase jumping and drew a glower from Theo.

"Damn, I knew the girl was good, but that was pure Granville. For a minute there, I thought I saw her granddaddy in those fiery brown eyes."

"She was something, wasn't she?"

"You bet she was. Granvilles are fighters. That old biddy Jocelyn Waitely never had a chance."

He gave Matthew a narrow look. "Is that why you're leaving town? Because you think Jocelyn upsets Natalie? Give the girl some credit, son. She's a Granville. She knows garbage when she sees it, and she knows where to toss it."

"I told you. Jocelyn isn't the only reason."

"Well, what are the other ones?"

"They're private." Matthew didn't want to be rude, but he didn't want to get into this with Granville, either. "They're between Natalie and me, and I don't plan to discuss them with anyone else."

He stared at the irritable old man squarely. "So if you need to kick my ass before we can settle down and talk business, let's get started."

Granville chuckled under his breath, and the angry look faded out of his eyes.

"I like you, Quinn," he said again, appreciatively. "Damn if I don't."

He forked a heaping mound of pancakes into his mouth. "So why did you call me here? What is this business you want to talk about?"

Matthew put his coffee cup down. "I wanted to tell you that Natalie needs some help. That place is falling apart around her ears."

He knew he was probably going to infuriate the old man, sticking his nose in where it didn't belong. But he didn't care. He wasn't the handyman anymore. He was just someone who cared about Natalie, and was not going to leave this town without trying to do something to make her safe.

"What kind of help?" Granville spoke around the pancakes.

"Money, of course," Matthew said. "Of which you have plenty."

"Well, I haven't got enough to straighten out that old mausoleum," Granville said. "Only God has that much. God and Bart Beswick. And she told Bart to take a hike."

"You don't have to make it perfect. Just make it better. Make it safe."

"It's not safe?" Granville's brows lowered. "I knew it *looked* like hell. But Nattie never told me it really wasn't safe."

"Well, it's not. It's damn dangerous. The stairs are rotting, the roof is about to fall in, the wiring in three of the bedrooms is just one sizzle away from setting the whole place on fire. I was only there a month, and I saw her nearly kill herself half-a-dozen times."

Granville raised an eyebrow. "Then why are you leaving?"

Good God, the old man was like a dog with a bone. He wanted to know why Matthew was moving out, and he wasn't going to let it go.

"If it's so awful, why not stay?" He raised the raffish brow even higher. "Sounds as if she needs a handyman pretty bad."

"A handyman isn't enough. Ten handymen wouldn't be enough. She needs money, Granville, and a crew of professionals. She tells me you're the only family she's got left. Maybe you should try to talk her into accepting the historical site designation. It might make it easier for her if she thought someone in her family wouldn't have apoplexy at the idea."

He gave the older man a straight, serious look. "But the most important thing is this. Before I go, I want you to promise me you'll help her."

He hadn't really meant to sound quite so adamant. He was trying to remain calm. Trying to postpone thinking about his own feelings until he was safely out of town. It was going to hurt, and hurt bad.

"I'm sorry," he said. "I'm just concerned."

But to his surprise, Granville didn't seem offended. He just wiped his mouth and sat back in his chair.

"What do you take me for, son? Do you think I haven't tried to give her money, time and time again? She won't accept it."

"That's ridiculous. *Make* her accept it."

Granville smiled. "Obviously you never tried to

make that little girl do anything she had her mind made up not to do."

He tilted his head, half-smiling as he absorbed the significance of that statement. "Which is a good thing, a damn good thing, if you know what I mean. But the point is, nobody can force Natalie to do anything she's set against doing. She's a Granville, and that's just how it is with Granvilles."

Matthew stood up. The old guy was just stalling now, playing games to make the conversation and the breakfast last a little longer.

Granville was no fool. He'd be out there in a flash, poking around, discovering what Natalie had tried to hide.

Matthew felt better, knowing that Granville would be watching out.

He'd said what he'd come to say. Now it was time to go. As he'd told Natalie, the longer he stayed, the harder it would be to tear himself away.

"Look," he said, laying down a twenty to cover their bill and the tip. "How you get around Natalie's reluctance to accept help is your problem. But don't tell me you can't do it."

He smiled at the old man and held out his hand for a goodbye shake.

"After all," he said, "you're a Granville, too."

BACK IN HIS ROOM at the hotel, he made one last telephone call.

The phone rang ten times at the other end before his sister picked it up, breathless.

"Hey, Maggie," he said. "Has the lunch rush started already?"

"Matthew! No, I just had my gloves wrist-deep in coleslaw. But how are you? Where are you?"

He waited through her usual enthusiastic surprise, her gushing expressions of affection, her litany of questions about his health, his happiness, his job, and whether he needed anything, anything at all.

Ordinarily, he didn't mind Maggie's mother-hen ways. They were as familiar and comfortable as an old jacket. And even though occasionally she overdid it, he knew how lucky he was to have family that loved him.

In prison, he'd seen too many empty-eyed men who faced the world entirely alone. If they got out of prison, they'd end up right back behind bars, because they simply didn't belong anywhere else.

Answering a few hundred questions was a small price to pay for knowing you weren't alone. Knowing that at least one heart was always out there, wishing you the best.

But today he was a little bit impatient. He had something to do that was going to be disagreeable, and he wanted to get it over with.

As gently as he could, he broke into the questions about whether he needed any new clothes, any money, any anything.

"Maggie, is Dennis around? I have to talk to him about something."

She didn't like the sound of that, obviously. He and Dennis had never really been friends. Dennis had always thought Matthew was too slick, too rich, too superficial. He tried to hide it, but he secretly thought Matthew had deserved to end up in prison, for being criminally self-satisfied, if nothing else.

Actually, he thought, Dennis might enjoy discovering that Matthew had come to agree with him completely.

"What do you need to talk to him about?"

"Put him on, Maggie, please. He'll tell you all about it later."

A silence ensued, then some whispering and shuffling as the receiver was handed from wife to husband.

"Hi, Matthew." Dennis turned away from the phone to speak to his wife. "Honey, I'll tell you whatever he says. Please go back to the coleslaw, or we'll have an angry mob here come noontime."

He returned to the phone. "Sorry. Maggie says you want to talk to me."

"Yes," Matthew said. "I thought I should tell you first, because it was really you who offered me the job at your new restaurant. I want you to know how much I appreciate that, Dennis. It's incredibly generous. I know you did it out of loyalty to Maggie, and I'll always think a lot of you for that. It's nice to know she has a husband who stands by her no matter what."

Dennis hesitated. He was smart, and Matthew could almost hear him thinking through the implications. "Okay. *But?*"

"But I don't think I'm going to be able to accept it." He paused, waiting to see if Dennis exploded in a storm of indignation, but the other end was silent, waiting, too.

"I have been doing a lot of thinking since I got out," Matthew went on. "And I don't honestly believe managing a restaurant is where my future lies. It's a good job, Dennis, better than I deserve. But it just isn't the job for me. I don't think I'd be good at it. Or happy."

Happy. It seemed funny even to be considering that. When he first went to prison, he had been so bitter, so disillusioned, that he couldn't imagine ever caring about life again.

He'd felt the same when he got out.

But he knew what was different now. Natalie had taught him to care.

In their few weeks together, she'd taught him so many things. She'd taught him that cynicism and bitterness are cowardly. That keeping your heart open, letting yourself care—even if it means getting hurt—is far more courageous than withdrawal or numb, despairing indifference.

So this was going to be the first courageous decision of his new life. He couldn't settle for a miserable life that didn't fit him. He had to keep searching for something meaningful.

"I'm sorry, Dennis. I know this sounds ungrateful, but it isn't. It's just honest. I think I'd be a failure. Miserable people usually are. And that wouldn't be fair to you."

"To tell you the truth, Matthew, that's pretty much what I always thought," Dennis said calmly. "But your sister thought she knew better, and I had to defer to her. She'd certainly known you longer."

He paused. "So. Any thoughts on what you *will* do? Is that summer thing going to turn into a full-time gig?"

"No, that job's already over. But I've enjoyed the work, far more than I thought I would. I used to do construction stuff, or odd-job handyman stuff, over the summers, you know. All through high school and college. I liked it then, and I've found it to be very rewarding this summer, too."

"Rewarding?" Dennis chuckled. "Not a lot of money in working with your hands."

"No." Matthew had to smile, thinking of the thousands he used to rake in every month. Sometimes he actually hadn't known what to spend it all on. He had earned more in one morning as a financial advisor than he had in a month as Natalie Granville's handyman.

"But you know what, Dennis? I think my love affair with money may be over."

"Good for you." Dennis's voice grew a shade warmer. "Well, I wish you the best of luck, Matthew. I want you to know there aren't any hard feelings here. If you change your mind, I'll always have a spot for you.''

''Thanks.''

''How about if I break this to Maggie for you? No point your paying long-distance for her to beg and cry and carry on. I know how she works, Matthew. I can make her understand it's for the best.''

''Thanks. But, Dennis. Be sure she knows—''

''How much you love her?'' Dennis laughed. ''She knows, Matthew. She knows. Just let me tell her you'll be coming for a visit pretty soon. That's what she really needs to hear.''

''I'll come,'' Matthew said. ''Tell her I'll come as soon as I've put together a definite plan for the future.''

The future.

For the first time in three years, Matthew actually believed he might have one. Maybe, with time, he could find a new career. Maybe he could make a decent living, doing something he could be proud of. Maybe someday he'd have a new life.

Maybe eventually it would be good enough that he could invite someone to share it with him.

But that rosy, optimistic picture had something wrong with it.

He didn't want *someone*. He wanted Natalie.

And by then it would be years and years too late.

TWO HOURS LATER, as Matthew's car neared the road sign for Vanity Gap, the struggle between his head and his heart began in earnest.

He needed to keep going. He needed to aim his car straight into the pass and not look back until he had reached the other side.

There was no earthly reason to turn right onto Blue Pine Trail. No reason in the world ever to go to Summer House again.

Except, his heart suggested…maybe he should just stop by and give Natalie his sister's name and address. Otherwise, how would Natalie find him, in case she ever needed anything?

What crap, his brain sneered. Need what? Someone to catch her when she fell? He'd be hundreds of miles away.

Someone to fix the wiring? He'd be hundreds of miles away.

A million dollars to repair her family home? What a joke.

So what could Natalie Granville possibly need from him? He didn't have anything to give her. Not a damn thing.

But his stubborn heart wouldn't give up. He had left so abruptly yesterday. It had been cowardly, not worthy of him or of what they had shared. He had left like that because he'd been afraid to be alone with her, afraid that somehow, with her smiles and her hands and her sweetness, she might be able to talk him into staying one more night.

Didn't he owe her a better goodbye? After everything she'd given him—his self-respect, new hope, fresh courage. Surely for all of that he owed her a real goodbye.

What he owed her, his brain retorted, was to leave her the hell alone. To let her forget about him as soon as she possibly could. To allow her to take her amazing beauty, her incredible strength, and all that love she had inside her—and give it to another man. A better man.

A man who had the strength, the courage, the *money,* to save her, instead of dragging his own battered soul to her door, looking for his own selfish redemption.

Blue Pine Trail, the sign on his right read.

And, suddenly, out of nowhere, he decided to ignore the entire discordant chaos of signals bombarding him from both brain and heart.

To hell with the logical debate. He had himself so mixed up he couldn't tell right from wrong anymore.

He decided to relax.

He decided to let his instincts take over.

It was, he thought with a smile as he turned his car smoothly to the right, practically a Granville moment.

CHAPTER SEVENTEEN

IT WAS THE KIND of china-blue day that made you believe summer would last forever. Birds walked openly on the lawn, drugged by the sunlight. Roses drooped heavy heads, red wax melting, dripping onto the green grass. The silver brook, which had been shrinking all summer, exposing silver-veined rocks and polished pebbles, was now so narrow you could span it with one stride.

People all over Firefly Glen stayed indoors, postponing outdoor chores until twilight, or until tomorrow.

Natalie sighed peacefully as she and Stuart walked slowly out onto the front porch of Summer House arm in arm. She knew it wasn't true—summer wouldn't last forever, because nothing ever did. But for once in her life she didn't really mind.

She knew, from years of living in these mountains, that one morning, a few weeks from now, she'd wake up and smell something different in the air. A different bird would be singing outside her window. One of the maple leaves would hold a suspicious auburn tint. Then two.

And, just like that, autumn would overtake them.

And then winter. Living in a place like Summer House, with broken windows, backbreaking heating bills and ancient, hoary plumbing, winter was always a terrifying prospect.

But not this year, she thought, with a sudden lightening of heart. Not this year, not for her.

Impulsively, she turned and hugged Stuart so hard he let out a small gasp.

"What's that for?"

"It's to say how happy I am. And to thank you for making it possible."

He smiled down at her. "As always," he said, "I'm delighted to be of service."

She rested her head on his shoulder, and the two of them gazed placidly out at the Summer House grounds. She couldn't remember when she'd been able to look at it without anxiety, without exhaustion, without its beauty being obscured by the thought of all she needed to do, must do, must somehow, somehow pay for.

And it was beautiful. Ravished, perhaps. Neglected, and a little weary. But still a thing of beauty. How lovely to finally be able to see it.

Because the day was unnaturally quiet—no one quite had the starch to run a lawn mower or a tractor—she heard Matthew's car coming up the driveway long before she saw it.

Funny, she thought, that she, who knew absolutely nothing about cars and cared even less, could perfectly identify the particular rumble of his engine.

But she knew it was his because her heart began to thump heavily in her chest. The sensation felt a little like hope, or perhaps the fear of hoping in vain.

As he pulled up to the front, she knew he could see them standing there on the porch together. Even from this distance, she felt his surprised recoil.

He obviously disliked the sight of her in another man's arms. Well, she could have told him he would. He could throw her away as carelessly as he liked, but that didn't necessarily erase the memory of her hand on his skin, her heart beating against his.

It didn't necessarily mean either of them would ever forget.

He got out of the car slowly, and walked up the driveway. She lifted her head from Stuart's shoulder and moved away a little. Not because she had anything to hide, but because, even now, she couldn't bear to cause Matthew any pain.

"Hi, Matthew," she said.

"Hi," Stuart echoed. "Good to see you, Quinn. I'm glad you didn't leave before I got a chance to say goodbye."

Matthew's eyes were deep and still. "I'm just on my way out of town. I stopped because I needed to talk to Natalie."

Stuart smiled. "Your timing's perfect, because I was just leaving, wasn't I, Nattie?"

When she nodded, he gave her a quizzical look. "Shall we tell Matthew our good news?"

She shook her head. "I think I'd like to tell him alone," she said. "I know you understand."

"Of course." Stuart smiled again. "Of course I do. Absolutely."

He leaned over and gave her a hug, not anything dramatic, but Natalie could see the stiffening in Matthew's shoulders.

With a wink and a sardonic salute to Matthew, Stuart trotted happily down the stairs and slid easily into his little sports car.

"Have a good trip, Quinn," he called. "See you later, Nat."

Natalie and Matthew both watched his car disappear down the long driveway, much longer than they needed to. It was as if, now that they were alone, they weren't sure how to begin.

She turned to him finally, with a strained smile. It was her house, after all, and she knew what was required of a hostess.

"I'm so glad you came," she said simply.

It was a ridiculous understatement, something Granvilles weren't prone to. But there really weren't any words that would adequately express how she felt, so it seemed pointless to try.

He didn't return the smile. "Are you?"

"Of course I am," she said. "Our last goodbye was hardly a goodbye at all. Why don't we go inside? It's getting hotter out here by the minute."

"No, that's okay," he said. "This won't take long."

"All right." She sat on the balustrade. She stretched her legs out along the marble, leaned her back against one of the honeysuckle-covered columns and looked at him. "What did you want to tell me?"

"I—" He shook his head, as if he weren't quite sure himself why he'd come. "I think I felt, too, that our earlier goodbye was…inadequate."

"That was thoughtful of you," she said politely, pulling off a leaf from the vine and wrapping it idly around her finger. "Especially since I know how eager you were to leave town."

He didn't quite look at her. He looked out onto the grounds, and his face was so dark it was if he disliked the very grass and trees he saw there. "Not, apparently, as eager as you were to—"

She raised her eyebrows, her fingers pausing, the leaf suspended between them. "To what?"

He moved away. "Nothing." He paced a few steps along the porch, then came back. "Stuart said you had news. Aren't you going to tell me what it is?"

She resumed playing with the leaf.

"I'm not sure I am," she said. "Not when you look like that. Why are you so angry? If I have good news, wouldn't you like to share in my happiness?"

"For God's sake, Natalie." He ran his hand over his face roughly. "Do you really expect me to?"

"Yes," she said levelly. "I do. As I recall, you said my happiness was very important to you."

"It is." He made a small, harsh sound. "It is, Natalie. I'm sorry. It's just that it's…so soon. It came as a hell of a surprise.''

''What did?''

''You and Stuart,'' he said. ''Together. Discovering that you and he have obviously made…an arrangement. Haven't you?''

''Yes, as a matter of fact, we have. But you obviously don't know what kind of arrangement it is.''

''I think I do.''

She hopped down from the balustrade. ''Well, you're wrong. Wait here. I'll show you.''

She was glad she'd left the papers in the front hall. It took her only a second to retrieve them. She came out into the bright sunlight and handed him the heavy document.

''Here,'' she said. ''This is our arrangement.''

He took the papers from her with a question in his eyes. ''What is this?''

''Just read it,'' she said. ''I have some work to do in the pool house. When you're finished, if you feel pretty rotten about what you've been thinking, as I assume you will, I'll be accepting apologies there.''

''Natalie—''

But she ignored him. It was a seventy-seven-page document, and she guessed that he'd need to read quite a bit of it to fully understand what had been done.

She might as well get some work done. She very much wanted the luxurious pool house bathroom to shine.

He must have merely skimmed the high points. Just fifteen minutes later, she was rinsing the cleanser off the Roman tub when she heard him walking up to the pool house.

"Natalie," he said from the doorway, as if he didn't feel entitled to enter. "Natalie, where are you?"

"I'm in here," she called out. "Come on back if you have any groveling to do. I'm busy."

He was still holding the documents when he entered the large bathroom, which she had been working on for quite some time this morning. It was practically spotless.

Not that he seemed to notice. He looked stunned and worried, and so handsome she had to sit down on the edge of the tub to be sure she didn't go weak in the knees.

"Natalie," he said. "Natalie, what have you done?"

"I've set myself free," she said happily. "I've turned over Summer House, and ninety percent of my inherited income, to the town of Firefly Glen. In return, they have agreed to be responsible for all taxes, maintenance and restoration."

She smiled. "I'm pretty sure I got the better end of that deal, aren't you?"

"But—" He came and sat beside her on the cool marble. "But Natalie, this is your home."

"Not anymore. Beginning September first, it's officially a Firefly Glen Historic Preservation Site. It will be open to the public five days a week, and they'll rent it out for society functions, and weddings, and tours and history students. I'll still have my nursery business, of course. But I'm going to have to start looking for an apartment.''

"When?" He kept leafing through the pages, as if he still couldn't believe what he'd read. "This didn't happen overnight. When did you do this?"

"I've been toying with the idea of applying for a historical designation for weeks. Ever since I called off the wedding to Bart, I guess. But pretty soon I realized I would have to do something even bigger. And that's when I thought of this.''

"But—" he said again. "Are you really sure, Natalie? Isn't this too drastic?''

She laughed and, bending over, carefully sponged down the snaking silver handle of the shower massage until it gleamed. *Hmm,* she thought. That might prove useful later.

She smiled up at him. "Actually, compared to marrying Bart, turning Summer House into a historic site doesn't seem drastic at all. It makes so much sense I'm surprised I didn't think of it sooner.''

"But all this—" He held up the agreement. "Are you sure you're legally protected?''

"Of course. Parker drew up the documents a week ago, and Stuart, who is a city councilman, you know, agreed to lobby the others. Some of them were pretty stubborn, I'll tell you that. I had to come up with reams of proof that Summer House had unique architectural and historical significance before they'd say yes.''

He nodded slowly, obviously putting the pieces together. ''All those hours at the library. All those dusty days up in the attic poring over old documents.''

She grinned. ''Right. And, after all that work, you know what finally clinched the deal? The discovery of the casino. Wasn't it clever of me to invite the whole city council, and even let them run their own gambling tables?''

He had started to smile, just a little. ''That was part of your plan all along?''

She sighed. ''I told you Granvilles aren't as naive as they appear. Anyhow, apparently a secret Roaring Twenties casino adds just the right touch of sex appeal. Now even that tightwad Mayor Millner believes Summer House will attract zillions of well-heeled visitors and tourists. They'll vote at the next city council meeting, and we expect it to be unanimous.''

He put his fingers in the corners of his eyes, as if the document had given him a headache.

''I just can't believe it, Natalie. You love this house. You care more about it than anything on earth.''

She looked at him. ''No, I don't, Matthew,'' she said softly. ''Not anymore.''

His eyes burned. ''Natalie, I—''

''Which reminds me,'' she said, standing up to gather some bath oils. ''Don't you owe me a serious groveling? Don't you want to tell me how abjectly sorry you are that you harbored such unfair thoughts about me?''

''I didn't—'' he began.

''Yes, you did.'' She pointed her sponge at him. ''I saw the way you looked at Stuart. I know what you thought.''

''Do you?''

''Yes. You thought that I had found myself another millionaire. You thought that I'd allowed a man I didn't love to buy me for the measly price of a few million dollars. And you thought I had done those things just two days after you and I...''

''I didn't really think it,'' he said softly. ''I just feared it.''

''Well, it was terrifically unflattering to me, and I expect you to be sorry.''

''I am,'' he said. ''It isn't possible to tell you how sorry I am—for that, and for any hurt I've caused you.''

She twisted on the water and tested it with her palm. Adjusting it a little warmer, she cast him a hard sideways glance. ''If you apologize for Friday night, I'll kill you.''

''No,'' he said. ''I'm not sorry for that. That was— perfect.''

She looked over at him. ''You know,'' she said, ''if you were to kiss me now, it would probably go a long way toward getting me to forgive you.''

Still he didn't move. Gosh, he was a tough nut to crack. She had to do all the work.

But she was willing to. He was worth it.

She came and stood in front of him. "Your performance will be marked down," she said, "if there's a noticeable hesitation."

He looked at her. "I don't want you to make a mistake you'll regret the rest of your life. I still have damn little to offer you. I'm starting over in every way. It may be a struggle. And this house. It's—" He touched her hand. "Whatever you say, I know you love this house. So much of your history is here."

"I feel responsible for it," she said quietly. "Love is very different. Don't you see, Matthew? Love is all about the present and the future. Love couldn't care less about the past."

He pulled her toward him with a groan, and he buried his face against her belly. She ached, a delicious pain, right under the place his face touched her skin.

She fingered his hair softly. "But guess what?"

He looked up. "What?"

"If we don't hurry, our bath is going to overflow."

Lifting his head, he tossed a quick look over his shoulder at the warm, aromatic, rising water. "Is that what you're up to? You're running a bath? I thought you probably didn't realize you'd closed the drain."

She began pulling her T-shirt over her head. She wasn't wearing a bra, which she figured might speed things up a little.

"You know, the way I see it, the biggest problem we're going to have," she said, her voice muffled by the cotton, "is that you persist in thinking Granvilles are too scatterbrained to live. Believe me, Mr. Quinn, when I fill a sexy bathtub with warm water and aphrodisiac oils, it is *not* an accident."

"I see." His eyes were twinkling. She loved his eyes. She shivered, thinking how very much she loved every single thing about this man. "And why," he asked, "are we taking a bath?"

She looked at him sternly. "You don't want to make love to me before I have a bath, do you?"

"Yes," he said. "As a matter of fact, I do."

She slipped off her shorts. "You'd better get those clothes off, then. Because I'm getting in right now." She shed her underwear, stepped into the warm water and slid in all the way up to her chin.

She had deliberately omitted bubbles, because she wanted to be able to see everything. She picked up the shower massage and turned it to jet pulse. She laughed, delighted.

"I don't know how we managed to overlook the obvious potential of this clever tub the other night," she said. "When you think what we managed to do with that armchair."

He leaned over and kissed her, kissed her so thoroughly that she felt a little drunk with it.

She sighed when he pulled away. "Matthew," she said, "see this shower massage? See what it can do? If you don't hurry up and get in here, I may not need you after all."

But he knew it was an empty threat, and he didn't allow it to hurry him.

Still fully dressed, he knelt beside the tub. He put his hand in the water and slid it across her leg, all the way up her body, and then retraced his path.

The oil made the water slippery and sweet, and she shivered again. It was unbearably erotic. Oh, why had she thought she could control this moment? She should have known he would take her silly flirtatious seduction and turn it into something strange and mysterious and sensual beyond endurance.

She still had so much to learn.

"I love you," she said thickly, caught in the magic of his hand. "It hurt so much when you left me."

"But I'm here," he said. "I am here now."

"Yes." She leaned her head back. "You certainly are."

He brought his hand up, and touched her chin with warm, wet fingers. "Natalie, why in heaven's name didn't you tell me what you were planning? Do you know how close we came to losing each other?"

"I wasn't sure until this morning that the deal with the town would go through." She dragged his hand back down under the water. Now that he'd begun, she couldn't bear for him to stop. "Mayor Millner kept straddling the fence, refusing to commit. I couldn't tell you until I was sure myself. I couldn't bear another parting, so I had to be sure."

She took a shaking breath. "I couldn't even be sure that finding an answer for Summer House would really be enough. I *hoped* that was all that stood between us, but how could I know for sure? You hadn't ever said the words, you see. You hadn't ever come right out and said you loved me.''

''I love you,'' he said huskily. ''God knows I haven't any right to, but I do.''

She felt some unseen tension inside her open up and finally relax, growing blissfully supple. Oh, she had waited so long to hear that sentence.

''Matthew,'' she began.

But he wasn't through. ''Marry me, Natalie. Let's start over together.''

She wondered if she might be dreaming. She leaned her head against his arm and made a warm sound of utter contentment. ''I could never have married anyone else,'' she said. ''I was waiting for you all my life, and I didn't even know it.''

''Be sure, Natalie,'' he said somberly. ''I don't know what kind of life I'm offering you. I can't promise where we'll live, or how. The only thing I can promise is love. But you'll never want for that.''

She looked up then. ''Won't we live here? We don't have to, of course, not if you hate the idea. But my nursery business does fairly well, and the people here have seen how good you are with houses. Parker was just saying he wished he could get your advice on renovating his law office.''

He smiled, not at all interested in Parker at the moment. Come to think of it, neither was she.

''We can live wherever you want. If we live here,

of course, Granville and I may end up having to kick Jocelyn Waitely's ass.''

She chuckled. "That's okay with me," she said, "as long as I get to help."

He kissed her again, and she could feel the intensity of the emotions rippling through him. She knew what those emotions were—she felt them, too. They were joy and disbelief, hunger and desire and a small shivering residue of fear.

"I almost left," he said, his voice dark. "Even at the very last minute, I almost didn't turn. I almost kept going. God knows where I would have ended up."

"You would have ended up here," she said, trying to make herself believe it, too. Anything else was unthinkable. "We were meant to be together."

"Even I didn't know where I was headed, Natalie. You wouldn't ever have been able to find me."

She tilted her head back, shutting her eyes sensuously as the warm water seeped into her hair, shivering as her breasts came up and crested the water.

"But you knew where I was," she said. "And someday you would have come back to me. You would not have been able to stay away forever. Someday, I would have looked up and you would have been standing there."

"Someday," he said. "Someday seems like quite a risk. It seems like a very long time."

She raised her head and smiled at him. "Well, I did have a small safety net in place. The truth is, you wouldn't ever have made it through Vanity Gap. The sheriff was waiting there, ready to pull you over.''

Matthew's hand paused. He looked at her, disbelieving. ''The *sheriff?*''

''Yes,'' she explained, wrinkling her nose. ''Actually, it could have been very exciting. If anyone saw him, it undoubtedly would have made the front page of the *Firefly Glen Gazette.*''

''But why on earth would Harry do such a thing?''

''Well, you see, I told him I would be heartbroken if you left town before you found out about the deal with the city council. Harry's a good friend of mine, so I told him how important it was to me.''

She watched him from half-closed lids that sparkled with drops of water. ''And besides, I told him you took something from me.''

He hesitated a moment, and then he burst out laughing. ''You little devil,'' he said, cupping water in his hand and splashing it over her.

''Devilish, perhaps,'' she admitted, blinking the drops away. ''But clever, huh?''

He shook his head helplessly. ''How could you do such a thing? The Natalie Granville personal protection squad has always been intensely suspicious of me. Now my reputation is ruined forever.''

He didn't look upset, though. He knew she was joking. He didn't bristle painfully at any casual mention of these things, not anymore.

He really was whole again, she thought. Whole and strong and everything she wanted.

His eyes were warm and confident. He was ready to tease her a little. "Now that you've done such a foolish thing, I guess we can't stay in Firefly Glen after all. No one will ever believe I'm not a shameless thief."

"But you are a thief, Mr. Quinn," she said, reaching out and grabbing the collar of his shirt, tugging him gently toward the water. She didn't intend to wait another minute.

"Oh, really?" Just like in the arm wrestling, he was letting her win. She was hardly exerting any force at all, and he was coming toward her, a hot, thrilling gleam in his eye.

"And what exactly did you tell the sheriff I had stolen? Don't forget, Miss Granville, you have already testified under oath that Donny Fragonard was the one who took your virginity."

"That's easy," she said. She felt her breath snag in her throat as their lips met. "You, sir, are the one who took my heart."

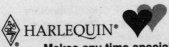

If you enjoyed what you just read,
then we've got an offer you can't resist!

Take 2 bestselling
love stories FREE!

Plus get a FREE surprise gift!

HARLEQUIN *Super* ROMANCE

The Special Agents

It takes a special kind of person...

Author Roxanne Rustand explores the exciting world of the DEA and its special agents. Dedicated, courageous men and women who put their lives on the line to keep our towns and cities safe.

Operation: Mistletoe
coming in November 2002.

Special Agent Sara Hanrahan's latest assignment brings her home for the first time in years. But old secrets and old scandals threaten to make this a miserable Christmas. Until Sara—with the help of Deputy Nathan Roswell— uncovers the surprising truth. A truth that sets them free to enjoy the best Christmas ever!

First title in Roxanne Rustand's *The Special Agents* series
1064—OPERATION: KATIE

HARLEQUIN®
Makes any time special ®